Elusive Destiny

Beatrice Holloway

TSL Publications

First published in Great Britain in 2013 by Bretwalda Books

Revised edition 2019
By TSL Publications, Rickmansworth

ISBN / 978-1-912416-51-6

Cover image: https://pixabay.com/en/milky-way-universe-person stars-1023340/

Acknowledgements

Again I am indebted to Anne and John at TSL Publications for their continued patience and help.

Many thanks also to Jenny Hunt and as ever, my supportive family.

One

'You have shamed us,' a stern voice rebuked.

Seventeen year old Matthew stood immobile in front of the twelve elders of the Senate. The elders were usually fair in their dealings with defaulters but as he looked at the stern faces he knew he would not get off lightly as he could see some were angry and others baffled by his behaviour.

'You took it upon yourself to change your destiny,' said another voice full of shock.

Matthew listened unmoved with bowed head and said nothing in his defence. Some of the men fidgeted, one or two shuffled papers in front of them and others turned to discuss Matthew's case. Snatches of their conversations ricocheted around the gathering:

'Far too young.'

'Disobedient dolt.'

'Deserves no chance at all.'

'Just a child, have mercy.'

But all agreed that they could not approach the higher authority, the true master, to help with the problem. It would seem like an admission of failure in their duty.

Matthew was unrepentant. In his mind what he had done was no less wicked than what others had done. What had upset these good people, he was sure, was the failure of their plans for him, that he had indeed shaped his own destiny, though not intentionally.

Peter, the leader of the elders, tapped on the table. Voices lowered until there was silence.

'We must deal with this matter ourselves,' he said, amidst a flurry of nodding heads.

Matthew waited.

'We cannot appeal to the higher authority,' Peter hesitated before going on, 'because I think, and I'm sure you will agree, we must have been at fault to let such a thing happen and possibly our own positions may well be questioned.'

More heads nodded and some gasped at the significance of Peter's words. None of them made any gain from their seat on the Senate, but nevertheless, it was a very prestigious and respected role. Each member valued his place, won on the merits of his own life and the unanimous selection by others. Each knew they could be replaced by equally esteemed men.

Peter went on, 'All of us must think, therefore, what is best to be done.' There was no sound for a few minutes until Peter said, 'Matthew, your destiny was designed for you. You chose to change this for the love of a woman, also destined for you as your everlasting soul mate, but your foolishness has altered everything.'

Matthew nodded, inwardly not sorry for his misdemeanour.

'I suggest ...' Peter hesitated and looked at the assembled group, 'that is, if none of you can suggest anything better ...' Faces turned towards him, hoping he had a solution, knowing that they themselves could think of nothing. Peter cleared his throat, 'I propose, my dear friends, that we arrange for Matthew to be given a number of lives until he has repaired the damage.'

The solution was greeted with sighs of relief from those assembled. 'It will not be easy Matthew, you understand?'

Matthew nodded again.

'There are some conditions. If you succeed, all will be resolved.' An excited muttering passed between the members of the Senate as they anticipated what Peter might have in mind.

For the first time in front of the Senate, Matthew showed a flicker of emotion.

'What ... what conditions? Is it ... is it a punishment?' he stuttered.

Peter's voice was full of sorrow but he gave a gentle smile as he answered, 'No, not a punishment.'

Again the members muttered amongst themselves and were surprised and pleased when Peter went on, 'If you live a life without breaking one of the Terms of Agreement, then all will be well. If you break just one, you will have to start again with a new life, say twenty years, perhaps centuries later. That is the best we can do for you.' Peter drummed his fingers on the table before adding, 'However, what you will suffer most is the keeping of your memory, you alone. So your task to win over the girl will not be easy.' He stood up and with an encouraging pat on Matthew's back, he added, 'You may go now. We all wish you the very best in this difficult undertaking.' The elders stood up to leave, questioning and speculating as to the possible outcome. It was obvious some thought that the task could not be achieved in a thousand lifetimes.

Matthew lifted his head and straightened his shoulders; his only thought was that he would be with his true love again. Bowing to Peter he said, 'Thank you. When are you thinking of returning me?'

Peter locked his fingers and tapped his lips for a few seconds before answering, 'Better start at sun up tomorrow.'

Matthew was delighted to be able to start so soon, convinced he would be able to meet the conditions and be with his true love at last.

Marion Knowles had broken a wrist and two fingers; a silly accident in the supermarket a few days ago. Someone came charging out of one of the aisles. Marion had stepped back quickly to avoid a collision, then tripped over a trolley loaded with tins. Onlookers fussed inevitably, the manager hovered unsure what to do or say, a first aider did her best but, as it became clear that there was a painful fracture, an ambulance was sent for.

Now she was sitting alone on a bench in her uncle's orchard at the end of an extensive lawn. It had always been called the orchard but this was a misnomer as there were only three pear and two apple trees, old and twisted with silver-grey lichen lacing the branches. It was obvious, looking at the well cut lawn and the flourishing roses nearby, that her uncle spent a great deal of time in his garden. Smiling to herself she recalled as a child how he insisted that she called every flower by its Latin name. Looking at the riotous colourful display now, she could only identify snapdragons as antirrhinums and geraniums as pelargoniums. There were rudbeckia, she was always attracted to their velvety brown and orange petals. Hidden among the regimented dahlias, the largest staked at the back, were the last of the blue iris.

Sitting quite still she watched as bees, one after the other laden with pollen from the lavender bushes, flew off. A glass of wine was gripped in her good hand and now and again she took a sip and followed this up with a satisfied sigh.

It had been a full day, the day of her cousin Rosemary's wedding, August 2008. As chief bridesmaid Marion didn't feel that she had done justice to the occasion. It was her responsibility to help the bride on her special day. Marion felt privileged and honoured when Rosemary had asked her. For the hen night she'd arranged a private viewing of *Seven Brides for Seven Brothers* followed by a champagne supper and this had gone without a hitch. True to tradition she had been there for Rosemary when she suffered nervous butterflies in her stomach. What she couldn't do and wanted to desperately, was to help Rosemary dress, help her from the car at the church and adjust her dress and veil. There seemed to be so many little tasks she was unable to fulfil. With the help of her aunts and two other bridesmaids she, herself, had been dressed, her hair set into a becoming style and her finger-nails polished. The sling had hastily been dyed the same colour as her lavender dress. With her finger tips just peeking out and resting high on her chest she had stood behind the bride at the altar and hidden the sling with the bouquet of flowers when they were handed to her. As the photos were being taken Marion stood valiantly behind the other bridesmaids, who reached to her shoulder. As the sling was hidden she hoped that the photos would be as perfect as possible.

Sitting quietly in the sunlight, Marion closed her eyes and sighed, and asked herself, is life too good? She kicked off her high heeled shoes, which, although really lovely to look at, hurt like hell. Shoes she could only afford because of her well paid job as an editor in one of London's publishing houses. In her wardrobe were a number of well fitting clothes with designer labels. She knew she had clear skin and a much envied English rose complexion, defined cheekbones and dark eyes. Eating good food in expensive restaurants was a joy. Also, as she was so busy, and to be honest didn't like household chores, she was able to employ someone to do her housework. What bliss she thought, to come home on a Friday evening to a clean and tidy home.

Sometimes she asked herself, am I being smug and is life too good? The best answer she could give herself was that by giving generous donations to charity and giving up time to help at the local nursing home for sick children, evened the score a little perhaps. She also made sure that her parents were not in need of anything to make their lives as comfortable as possible. Since her father had retired from law, Marion knew that his pension was more than adequate, but she also knew that it was the surprise treats she arranged like theatre tickets and weekend breaks that gave them so much pleasure. She experienced a brief moment of shame for her patronising state of mind, and chided herself. Could I do more, she wondered, to somehow balance the good life I am enjoying? The answer she felt was, at present, no.

Two

Everything seemed perfect, but for some reason she couldn't understand, she often felt something was missing from her life, something that at times brought her overwhelming sadness. All around her was quiet and still except for the soft gentle buzzing of the bees. She put her wine glass on the ground and, nursing her aching arm, and with her eyes closed, she began to relax in the warmth of the late afternoon sun, but was suddenly jolted out of her reverie.

A man's voice said, 'There you are, at last. This time I thought I'd never find you.'

At the sound of the voice Marion's heart filled with unexpected and overwhelming joy. It was as if she'd come to the end of a long search, that an unknown lifetime of sorrow she was barely aware of had been lifted from her. Her eyes flew open and she was momentarily blinded by the sunlight. Once she had adjusted to the glare, she saw a man, of about thirty years of age she thought. His jacket was hooked on his finger and hanging over his shoulder and his tie was loose. He was hunched down in front of her, his face level with hers; a complete stranger. Although he had a wide grin on his face she could see his relief that now, finally, his search was over; although she wondered briefly what it was he was seeking.

'May I?' he asked as first he stood up from his crouch, then sat down beside her on the bench.

Marion nodded, and said, 'You seem to know me, but I'm sure I've never met you before.'

The man ran his hand through his hair before answering, 'I'm Matthew Hope, the bridegroom's cousin.'

'And I'm the bride's cousin.'

'I was hoping that this time you might remember me.' Blue eyes gazed at her with expectation, 'No? Well, they said you wouldn't.'

Marion laughed quietly, shaking her head in bewilderment. Looking into his tanned face it seemed quite ordinary, the mouth a tad too wide, laughter crinkles around his eyes and a few freckles scattered about his cheeks. He lifted her half empty glass and took a sip, laughing as she started to protest.

She said after a little hesitation, 'Oh, go on then. Help yourself. I've really had enough anyway.'

'Thanks. Now tell me, what have they called you this time?'

'What do you mean this time and, who are they?'

He gave a little groan. 'It really isn't fair. They, the Senate, said you wouldn't remember, not ever, but it would make everything so much easier if you could. Every time we meet up I work so hard to get you to remember. I suppose they knew it would make everything more difficult for me.' As an afterthought, he added softly, 'And you.'

'Remember what?' Marion was getting a little uneasy as she listened, but she was also curious. This man seems so at ease with me as if he has known me all his life, she thought.

'So, what is your name?' he asked again.

'Marion.'

The sound of his laughter echoed around the garden.

'Marion,' he repeated.

She stood up quickly and turned to leave, 'It's not that funny. It's a good name, taken from the old Hebrew name of Miryam. My mother told me it means "Star of the Sea". You really are so unbelievably rude.' Picking up her shoes, she began to walk smartly away, saying, 'I really don't have to stay and listen to you making fun of me. What have I ever done to deserve your mockery?'

Matthew stopped laughing and patted the seat beside him as he said, 'Please, sit down. Stay a while longer. I'm so sorry to have offended you. Truly I am.' He raised his eyebrows slightly before adding, 'Got yourself into a right old tizzy. For a moment, I thought you were going to stamp your foot.'

She gave him what she hoped was a scathing look, dropped her shoes and sat down, cradling her aching arm, knowing that she didn't want to go away, wanting to know more about this man.

'My name's Matthew, but I've already told you that.' He held out his hand to shake hers. 'Marion.' He seemed to be testing the name out. 'Marion,' he repeated quietly. Smiling at her he said, 'Every time I seek you out ...'

'What?'

Patiently he went on, 'Every time I seek you out, your name always begins with "M".'

'What do you mean?'

'Well, last time you were called Martha, before that Mary, then there was Madeline and ... Oh, the list is endless.' He looked keenly into her eyes as he said softly, 'Your real name is Magdalena.'

'You're mad,' Marion laughed, 'but it's the best chat up line I've ever heard.'

'Oh, there's more, lots more. Want to know?'

'Go on then, until we're called for supper. I suppose you're staying on for supper?'

He nodded. 'So, I'd better start at the beginning.' He took a deep breath and surprised her by saying, 'Around the year twelve hundred and fifty ...'

Marion raised her eyebrows and he bit his lower lip and nodded, adding, 'Honestly, my memories are that good, but of course they told me it would be.'

'Who?'

Matthew linked his long fingers together, then unhooked them before resting his hands on his knees. 'As I said I'll start at the beginning. Ready?'

'Oh, go on then. It had better be good.'

'Long ago I unknowingly altered our destinies.'

'Our destinies? Oh come on. You're making this up.'

'No, I'm not. Please, just hear me out.'

Marion shrugged her shoulders. 'I'll listen, but don't expect me to believe you will you?'

He leaned towards her and looked intently into her face. 'All I ask is that you listen to my explanation. When I have finished you can make up your mind about the truth of it all, and the truth is what I shall tell you.'

Marion smoothed her skirt with her good hand and, gazing back at him, said, 'You're serious about this aren't you?' With a flippant wave of her hand she said, 'Alright, I'll listen to what you're going to say. Just don't expect me to believe you.'

Taking a deep breath, he began again. 'As I said, because I changed our destinies the Senate ...'

'The Senate? Who or what are the Senate?'

'Yes, I'd better explain. The Senate is made up of twelve men who shape the destinies of everyone.'

There was a little exasperation in Marion's voice as she said, 'Is this a dream or are you making it all up as I suspect?'

'I know it's hard for you to believe. Let me try to convince you.' Even though she nodded for him to continue he could see doubt in her face. 'For my interference they, the Senate, decided that I should live my life over and over again until I have lived one without breaking any of the commandments.'

Marion was quiet for a few moments. The sun was lower now and, although she was convinced he was spinning a tale, Marion found herself intrigued and wanting to know more.

They heard a voice calling them for supper. They stood up together and Matthew picked up her shoes and guided her firmly with his hand on her elbow. She was unexpectedly thrilled by his touch. In stocking feet she walked slowly back to the house with him.

Stopping suddenly in her tracks, Marion asked, 'But why? What had you done that had been so dreadful?'

He stood beside her in silence for a moment, his toe nudging a stone on the path. They heard her Aunt Amy calling again. 'Come on, they're waiting for us. Tell you later perhaps,' he said. There was sadness in his voice as he went on, 'But I think the answer might upset you. It will certainly surprise you.'

'Oh you! It's only a tale, but I'll confess I'm very keen to know what happened.'

They sat together for the buffet supper her aunt had provided and talked to other guests from their respective families. There was chatter and laughter all round them, people who only met at family gatherings greeting each other. Glasses were being refilled; elderly guests closed their eyes, hoping no one would notice. Belts were discreetly loosened and children raced around the lounge and garden with the family dogs joining in pursuit. Marion was happy.

Somehow she felt safe, as if Matthew's presence had enveloped her, protective somehow; but from what, she wondered? I have nothing to be afraid of.

When her aunt came over to the couple, she looked at Marion. 'Well our Marion. You've brightened up a bit, what's brought this on?' she said. 'Last time I looked at you out in the orchard on your own, you looked as if the world was about to fall apart.'

Marion laughed, 'Oh, I expect it was before I took my painkillers.' She half heartedly lifted her injured arm, 'This is quite painful at times,' then turning to Matthew she said, 'Do you know Matthew? He's Dominic's cousin.'

'Yes, yes, I do. Matthew Hope isn't it? Staying at The Bell in the village overnight aren't you? Just so sorry we couldn't put you up, but as you can see,' she said, as she shooed some over-excited children away, 'we are about to burst out of the walls here.'

Matthew gave a quiet chuckle and raised his hand as if to brush away her worry and told her he didn't mind a bit staying at the local pub.

'You said you were leaving tomorrow to catch the two twenty train, so we'll have an early lunch, Marion, although you are welcome to stay as long as you like. In fact I'll probably miss Rosemary so much, that I'd be glad if you would stay on at least another day. You can't be doing much for yourself with a broken arm. How about it?'

Before Marion could answer there was a buzz around the room, and Rosemary entered the room on the arm of her new husband. They had come to say their goodbyes to everyone as they were leaving for their honeymoon, kissing, shaking hands and giving thanks for all the presents.

Once the couple had left, the atmosphere in the house seemed to alter; Aunt Amy was wiping away tears while she was beginning to collect up glasses, some still half full, the crumpled napkins and used crockery. The guests who were leaving began gathering their belongings and children. There were more hugs and kisses as goodbyes were said and promises made to keep in touch.

When only a few people were left, including Marion and Matthew, Aunt Amy came over to where they were standing at the open French doors getting a little fresh air and asked Matthew if he would like to join the rest of the family for a walk in the morning.

'A brisk Sunday walk after church,' she suggested, 'a couple of miles or so to the village inn across the fields for morning coffee.'

Matthew put his arm around her and dropped a kiss on her cheek. 'I'd love to,' he told her. 'Will we be taking the dogs?'

'It's the dogs that will be taking us,' was her brisk reply as she moved away. 'We'll pick you up from the pub about a quarter to ten, okay?'

Matthew put his thumb up in reply and turned to Marion. 'If we walk together tomorrow, I can give you the answer to your question. Will that satisfy you?'

'Your story? Time for you to be able to dream up something dramatic over night, I'm thinking. Aren't you the lucky one?'

He laughed as with a half smile he shook his head, knowing that she wouldn't believe him.

Three

Matthew was waiting outside the pub for them as arranged and he raised his hand when he saw the group approaching. Marion felt a rush of happiness when she saw his tall frame leaning against the wall. She was impressed to see him wearing a plain, short-sleeved cotton shirt over slacks and sensible walking shoes. His sunglasses were pushed up to the top of his head. After greeting everyone in turn, he pulled down his sunglasses and fell into step beside Marion.

The group set out along the stony path alongside the hedgerows bordering the fields ready for harvesting. The dry, bearded barley heads rasped gently as they passed by. The sky was blue and cloudless and the air still and warm. Hills in the distance seem to shimmer; sunlight was reflected off the white-washed walls of lone cottages dotted about the hillside. Sheep were steadily cropping their way across the surrounding fields, their occasional faraway bleating just audible. There was an abundance of wild flowers and Marion was delighted to see blue cornflowers and bright red poppies mixed in with the dusty ripened grain. They were standing straight displaying their colours, finding their own defiant stance in the field as if mocking men's efforts to eradicate them. She was secretly glad that they had escaped the fate of many wild flowers, that of persistent herbicides.

'Sleep well?' she asked. She immediately felt silly asking such a mundane question, but couldn't think of anything else to say. It didn't help that she was feeling a glow of warmth at being close to him again; close enough to smell his fresh aftershave.

'I did. It was a long day yesterday.' Looking down at her he asked, 'How's the arm? Not so painful? I saw you wince once or twice yesterday, and I wished I could have taken the pain away for you.'

'Oh, it's much better, thank you. Just glad it isn't my leg. I wouldn't be here if that was the case,' and gave a little laugh at her silly joke. As they walked, Marion asked, 'What do you do for a living, Matthew? Anything exciting?'

He frowned a little before answering. 'Not really exciting, but challenging enough. I'm a representative for Spencer's Engineering. They make components for irrigation plants, that sort of thing, mostly for central Africa. I go all over the world, mainly trying to bag lucrative contracts and, as I'm also an engineer, I often oversee the installations. Mostly they are in remote places and difficult to get to, but usually there's a small plane that the firm charters so I don't have to travel for days over land. That would be more than uncomfortable in the heat in some places.

'When I arrive at the proposed site I'm always dismayed and saddened by the lack of water. Everything so dried up, even the people. I don't know how they manage, although they appear to be happy enough.'

Marion was impressed with his empathy for the people, and she felt a warm glow, thinking of his caring attitude.

'It's the children I enjoy being with. At more than one place they were so curious and kept asking endless questions, wanting to help. They saw no danger in clambering around the site. I always make sure I take plenty of ball point pens and colouring pencils with me. As there is always plenty of scrap paper in the office I am able to draw diagrams for them and of course they loved to draw and copy the letters for themselves.' He laughed as he said, 'Like the world over, the boys always drew cars and mechanical things and the girls houses and fairies. Well, I call them fairies, but they told me that they were drawing happy spirits.' He smiled as he was remembering. 'They brought presents for me in exchange, usually slices of fruit, and were never happy until I'd eaten some. Then I'd chase them and tickle them, they loved all of that. I was someone having time for them, boys and girls, although the girls were shyer.'

Seeing the look of surprise on her face he said, 'I see you're suitably impressed. In fact I have to be back in London tomorrow evening, get packed and be ready to fly to Nigeria early on Monday, calling in at Amsterdam first to meet up with some colleagues. Together we fly on up into the north of Africa. Matthew paused and said, 'Now your turn, what do you do for a living? Something glamorous, I shouldn't wonder.'

'My job? I'm an assistant editor of a publishing establishment called Bulmer and Gibbs. I don't expect you've heard of it, but it's doing well at the moment. Mostly non-fiction stuff. Quite exacting at times, but with a secretary taking care of the more mundane tasks I'm always able to keep on top of my assignments.

'I'm paid well. Enough for two good holidays a year that others only dream of, usually somewhere warm and exotic.' She smiled as she remembered being in Bali last year; the soft, white sandy beaches; the mystic mountains with holy temples at their base, the many diverse cultures and the friendly welcoming people. Next year the plan was to visit Malaysia.

Coming out of her daydream, she turned towards Matthew, 'Now tell me,' she said, 'what sort of story have you dreamed up for me today? Come on, I'd love to hear where your imagination has taken you.'

Gently protecting her arm, he helped her over a stile before answering. 'I shall tell you only the truth and hope we will still be friends at least when I have finished, although, to be frank, I would value more.' His heart beat a little faster. He longed to be alone with her and take her in his arms. He turned away from her briefly so that she couldn't see the telltale blushing he was experiencing. He realised it was too soon, he had to be gentle in his approach to her. The waiting was going to be hard, but he had found her and told himself he must be patient.

Marion wasn't sure what he meant by the last remark. It seemed to her that he was hoping for more than friendship, more, she knew, than she was willing to give. As they fell a little behind the rest of the walkers he began to tell her his story.

'Remember, I'm talking of Henry the third's time, the thirteenth century.' Marion nodded.

'It so happened that I was then just a lad of twelve working in your father's stables ...' He was surprised when Marion stopped walking and he had to turn back to be at her side. 'What?' he asked.

'What do you mean by your father's stables? Surely you're not going to tell me I was there?'

Matthew laughed, 'Of course you were there. Haven't I said our destinies have been planned for us?'

There was a look of bewilderment on her face.

Matthew knew it was going to be difficult for her to understand. 'Let me go on telling you. It might be easier to grasp as I go on.'

There was the slightest nod of her head and Matthew began again.

'He, your father at that time, had,' Matthew counted off on his fingers, 'pack horses, a couple of palfreys, you know just for riding, a cart horse for the farm work and a charger, his favourite war horse. This old boy was kept to remind your father of his jousting days. He was a knight you know,' Matthew smiled at Marion. 'I was told he was pretty good. That's how he won your mother's hand in marriage, so they said. He was quite tall for the time, around five foot eight, had a good figure, not overweight like so many of the gentry, but definitely fatter than I was or the others about the yards and fields.' Matthew bent down and picked a trailing purple vetch before going on.

'My father was a favourite groom and used to attend the jousting tournaments with him to look after the horses. At the time the church did their best to ban tournaments. In fact King Henry supported the church ruling during his reign but few took any notice. It was a way of improving battle skills, you see. Of course, to be a knight meant that chivalry was also part of their code.' Steadily walking beside Marion he stopped for a moment and raised his glasses. Marion stood alongside him. 'The fields were different in those days,' he said as he gazed around. 'The fields were more open, no hedges and many more flowers like poppies and cornflowers.' As they continued to walk, Matthew took up his story again.

'The king's support of the church was only a token acknowledgement; my father used to say that jousting also meant revenue for the King. He artfully charged the patron of the event, a long ago form of taxation, don't you agree?'

Marion looked over the top of her sunglasses, 'If you say so. You can be sure either the government, or in those days the king, will get some of your wealth somehow. But go on with your story, I'm enjoying the walk and having someone to talk to seems to make it more interesting, especially if they are telling you a tale or two.'

Matthew blew lightly through his lips, and then chuckled as he continued. 'I knew making you believe what I'm saying was going to be an uphill job, but with your blessing, I'll go on. I'm setting the picture for you, see?'

She smiled and shrugged her shoulders. 'Right, I'll do my best not to interrupt again,' she answered.

Matthew stopped and broke off a few more wild flowers as he said, 'The tournaments were arranged by Earls or Barons who used to send out men to advertise the event, usually held in fields near their castle grounds with some sort of boundary.' He grinned as he said, 'No text messaging in those days. The knights were known as tourneys and fought each other with no intention of killing their opponent, and there was much grief and regret should someone die. Hope I'm not boring you?'

'You seem to be very well informed, I must say. A graduate in history I think?'

'No, my lady, engineering is my calling, and I tell you I was there.'

Marion rolled her eyes and shook her head from side to side.

'Okay, if you say so.'

'The loser of the battle had to pay a ransom and father said that many of the knight's entourage made heavy bets. When the jousting was over it was the women who typically gave the prizes at such tournaments. Sleeves and veils were the most popular favours granted as tokens and often fastened to the lances of the champion. One day your father won your mother's favour and consequently her hand in marriage.'

The walking group had stopped, and all were admiring the sleepy swifts drifting over the hills. Marion and Matthew caught up with them, and heard that they were not too far away from the promised cup of coffee. Matthew didn't say anything more whilst they were in the company of others. In fact he left Marion to go and speak to other members of the party, and suddenly Marion felt alone, self doubts came for no reason and quite unexpectedly. What is happening to me, she asked herself? I set out happily this morning and now ... now Matthew had left her; only for a short while, but she was experiencing a sense of being lost in a confusion of unbidden thoughts. It wasn't the first time. At other times she'd felt a yearning for something, but she didn't know what. Worst of all, were the times she felt as if she were weeping deeply, internally, as if her heart was broken.

Trying to analyse her present mood, she thought life could not get any better. I have a lovely four bedroom house almost in the centre of London and a good job nearby. She knew these feelings weren't caused by Alex and in any case he'd be back tomorrow. It was something else. Something she couldn't understand and felt she could never explain to him, these forlorn moments in her life. Even to herself she couldn't put into words the distress at these fleeting moments.

Sitting down with a cup of frothy cappuccino, smothered in chocolate dust in her good hand, she was glad when her aunt sat down beside her, a little out of breath, to tell her that Rosemary had telephoned earlier to say they had arrived safely in Portugal.

'Of course,' her aunt said, 'I wasn't worried, but it was good of her to put my mind at rest.' She reached into her shoulder bag for a tissue, gently blew her nose and, looking a little sheepishly at Marion, gave a little sigh as she added, 'Oh, dear, will I ever get used to being redundant as a mother?' she laughed.

'Now, aunt,' Marion chided as she put her arm around her, 'you know the old saying "lost a daughter and gained a son".'

'Well, he's a lovely boy, I must say, and I'm very fond of him, so I'll settle for that and as long as he takes good care of her and brings her home often then I think I'll be satisfied.' She stood up, smiled at Marion, then called the walkers together for the homeward amble. Marion agreed immediately when Amy turned back to her and suggested she bring Matthew back for lunch before they both set off home.

It was when Matthew fell into step beside her for the return journey that immediately her mood lifted. In his presence again she felt safe. No, she told herself, that is not the right word, but I do feel better.

'Aunt suggested you might like to have lunch with us before you leave this afternoon, unless, of course, you're in a hurry to get away,' she said.

Obviously delighted and still clutching his untidy bouquet of wild flowers, he said, 'Splendid, a little more time for me to tell you of some of my many lives. Shall I go on or have you had enough for now?'

'Oh, please go on. I still don't know why your Senate people want to punish you yet.'

They fell behind the others and Matthew, after adjusting his sunglasses, began, 'Where was I?'

'You were telling me how the knight won his lady,' she reminded him.

'Oh, yes. Your mother was beautiful, and popular with everyone. Every year she made sure there was a lavish harvest supper once the fields were cleared, and again at Christmas. She always asked after the new born, sometimes bringing a wooden bowl of broth for the new mother. A very kind and thoughtful woman, and she was well liked among the villagers. So was your father, but he had a fierce temper on him, and could sometimes be quite harsh in his dealings with the workers about the estate. Whoops,' Matthew said as he stumbled, 'hold on a moment,' and handed the flowers to her as he bent down to retie his shoe lace.

Marion gazed down on his head noticing the clean, dark hair with a hint of a bald spot on the crown and she knew that, like her father, at some time he would discover it and probably be upset.

Straightening up, Matthew went on, 'One day when you were nine years old your father bought you a lively colt. Your mother brought you out to the stables. My father lifted you onto the horse. Your mother instructed that I should lead you around the smallest field until you could handle him properly. Then I was to escort you around the estate, you on your pony and me on one of the older nags. I was really cross about this, and told my father later that I was twelve and a man and not a baby minder. I was so indignant about this chore. He cuffed me and said I was to do as I was told or lose my place.

'You came every day with your mother, and one day you were so pleased to see me that you ran and put your arms around me, calling my name. Your mother was furious. I remember her saying, "Magdalena, do not touch that boy, ever. Do you understand?" Then she looked at me, I don't know what she read in my face, but her voice softened a little as she said, "He cannot bathe every day like you dearest, he may be a little dirty and smell very unpleasant".' Matthew laughed as he added, 'A little dirty, she thought. Of course I was dirty. Who wouldn't be, working with horses all day, cleaning them and cleaning out their stalls? Mind you, I did get to swim in the river now and again in the summer months so that helped to freshen me.'

He looked fondly at Marion and smiled. 'Such a pretty little maid, but so naughty. One day you fell off your mount and I had to lift you back into your saddle. As soon as we got back to the yard you were so excited, and told your mother that you had fallen and I had picked you up. She instructed that I should receive two lashes for touching you and then my father cuffed me. What was I supposed to do? Leave you on your bottom and walk home without you? This happened three days running. It was too far to run to the stables for my father. I couldn't understand it at first, and then I got wise to you. "I know your secret, miss," I said to you, "but if you were to just slide off your horse we could walk a little way, then I could lift you back without you telling anyone, and then I wouldn't get beaten would I?" You said you were sorry. Seems what you wanted, was to talk to me and from that day on that's what we did; walked a little, played childish games; you loved to chase the chickens. We talked a great deal and became the best of friends.

'On one of our walks you told me that our initials were the same, "M". You showed me the letter in the dust on the ground, drawing it with a twig, and I practised writing this and, with your encouragement, I carved intertwining "M"s on a tree on the river bank, and joined them at the bottom so that they looked like a heart.' Matthew stopped to pick another flower.

Marion said, 'I do believe you are a writer and you are testing out your next plot on me. Someone must have told you I was an editor. True?'

'I had no idea what your profession was until you told me, but what a good idea,' he laughed. 'If only I had the time to write. It's all in my memory, I'm afraid, and you, you should consider yourself lucky that you don't remember your past lives.'

'Don't think it can't be done,' she countered. 'I've heard some-one in London can take you back into the past through hypnosis. I could go to some of those regression sessions if you like, get someone to help me unearth my buried memory, then we …' Marion paused when Matthew stopped walking, 'What?' she asked.

'Wait,' he said. Taking her by the shoulders, he raised his sunglasses and looked into her eyes. As she looked back at him she could see he was disturbed by her suggestion. He stood for a moment, quietly thinking before he answered, 'Don't ever do that. Promise me. You may find it all too painful.' Nothing was said for a moment or two. As he took his hands away from her he said, 'That is why the Senate insisted I kept my memories; to cause me pain. I don't want that for you.'

Marion knew for certain that she would never seek to know her memory. Somehow she felt she had to take account of Matthew's obvious distress and insistence.

They began walking again and he said, 'Now, no more inter-ruptions or I shall never finish. Agreed?'

Marion nodded.

'We, Magdalena and I, were out for an hour every day, some-times longer. Like all children we played, chasing and hide and seek and, best of all, racing the horses. You always won, of course, you had the younger horse. We never told anyone of this, always returning back to the manor house very sedately, you leading and me on the old plodding horse behind, dressed in a cast-off aketon, a sort of padded waistcoat on which your family crest was embroi-dered that once belonged to one of your father's squires. All too soon you were a beautiful lady of fourteen and I seventeen.

'One awful day your father returned from one of the tourna-ments he'd attended, no longer a participant in the jousting, but he still enjoyed the events. Anyway, he came home that day, having been away for almost two months, full of news. My father said your father was grinning and hailing everyone with a cheer on their journey home, partly because of his news, but mostly because he had been overindulgent with ale. One of the housemaids told me why. It seems he had found you a rich husband; one who owned a castle with plenty of land. Your mother, it was said, protested, saying he was far too old, he was fifty-three I think, that he was too fond of wine and womanising and lived over a hundred miles away. The little maid said you were in tears as was your mother, but your father was adamant. You were to marry next summer. There were whispers around the estate that your father had lost a bet, and you were the prize. I'm not sure of the truth of this, but then everything turned nasty. Nothing was ever the same again.

'All the courtesy and chivalry required by a knight were forgotten by your father when you refused to marry the wretched man. You were locked in your room. Next day I waited in the yard as usual and was told that you would no longer be permitted to ride. I was distraught at this, and it was then that I knew I loved you. Oh, I knew nothing could ever come of this, you being a lady, but I resolved to be near to you always as a devoted servant of some sort.

'After a week of your defiance, your father said that you should be beaten into obedience. Two lashes would be enough, he said, and he instructed one of the womenfolk to carry this out forthwith. Your screaming was heard all round the yards, everyone was shocked, and I was very, very angry. My father was aware of my frustration and anger, and cautioned me again and again to guard myself.' Matthew was quiet for a moment, and Marion, walking beside him, said nothing, knowing somehow he was reluctant to go on.

Matthew sighed resignedly and hesitated before saying, 'Yes, I was more than angry. One of my jobs was to release the horses into the field early every morning. For days when your father came for his horse he was sullen and bad-tempered with everyone and everything. On the morning after your beating he came across to the stables, quite happy as if nothing untoward had happened. He seemed confident, and I believed from his improved mood that you had been forced to surrender to his wishes. It was then that

I …' Matthew stopped and then dropping his voice said, '… it was then that I took up a stave and hit him across the back of the head. He fell motionless in the narrow doorway. Never made a sound. Instead of releasing the horses one at a time so that they didn't jostle at the doorway, I quickly lifted the bar to each stall, one after the other. Of course the horses knew the routine and, anxious to get out, they milled around the doorway where your father lay. When they were all finally out I looked down at your father's mangled body. I could see at once that he was dead. I had allowed that to happen. I was half glad and at the same time mortified by what I had done. Without thinking, I left the bloodied stave leaning on the wall and ran away into the woods. The stave gave me away, of course. Everyone must have guessed it was I who had cracked his head open, and search parties were sent out to look for me, but I was never caught. It is possible that the villagers didn't look too hard. I like to think that.

'It was fine outdoors in the summer months, plenty of berries and corn in the fields. At nightfall I was able to help myself to milk from the animals, sheep and goats mainly, and there was water from the river. Often I saw someone I knew in the distance, the shepherd, people working in the fields, the priest visiting, probably consoling someone after a death, and once the midwife, so in a way I was aware of the local news.

Once the winter months set in I had a terrible time, of course. There was a keen, remorseless wind from the north, day after day, from which I never seemed to escape, and I was in my summer tunic. There was little food about; how I longed for my mother's hot broth. The animals had been taken into the barns. This happened only when it was thought the winters were going to be harsh, so I knew I was probably in for a hard time. I ventured into the stables once or twice for warmth, lying close to the horses after I had eaten an apple or two from the store in the roof space. I was too scared to stay long, and fled as soon as daylight came. I even took a coarse blanket thrown over one horse to keep it warm, and wrapped it around myself, but it gave little comfort.'

Marion held her hand up to stop him. 'If, as you believed, the people knew you were still around, why didn't they leave some food out for you? I mean your parents must have been beside themselves with worry.'

'They were poor, very poor. Everyone was poor, and food was always scarce, more so in the winter months. At the time I thought if I showed myself to them, my father would have killed me with his bare hands.'

'Why? Surely he wouldn't have? No matter what, parents usually stand by their children.'

'He would have lost face with the neighbours and, worse still, lose his employment. How he kept it I don't know after what I did, but I sometimes saw him around the stables. How I longed to call to him. Without his work he would be unable to stop his family from starving. I missed them dreadfully, I was so lonely.

'Oh, Marion, you cannot imagine how the cold can make you ache. Every night there was a frost, lovely to look at, but so penetratingly cold. Few people ventured out and to see smoke rising from the cottagers' chimneys was a form of torture in itself, and I longed to be close to my father's hearth. The day the snow finally came I curled up to sleep under a hedge. Sleep was my only escape from misery.

That was when I found myself before the Senate. I stood before them, and heard their sharp words flying across the room, like excited wasps around an abandoned jam sandwich. Their voices criss-crossed each other as they pointed at me and called out,

'Never happened before.'

'Unfair after all our efforts on your behalf.'

'What were you thinking of?'

'Why you ever came here I'll never understand.'

'Spoiled, spoiled all our plans for you.'

I was convinced I was to be sent to Hell. Hellfire and damnation was always being quoted in the village church for wrong-doers, even for the mildest of misdemeanours. Then Peter came up with his ideas and - well I've already mentioned that.'

Matthew slowly shook his head and smiled at Marion as he said, 'Just a sad little youth really, out of my depth.' He straightened his shoulders and stepped out a little more briskly so that Marion had to do a little run to keep up with him.

'What happened to Magdalena?' she whispered breathlessly when their steps matched again.

'I overheard a charcoal burner worker in the woods tell another that your mother died quite soon after your father, from a weak heart – unable to take the horror of her husband's death. My conscience told me I had caused another death. Magdalena, the fellow said, had entered holy orders to become a nun, so I knew you were safe for life and not the wife of some dreadful reprobate.' He glanced at Marion, gauging her reaction. 'So now you know, I am a murderer.'

Marion could see Matthew was more than upset, saddened by the telling of his past, and to be honest, she almost believed him. She said, giving him a little nudge with her elbow, 'Come on, cheer up. It's only a story to entertain me.'

Slowly he shook his head.

'If only. It seems I can never make amends for that dreadful deed.' By now he had quite a bouquet of wild flowers and with a bow he presented them to her. 'For you, my lady, just as I gave them to you all those years ago.'

With the delight and respect that the occasion demanded, she bobbed a curtsy.

'Thank you, my liege. I shall treasure them for as long as possible.' By this time they were back at her aunt's house. After a glass or two of wine during lunch, Matthew was looking less depressed.

It was Matthew's idea that they should travel together to London. 'I can help you with your bits and pieces and we will be company for each other.'

Marion didn't need to think twice about this proposal. It was after all a very long journey back to London. 'I'd like that,' she replied 'and there'll be plenty of time for you to tell me more of your story.'

Matthew grinned. 'Good idea, perhaps this time I can get you round to believing me.'

'I doubt that,' she retorted, 'but truth to tell, so far it has all been very fascinating.' Together they went to tell Aunt Amy of their plan to travel together and she thought it a good idea.

'Well, it would have been great if you had stayed for a day or two Marion, but as you say, Alex is home tomorrow, and Matthew will be a great help on the train. I'll pack you something to eat on the journey shall I?'

Putting her arms around her aunt, Marion said, 'That will be just great, thank you. I have enjoyed the weekend so much. I'll keep in touch. I'll phone to let you know I'm home safe. All right?'

Matthew took her good elbow and asked, 'Who is Alex?'

Before she could answer a shrill child's voice called, 'Auntie! Auntie Marion, can you push me on the swing for a little while?'

Half laughing, she turned to Matthew and said, 'Sorry, would you excuse me for a moment? I'll see you later.'

He watched as Marion crossed the lawn to the child, the sun catching the rippling waves of her fair hair swaying around her shoulders. As she walked he heard her call out to the child. 'I'll do my best sweetheart, but with only one hand you'll have to be patient.' Watching, Matthew felt his undying love for her in his heart.

Four

Fortunately, on the train they had a first-class compartment to themselves and, seeing her questioning look, Matthew said, 'I hope you don't mind, but I took the liberty of upgrading your ticket.'

Marion's eyes widened and she gave him a smile. 'Great, thanks. It's a long time since I travelled first class.'

He grinned back at her, seeing her hug herself. 'My pleasure,' he answered, seeing her delight. 'Thought we would probably have the place to ourselves the best part of the way, all the way, if we're lucky, seeing as it's Sunday. Give us a chance to talk.'

Marion kicked off her shoes, more from habit than anything else, rubbed her feet with her free hand and settled herself into a corner seat. He's right, she thought, it will be a long journey. Each time they had been together over the weekend, there had always been someone nearby. This time she was really alone with him. She couldn't explain why she felt so anxious. She picked nervously at her skirt, then speaking rapidly as if to cover her unease, she said, 'I always think a train journey gives a person time to relax. You know just looking out of the window, catching up on reading, or better still a chat if someone is with you. Why, you could doze off for a catnap if the fancy takes you, there's little else to do. It's as if you're a prisoner doing time, but far more pleasant, of course.

And then there's arriving, though these days trains seem to be constantly delayed. Working on the line mostly is the general excuse. There is something quite satisfactory in arriving wherever one sets out for, don't you think, especially going home, no matter where you've been or how marvellous a time one's had?' I'm gabbling, she thought, whatever must he be thinking?

Matthew sensed she was nervous and wasn't sure how to reassure her. After putting their cases in the rack, he took off his tie and jacket, saying as he did so, 'You're right, this is a particularly long journey from Scotland, so we might as well be comfortable.' He sat down opposite her. Absent-mindedly, he pulled out a newspaper from his briefcase, but before he had even read the headlines, Marion stopped him, and almost snatched it from him.

'Hey, none of that. Come on, you promised to tell me more of your stories.' Matthew gave a slow smile, one that gently turned Marion's heart over and she was bewildered by her response.

'Do you actually know the Terms of Agreement I'm talking about?' he asked.

The warmth of his smile relaxed her. 'Of course I do. What do you think I am, a Philistine?' She smiled back at him as she began to quote, 'Thou shalt not ...'

'Okay, okay. So which one do you want to hear about first? I can offer ...'

'How about,' she paused for a moment, 'how about Thou shalt not bear false witness? Got something on that?'

Crossing his knees, Matthew leaned back in his seat and tapped his chin thoughtfully.

'Oh yes. Now then, miss, I'll tell you again. This really happened, somewhere around the early eighteenth century. I do believe this event will keep you interested for a while.'

Marion hugged herself. 'Oh good, I love stories from the past. Go on then, get started.'

Matthew gave a small laugh and began.

'In the year 1729 I was a young man of twenty-three. My family, mother, father and five sisters were very poor. My favourite sister, Sarah, was like a second mother to me until she went as a maidservant to a large house in London. We lived in Cripplegate, a crowded smelly environment, and all the young people did their best to leave by one means or another, including myself. At the time I know my parents were proud of me, their only son, leaving home and seeking work. I walked into the countryside, mile after mile, doing odd jobs as I went.

'For a short time I was a labourer, digging ditches, cutting hedges and such like, but I couldn't get used to the open fields or the expanse of space. All the sounds were unfamiliar, especially at night, foxes with their strange bark, especially mating times, owls, scuffling of creatures in the walls just like at home, but others unknown to me. And then there were the smells, so … shall we say, pungent. I never got used to them, even though I had to sleep on hay in the cowshed, being a single lad. It wasn't long, just a few weeks, before I returned to London, utterly disenchanted with the countryside.

'Like all the youths of the time there was little chance of bettering oneself if one was unable to read or write or basic accounting in London. After a while, along with some friends, I found myself a member of a gang. Nothing notorious, just lads mooching about and making a living of sorts. Well, to be truthful, making a living somewhat dishonestly.'

'Just like some of today's youth then.'

'I wouldn't …' Matthew glanced at Marion's face and saw that she was about to interrupt. 'You're going to say something like, why did I give up? Why didn't I earn an honest living, live by the good book, as my father called it? I was twenty-three and, to be honest, had given up hope of finding a girl or love. I was often hungry and, I'll admit it, I was bored and longed for excitement.

'The gang worked together, one distracting our chosen victim while another picked his, sometimes her, pockets, or, with luck, a well filled purse. Books, lace edged handkerchiefs, the odd brooch or bracelet were easily lifted. We sometimes waylaid and robbed the wealthy. We also robbed whoever chanced their luck down alleyways after dark and made themselves an easy target. Of course, we didn't use any physical violence. The size of the gang was enough to frighten anyone into handing over their belongings. On rare and desperate occasions we broke into one of the larger houses. When the owner was absent, we were tipped off by an ex-member of staff – usually one who had been dismissed for a minor demeanour. We helped ourselves to the silver plate and jewellery. Everything had some value, and we often felt cheated by the fence, but he could well have turned us in to the constables if we complained. Money was the best prize, a gold sovereign would keep us all in beer for days. How we celebrated! Landlords asked no questions, glad of any coinage themselves. Drinking in ale houses and er ... well, meeting up with, shall I say, ladies who gave their favours willingly for a gin or two.' He smiled at Marion, before saying, 'You were never one of them, my dear.'

'I should think not,' was her indignant reply. 'Whatever would Aunt Amy say?' Looking at him thoughtfully she went on, 'You know, you had already broken one of the rules. I mean, by stealing. Didn't it occur to you that your case was already lost?'

'To be honest, I didn't think it counted. But you're right, I had already spoiled my chances in that life, but my memory hadn't been woken at that time. Thinking about it, I believe the Senate overlooked my thieving, knowing that there would be a much more significant test they had set up for me later in that life. I also believe that if I passed that test, then they would use thieving as an excuse to haul me back.' He sighed, 'I tell you, Marion I'm sure they intended me to fail forever, but not this time. My life this time, now, has been almost exemplary.'

He smiled at her as he said, 'It was around that time of easy thieving that I first saw you in this particular life. Selling flowers you were. "Straight from the countryside. Flowers, flowers," you were calling. As I passed by you offered me a nosegay, which, as I had a half-penny at the time, I bought from you. Then you smiled, a warm full smile, as you thanked me. I asked your name and you told me it was Mollie. The M again. After that I saw you quite often in the streets, calling out something like, "Country flowers for milady."

'Always though, after that first time, you gave me a flower for free, and I paid you with a kiss on the cheek, not that you were bold, but your returning kiss gave me hope. I'd meet you, I mean her, some evenings and we would walk and talk. I drew our MM emblem in the dust on a shop window one evening. Mollie was so impressed, thinking I knew my letters, but truth to tell that was all I could muster. I taught her how to write her own initial, and she really thought she was smarter than the rest of the flower girls. It was a happy time for both of us. I knew though, that her work was very tiring and there were days when she didn't earn a penny. She told me she got up with the sun and gathered the flowers, breakfasted on bread spread with honey and a drink of milk. She then walked four miles into London. In the winter months she sat with her mother and spun sheep's wool they found entangled in the hedges. It was something the farmer allowed them to take, and they made a little money from their efforts.

'In a short while there was a sort of understanding between us. We didn't make any firm plans to marry, but that was always my intention. We thought it best to live in the country where I knew you, or Mollie as you were then, would be happiest. I know my sisters, except one, opted to live near mother. When the babies came along mother was always there, and looked after the youngsters when the girls went back to work. I wanted that sort of loving support for you too, although I'm sure my mother would have looked after you just the same had we decided to stay in Cripplegate. You told me of a cottage attached to a farm and we could have it, provided I worked on the farm.'

Marion frowned, as she said, 'But you left the countryside. You said you didn't like the noise and smells.'

'It was different now I had found you, so I was sure everything would be more bearable. What was more important was that a job had been promised. It appears that you were very popular amongst the locals, and known to be an honest girl so everyone trusted your judgement. I suppose they meant you would choose a sensible husband.' Matthew paused for a few moments before saying, 'I don't think I was that sensible, but I loved you wholeheartedly.' Matthew chuckled 'I took you to meet my mother and she loved you at once. She told me afterwards she was sure that you would put an end to my wicked ways.'

Marion raised her eyebrows, 'Like what?'

'You know, thieving mostly.'

'Right.'

'I had found you, but then ...' Matthew hesitated then picked up his story again, 'One or two of the gang members sometimes got caught. We all said it was their own fault, careless, gave themselves away. Talking too much and too loudly when drunk, was their downfall and there was always someone willing to turn King's evidence for a shilling or two. Not many did that though, tell of what they knew, because once they were found out by any villain, their death was practically assured.

'For those who found themselves before the magistrates there were a variety of punishments, depending on which judge was presiding. Mostly my friends were fined, usually around three shillings. Well, between us that was fairly easy to find. We just sought out an unsuspecting victim when it got dark, and paid the fine the next morning. Others got hard labour working on ships, known then as hulks, on the Thames. Before hulks became prisons, the rigging, masts, all things that aided sailing were removed. The sentence of hard labour could be months long. Prisoners were taken from the river bank to the ship, so we were able to snatch our friends from the working party when they returned at nightfall. We made sure they vanished, gave them enough food and a few coins to leave London.

'Another time, when one of the lads was put in the pillory we all went along to laugh, and throw rotting vegetables at him, telling him if he was hungry to catch them in his mouth. That was Timothy, The Mouse we called him. He was quiet in his speech and so quiet in his thieving ways. We were not so pleased to see one of our members thoroughly whipped. His back took ages to heal, and, to be honest, we gave up our bad ways for a whole summer for fear of a sound whipping ourselves. Thieving was easier in the dark nights of winter anyway.'

Matthew paused for a moment, ran his fingers across his chin a couple of times before going on. 'One day Sarah came home covered in ugly bruises about her face, her bosom and arms. It was quite common in those days for men to beat their women, although they could be imprisoned if a complaint was lodged with the magistrates. Most women didn't complain. They needed to feed their children and if their man was imprisoned they could well starve. Without someone providing even the meanest food, women could find themselves in the workhouse. Workhouses were founded to provide for the poor but dreaded by everyone. There were deliberately harsh measures to deter those desperate for food and shelter. This was doled out in return for long tedious hours of work from the inmates. Not only that, they had to wear workhouse clothing which stigmatised them immediately, almost as if their failures were of their own making. Even worse, mothers would often be separated from their children. So you can imagine their dilemma. In any case, many were probably too scared of the fellow and feared what might happen on his release.

The whole family were horrified to see Sarah's bruises and mother wanted her to stay home, but Sarah, like all of us, needed the work for the little money it provided and a roof over her head.

'It seems, although only fifteen, she had become involved with Richard Payne, who was a villain of the highest order. A bullying leader of a rival gang, who showed no mercy to the souls he battered and robbed. In fact he had a pistol with which to threaten folk and I, along with others, was convinced he had killed more than one unlucky person. My gang thought it best to keep as far away from him as possible. It was rumoured that he had married bigamously. How true it is I don't know, but I heard that one day his legitimate wife turned up at his lodgings where he had taken his second bride. As you can imagine there was a right set-to and no one knows how but the first wife ended up dead. There was no conclusive evidence as to how she died. It was said she fell and struck her head. Payne swore on oath that is what had happened, as did his second wife. She, poor soul, was too awed at the time to say otherwise, I suspect.' Matthew paused and looked out of the window, gently rocking to and fro.

Marion leaned forward in her seat. 'You don't have to, you know. Go on telling me these stories. I see that at times they seem to, I don't know, upset you.'

He turned to face her and took her hand. Marion was thrilled by his touch but gently drew her hand away.

'That's part of the deal, don't you see?' he said. 'I remember all the awful things I've done in the past. This time,' he looked deeply into her eyes, 'this time, in this life now, with you, I think I'm going to make it. As far as I know I have obeyed all the rules, even as a child.'

'I don't see how,' she retorted. 'Already you've told me a lot of … of, I won't say lies, but certainly a great deal of make-believe.'

'We shall see. Shall I go on or would you rather …?'

Marion nodded, 'Yes please. You've got to where Sarah came home with bruises.'

'A few weeks later she came home to tell us that she had married Payne. Horrified, I asked her how this had come about, as I was sure that he already had a wife somewhere. Sarah told me that, as she now had a child in her belly, she had begged him to marry her. It seems he made false marriage promises to her by getting a bogus preacher to marry them swiftly.

'It was a few weeks later when I was supping ale in a tavern, I found out that the preacher was one of his gang dressed up to appease Sarah's wishes for marriage. There was much laughter when the fellow told his companions of this bragging that he was "A man of God". Needless to say, I was more than angry. I longed to batter the brute, but could do nothing about it, fearing for my own life. To be honest, I didn't like the way things were going and, whenever I could, I'd go round to their lodgings and keep an eye on Sarah, and to see what else the devil was up to.

'Anyway, one day, like the first wife, the second one turned up. Seems she was a large outspoken woman. I wasn't there that time so didn't see her. How I wish I had been. As Sarah knew nothing of this woman's existence, she told me that at first the woman started shouting and swearing at her, demanding that she leave her husband alone, calling her a whore. Sarah told me she was horrified, but the woman then attacked her. There was much beating and screaming from both women until, finally, the brute held his second wife down on the floor, pinning her two arms with one hand and covering her mouth with the other.' Matthew paused and chewed on his lower lip for a moment before saying, 'Marion, what that devil did next was beyond any reasoning.' Matthew stopped and Marion, watching him, saw him swallow nervously before continuing.

'He ... he ordered Sarah to pick up a knife from the table, a silver one, Sarah told me later, one he'd stolen from a country house a few days earlier, and told her to kill the bitch, all the while shouting at her that she'd be next if she didn't hurry. She was so afraid and, in order to save her child and herself, she picked up the knife and ... and did as he bid.'

Marion was shocked at the brutality of the tale. Matthew was saddened by his memory. Both sat quietly for a few moments the only sound being the monotonous clattering of the carriage's wheels over the rails below.

Marion longed to put her arms around him to give some measure of comfort, but with only one arm this wasn't possible or prudent. Instead she said to him softly, 'Oh, Matthew how awful for you.'

She told herself not to be so silly, listening to his tales and allowing herself the emotions they evoked in her. She thought, soon I'll believe them if I'm not careful. Taking a deep breath she asked, 'So what happened in the end?'

'In the end, Payne was apprehended. Seems the woman's children, none of them Payne's, raised the alarm as she had never left them before. The evidence pointed to him even though he denied it again and again in court. On the day of his trial I sat with Sarah, trying to give her some comfort as she was still afraid of him despite his being heavily guarded in the dock. Also, the courts were vile, even though they were sprinkled with herbs and flowers to mask the dreadful smell of the unwashed prisoners and others. I was afraid Sarah might faint and draw attention to herself.

'Interestingly, it was thought that the scattering of herbs would also prevent the spread of disease in those days; there were always so many people crammed in the courts to hear what was going on, so epidemics of one sort or another were pretty frequent. The public seemed to thrive on verdicts and were gleeful when really harsh punishments were handed down, sometimes quite unfairly I thought. Most cases took only a few minutes for the judge to decide.

'When questioned, Payne denied everything and pointing his shaking finger towards Sarah, told the judge it was she who had stabbed his beloved wife. The whole court fell silent and turned to look at Sarah when he said this. He was showing his true colours at last, accusing an innocent woman, as they thought, to save his skin. I was sitting close beside Sarah and she turned white and began to shake.

'Then pandemonium broke out. The common people knew him for what he was, a bullying, lying cheat, and they jeered and shouted their disgust. The judge had to bang his gavel three or four times, and threatened to clear the court before order was restored. The prosecutor asked Sarah to stand. She was no more than five feet four and far gone in her pregnancy. The counsel turned to the jury and I'll never forget what he asked of them. "Does this woman look capable of stabbing Mrs Payne? Mrs Payne of some larger dimensions than this weak woman you see before you now?" The jury could see his point. When Sarah sat down again next to me she was still shaking and weeping. I whispered to her to slip away quietly, to make her way home and to stay out of sight.

'I then motioned to the prosecutor, and asked if I could give evidence. He agreed, but as I took the stand Payne looked me straight in the eye, and drew his forefinger across his throat, his way of warning me that I would be sorry. To be honest I felt a chill as he did that, but then I didn't care. I knew what I was going to say. I had seen him thrash people almost to death and I wanted to protect Sarah. I stared back at him and gave him the Archer's salute. The crowds loved that; gave a loud cheer.'

Marion interrupted. 'Hold on. Archer's salute?' There was a look of puzzlement on her face.

Matthew gave a discreet cough. 'I would show you but ...' he hesitated. 'You know, the two finger gesture.'

'How come Archer's salute? I've not heard it called that before.'

'When archers were victorious they would raise the fingers they used to pull back the bow to shoot their arrows. Sad to say, when they were captured by their enemy, the first thing their captors did to them was to the remove those two important fingers, making sure they could never use their weapons or cock a snook at their foes again.'

'Ah! Yes, I've heard something like that before.'

'Shall I stop or ...'

'Don't you dare!'

'Honestly, Payne seemed to crumple before my eyes. He knew he was done for. I laid my hand on the Bible, and swore I was telling the truth.' Matthew sighed. 'I told them that I had, in fact, seen Payne pick up the silver knife and plunge it into his wife's chest. As I looked at Payne, I saw his shoulders drop and his head dropped forward as he closed his eyes. He said something like, "I'm done for now," and for a brief, very brief, second I felt a little sorry for him. We both knew he was going to hang.'

Marion put her hands together in her lap and looked down at them before saying, 'So you did in fact bear false witness?'

Matthew's eyes flashed as he fiercely replied, 'At best Sarah would have been deported, probably to America, on the birth of her child, who would have been taken away from her. At worst she could have hanged. What choice did I have?' They both sat quietly for a while lost in their own thoughts until Marion broke the silence by scrabbling about with her good hand in her holdall.

'Come on Matthew, let's have something to eat,' she said. 'There's some smoked salmon sandwiches in here, or perhaps you'd prefer the ham?'

They ate some of the food, and each had a carton of orange juice. As Marion struggled to get the straw into the hole he took it from her and neatly punctured the carton. Afterwards, Marion tried to repack the bag, but Matthew took over from her.

'I'll do that. No need to struggle.'

When all was safely away, and they were both relaxed, Marion said, 'What happened afterwards, Matthew? Did Payne hang? That would surely trouble you all your life.'

'Yes, the poor fellow did hang.'

'Well, you had little choice that time, I must agree.'

'You know, each time I fail to keep the laws, the Senate arrange for me to return to them, quite quickly. No need to stay on earth any longer, they reckoned. I knew at once, my life would be ended as soon as I put my hand on that Bible. Naturally I was fearful and, of course, I never got my soul mate.' Then softly he added, 'Not until now.'

'How? I mean, how did they get you back?' she asked.

'Thankfully, they, the Senate, nearly always make my death quick and sometimes as pain free as possible.'

'How? How after …?'

'After breaking the false witness crime? I went to watch Payne hang on a very cold, wet and blustery day and waited about for hours. Sounds macabre, doesn't it? I wanted to put Sarah's mind at rest now her babe had been born. Until that moment she really thought he might escape and come after all of us.

'Believe it or not, the next day I caught a chill and was delirious for nearly a week. My sisters and mother took turns to bathe my face, trying to feed me gruel or soup and hoping I would recover. Despite their efforts I died of pneumonia a few days later. See, as easy as that.'

'And so you went back to the Senate?'

'Yes indeed. Some, of course, jeered and told me that I wouldn't ever succeed. Others were a bit more sympathetic, realising that the task was indeed difficult. Peter put his arm around my shoulder and said I was to try again. He said that to me each time I returned. I believe he was the only one who really thought I might succeed.'

The train pulled into a station and they both stood up, glad to stretch their legs and open the window for some fresh air. They watched as luggage was deposited on to the platform, followed by weary travellers, and new passengers came aboard. They were quietly glad that no one joined them in their compartment for their onward journey.

Five

Once the train was on the move again, Matthew said, 'You know Marion, I believe the Senate never intend for me to win you. We have known each other in each of my lives, sometimes just a week or two, sometimes longer. In others, I only had a fleeting moment of your presence. There's something else too. They, the Senate, seem to deliberately set up situations where I have to do the wrong thing for the good of someone else.'

'Oh, so there's more?'

''Fraid so. For instance ...' Marion waited as Matthew was thoughtful for a few moments.

'I'm not sure that I've made it clear that you, Marion, are the same girl in every event I tell you about. You are always Magdelana to me, but your name changes each time and always begins with an M. Is that clear? I mean it's a bit difficult to explain.'

'Yes, Matthew, I understand, but ...'

'I know. I know you think it's all in my imagination.' He shrugged his shoulders. 'Oh, well, I'd better get on with the next life story hadn't I?'

Marion nodded.

'Do you know the silly little rhyme that goes like this: "The lightning flashed, the thunder rolled, and all the earth was quaking, The little pig curled up his tail and ran to save his bacon"?'

Marion laughed. 'No, I've never heard that before, but it's quite enchanting.'

'My mother used to tell it to me when I was a boy. She told me that when she was a girl at school every one of her friends had an autograph book. The one I've just quoted was an entry in her book. Another one went something like this, "Your future lies before you like a field of virgin snow, be careful how you tread for every step will show".'

'Very cautionary and how very true.'

'Anyway, on this occasion the first saying kept going through my head over and over again. It was in nineteen sixty-two when I was with Tony, a friend from infant school, his wife Teresa and his cousin Stella. Tony and I went through school and university together. His parents were much wealthier than mine, but we understood each other, and had a great deal of fun. When we graduated, my parents rewarded me with a secondhand motorcycle. I was thrilled to bits with it, and, with Tony perched behind me, we explored the seaside towns in the south every weekend.

'Tony's parents gave him, amongst other gifts, a Caribbean holiday, and he invited me along. We made plans to try our hand at sailing and hired a small yacht. Sailing in the gentle breezes of the Caribbean was heaven. Have you ever been there?' he asked.

Marion shook her head.

'You must go one day. I promise you, you will be amazed. Some islands, like Bermuda or Jamaica, have the most fabulous beaches, fringed with palm trees and the clearest of warm, blue water.

'There was a lifting of my heart when I saw you in the hotel foyer. At that moment I just knew you were Magdalena. It was obvious you were from England, even if I hadn't read the labels on your luggage. You were so pale, and I understood later that you had been unwell. This holiday was to get you fit again. I was surprised that your parents were with you, but hey, that was fine by me.

'I introduced myself and my friends to you, and your parents that first evening. You were so shy, or perhaps the illness had made you a little reticent, but you smiled as you murmured your "hellos" to everyone. Your parents introduced you as Marcia. You were a quiet, gentle girl and it was obvious you were wary of meeting new people and making friends. I knew I would have to be very careful if I was to win you. I asked if you played tennis, and when you nodded I suggested we had a game early the next morning. You looked to your parents who smiled and nodded approval. It was as if you were asking their permission, but I realised you were all a bit anxious of taxing your strength. They needn't have worried, you had so much energy. You beat me fair and square in our match and, my goodness were you smug? Still, I suppose you had every right to be. I could see that you were exhausted at the end, though. The next day we had arranged to go swimming in the early morning then have breakfast together. I remember doodling on a paper napkin and, without being conscious of it, drew the MM sign again. Proof, I thought, that Marcia was the one.

'Your parents had suggested the four of us meet up with them for dinner that evening. They looked at you and you looked so happy. I was sure that you had engineered this. I hoped that after the evening it might signal to everyone that we were about to be a couple. I was so looking forward to knowing you better and winning you over. I thought to myself, I've been so conscientious throughout this life, surely this time I'll be with you forever.' Sighing Matthew said, 'But it was not to be.

'As I said, arrangements had been made to go sailing. We had anchored about two miles off-shore and had been sunbathing on deck. Me and Tony were in shorts and baseball caps, and the girls in skimpy bikinis, just coming into fashion. The wind-up gramophone was on, and we all sang the popular songs being played at the top of our voices. We had the ocean to ourselves so we really let ourselves go. Songs like "Twist and Shout" and of course, "Itsy, Bitsy, Yellow, Polka-dot Bikini" and teased anyone who went off-key. Tony had a gift of making up his own words, naughty ones to amuse us, and we laughed at his cleverness. Teresa pretended to scold him but he carried on just the same and ended up singing on his own, "They're Coming to Take me Away. Ha, ha." Stella had muttered, "The sooner the better," and set us off laughing again.'

'I know those songs well,' said Marion. She began to sing, "It was an itsy, bitsy, teenie, weenie, yellow polka-dot bikini that she wore for the first time today".'

He joined in and together they sang, 'An itsy, bitsy, teenie, weenie, yellow polka-dot bikini, so in the locker she wanted to stay.' Together they clicked their fingers as they sang: 'Two, three, four, stick around we'll tell you more.' They fell back against their seats, laughing and out of breath.

'People will think we're mad,' spluttered Marion.

'If anyone heard us, which I doubt, I bet they'd join in,' he replied.

Once she had stopped giggling, she told him to go on with the story.

'Right,' he said, 'so, we were having our lunch on the deck. The girls had made some sandwiches along with slices of quiche and fruit and I opened a couple of bottles of wine. It was quite a feast, all very relaxed, and we were enjoying ourselves no end. We had waved casually to the crew of a small fishing vessel that had suddenly appeared and had stopped nearby, and the six men grinned and waved back.

'We watched as they threw their nets over the side, and clapped when they hauled them back into their vessel full of wriggling silver fish. It was obvious they were showing off, bowing to us and laughing, even throwing some fish to us but they were just too far away and unable to reach us. Everything seemed perfect.

'After lunch the girls cleared up and settled down to thumb through their pile of magazines. Tony and I pulled our caps down over our eyes, and dozed and the fishermen got on with their business. We were surprised when after an hour or so, they drew alongside and before we knew what was happening, they had boarded the yacht. We'd all heard the thump of the grappling hook they threw. I thought the yacht had hit something in the water; you know, a log or a crate something similar that had drifted out from shore. As they jumped onto the deck, the yacht rocked violently for a few seconds, and then we realised their intention. Silly, amateur sailors we were. They had caught us unaware. Needless to say the girls were terrified. Gone were the men's friendly smiles, which were replaced with grim, menacing determination. We had nothing to defend ourselves with. We knew, or rather thought, that we had no need for any weapons as we believed we were in safe waters. We were helpless. None of us ever dreamt that such a thing could happen. The pirates were unbelievably ruthless. They pushed and shoved then forced us, wielding machetes, into the inflatable life raft. We begged and begged, but they did not allow us time to collect anything that might have been of use. We were just callously cast adrift.

We drifted without a compass for two days and our few emergency supplies in the life raft, two packets of biscuits from the local store, had gone.'

'Biscuits!' Marion was astounded. 'Who on earth decided biscuits were emergency rations?' she queried.

Half laughing, Matthew replied, 'Tony had a weakness for biscuits. He just chucked them into the raft when we boarded earlier. I think they were supposed to be hidden from Teresa. She said too many sweet goodies would make him fat; he did have a sweet tooth.'

Marion watched Matthew smile to himself as he remembered,

before he went on.

'On the second day we thought we saw a smidgen of a coast-line. Tony couldn't remember if the horizon was three or five miles away, but he told us that if the currents were favourable, we could be on land by nightfall. How our spirits lifted at that moment. We hugged each other, telling each other to cross our fingers, and that we would be safe in a matter of hours.

'The harshest enemy was the blazing sun, all of us were so badly dehydrated and burned. Honestly, you could feel your skin splitting. At night it was the bone-chilling cold that was our foe.' There was a short pause and Matthew bit his top lip before continuing.

'As I said, we were all elated on the second day. Suddenly it rained. Salvation, we thought, and we were overjoyed. At first the needle-like feel of the rain on our badly cracked skins was a relief. We held our heads skywards with open mouths to catch the rain to quench our thirst, but then it turned into a relentless, cruel infliction. It stung our open wounds. It was as if we were being whipped and we curled ourselves up, trying to escape the pain. The rain began to make puddles in the bottom of the raft and we realised that we had to bail the water out with our hands. This was an impossible task. We were so exhausted.'

Marion, carried away with the story, gasped, 'That must have been absolutely dreadful. I'm afraid I'd never be brave enough to endure anything like that.'

Almost tenderly Matthew looked at her, saying, 'Thank goodness you didn't have to. But Marion, that was not the worst we had to suffer. By late afternoon there were other elements as well as the sea that terrified us. First it was the wind. As it increased and howled around us we had hoped it would blow us towards the land we had seen earlier, but we couldn't see now. The waves were whipped to a frightening height and we were lifted up to a heart stopping crest, then plunged into a deep trough. To add to our anguish, the sky darkened quickly with black, rolling clouds lit up by continuous vivid, blue lightning, all followed by unbelievably terrifying cracks of thunder. I can't begin to tell you of the terror we all felt. I no longer considered myself a man, I was a quivering coward. The girls were relying on us men to save them, and we were as helpless as babies ourselves. We all prayed for our lives over and over again.

'Night time came and still the storm had not abated in its

ferocity. Tony, holding on to the sides of the boat, was gripping unconscious Teresa, his beloved wife, who had slipped to the bottom of the boat between his legs, which he twisted securely around her body. He heard me begging Stella to answer me, and when I had no answer – here's the bit where I break another of the conditions – I screamed obscenities to a God I knew wasn't listening to our prayers. Words you have probably never heard of, words I'm too ashamed to recall.

'Tony must have known that we were doomed, that there was no hope of safety and certainly no hope of rescue. He began his own quiet prayer. I could barely hear him, as he murmured it over and over again until he too sank into merciful unconsciousness. Tony had been repeating a simple rhyme that his mother had taught him. "Now I lay me down to sleep, I pray the Lord, My soul to keep."

'It was to be another hour before I too succumbed. Death was inevitable. Strange that, don't you think? I cursed God over and over again and Tony asked for peace.' Matthew was quiet, 'My fault, of course, calling on God in vain, not to mention cursing him.'

Marion longed to put out her hand to comfort him, but instead she said, 'You get so involved with what you tell me. Don't make it so hard on yourself.'

Matthew gave a fleeting grimace as he answered, 'But don't you see? If I hadn't started calling on God in vain, we just might have reached that land and been saved.'

'Against those odds! It was very unlikely. What's more, I don't think you called in vain. As you said, your prayer just wasn't heard. I'll say it again, don't be so hard on yourself.'

'Could you not just for once believe me? Just a little glimmer of remembrance would help.'

Marion smiled, 'Nothing Matthew, I remember nothing at all, and I'm sticking to my belief that you're telling me stories, very clever ones at that, I'll admit.' As an afterthought she added, 'I suppose the Senate were smirking again?'

'One or two, but on the whole I think they saw I was at least trying. Peter reminded me that my destiny was to be with you.' Matthew gave a weak smile and said, "Nearly, but not quite there yet". This time? Who knows? But I'll tell you one thing, I'm pretty certain I'm close to winning.'

Six

Marion winced as she adjusted her sling, 'Could you fish in my bag for the paracetamols and the bottle of water?' she asked. 'I think it's time I took something to ease this nagging pain.'

Matthew dug deep into her bag, unscrewed the cap off the water bottle and tipped two tablets into her hand. Marion took the tablets, gave her thanks and said, 'You know, your stories are so plausible that I can almost believe them.' She laughed when she saw the look of surprise and hope on his face. 'I said almost.' She pulled a paperback out of her bag and settled to read, saying, 'You could nod off now if you like.'

'Me? Nod off? I'd rather just keep looking at you,' he replied. Marion took no notice of this compliment, so he picked up the newspaper and together they sat reading, the silence only disturbed by the rustle of the paper.

After ten minutes or so Marion, unable to turn the pages without difficulty, said, 'You know, Matthew, the Terms of Agreement you have broken so far in your stories are not so dreadful, are they? I mean, have you committed any of the more serious ones?'

'Yes I have, I'm sorry to say.' He sat up straighter and said, 'I could tell you of one in particular if you like. Want to hear more?'

'Why not?' she answered.

Matthew stretched his long legs, folded his paper and settled himself comfortably and began by saying, 'Let me explain about my adultery. My marriage was an arranged affair, made between us during our childhood by our parents. I liked the girl well enough, we had known each other since childhood, of course, but there was never any real passion between us. I knew at the time what I was doing, but as I was gone thirty I just gave up hope of ever finding true love and thought, what does it matter now?'

Marion tutted. 'Adultery, you say. I'm surprised at you. Tell me more, if you please.'

Matthew cleared his throat.

'So, what time is this going to be in?' she asked.

'Around the seventeen nineties I'd say.'

'Right, I do like to establish times and settings. Isn't that the beginning of the Industrial Revolution?' When Matthew agreed with a nod, she wriggled herself into a comfortable position and ordered, 'Carry on, if you please.'

'On this particular occasion, I had stormed into my lodgings in Bloomsbury, London. I threw off my clothes and scratched frantically as I was itching madly from fleas, convinced I'd caught them from the unsavoury lot I'd just been preaching to. Did I mention I was a bishop? I was responsible for a small diocese in Gloucestershire, no more than seven or eight parishes.'

Marion shook her head. 'I did wonder when you said you'd been preaching.'

She giggled when he piously put his hands together and nodded solemnly.

'To go on. I yelled for Bolton, my manservant. Within seconds he crept into the room. Bolton was always quiet when undertaking any task and his ability to see all, hear all, hold his tongue and be discreet when I had visitors, ladies in particular, was something I greatly appreciated.'

Marion raised one eyebrow but said nothing.

Matthew, embarrassed and trying to justify his behaviour, said, 'After all, at that time the Prince Regent, later George the Fourth, spent more time with his lover Mrs Fitzherbert than with his wife. A blind eye was turned by most to his debauched lifestyle, and the huge debts that he ran up gambling at cards and racing, and generally living his life to the full.'

Marion couldn't believe what she was hearing and protested, 'Surely not a man of the cloth? Is that how they behaved in those times?'

Matthew nodded as he replied, 'Well, not all of them of course. Many were honourable and extremely devout, but as in most professions some, including myself, enjoyed what life had to offer. I saw many of the gentry and their ladies follow the Prince's example, being openly indiscreet as far as I could see. Gambling didn't appeal to me. My needs were few. I had a wealthy background, so I never fell into the clutches of moneylenders. Greedy, shifty fellows all of them, some often found themselves in court on a charge of blackmail.

'Mistresses were never acceptable to some wives, of course, but a good enough practice for princes and lords, and, in a few cases, their ladies, so I thought why not me? My wife was miles away, and it was very unlikely that she would ever find out. I had reasoned that because I was away from her and my home, I was entitled to seek comforts wherever I could. We were happy enough, but despite desperate efforts on my part when I was at home, my wife had not produced an heir and this was becoming a serious contention between us.

'I digress. I spent Spring, Summer and most of Autumn in Gloucestershire. As bishop I had many duties, but I er ... left most of the work to the churchwardens of the parishes under my jurisdiction.'

'Matthew,' Marion burst out, 'I can't believe that is how you behaved as a bishop. I mean, surely your duty was to all parishioners?'

'Oh, I did my duty on the Sundays when I was invited to preach and I presided at regular parochial courts.'

'As opposed to law courts do you mean?'

'That's right. The church was obliged, through charitable aid, to assist the poor of each parish by means of a local taxation. Each parish was responsible for their own destitute people. They, known as the Select Vestries, used their power of enforcement to levy a tax known as the Church Rate. I was able to insist on certain expenses from this, but ...' he stopped when Marion tried to protest.

'But,' he continued, 'I was not alone as other members were obviously more corrupt. Paid their taxes and then clawed it back with claims for expenses. I realise now that the poor, indeed, stayed poor.' He could see Marion was perplexed and he smiled at her, 'You're shocked, aren't you? I'm just telling you how it was then.'

'I always thought that the clergy in particular endeavoured to do the right thing.'

'Sorry to disappoint you, but well, read the newspapers, nothing much has changed, has it? It seems to me that in all walks of life corruption appears occasionally.'

Marion was thoughtful for a moment or two before asking, 'So what were the duties you neglected and left to your wardens?'

Matthew laughed, 'All the boring stuff, like keeping the accounts; the income and expenditure needed to keep their own church in good repair, for instance. Another of their duties was to present to the church courts twice yearly, any misdemeanours of the parishioners, in particular any impiety or immoral behaviour. I was often greatly bored at these courts. Really petty faults, like missing a church service, disputes between neighbours and, men in particular, blaspheming. It was serious business nevertheless.'

'I wondered what the parochial courts dealt with,' Marion remarked before adding, 'So, go on then, tell me about your adultery.'

'As I said, I spent most of my time in Gloucester, mainly hunting with the Lord of the Manor. We were of the same age and became firm friends. It was he who suggested that I visit London with him in the winter months. That was when society began its party season. I rented a newly-built house in Bloomsbury Square, and took a number of servants with me. I could have stayed with my friend, who had his own house of course, but I preferred to maintain my privacy, especially when I was at my prayers, which he scoffed at, and I was sometimes anxious at his daring to ignore his soul's well-being.

'We partied three, four days a week, sometimes more. He was very popular, and I suppose you could say I was lucky to be counted as one of his friends. One evening, I was introduced to one of the London bishops who suggested that I might like to preach to the good people of East London occasionally. He laughed when I said he might care to preach to the good people of Gloucester in return. "No fun to be had in the country," he said to me. I told him of the excellent hunting, mostly of deer, and the occasional visits of strolling players, but he declined.

'I was guided by my conscience, and decided that I would make a few visits to justify my absence from my own churches and home, or maybe as a penance for the sort of life I was enjoying, I'm not sure which. I made no more than three visits.

'I'd travelled to London by stagecoach so had no transport of my own. I hired a horse and set out for one of the places on this particular day. It was surprising what a difference just three miles travelling can reveal. In Bloomsbury the streets were swept often and were fairly clean, but as I travelled eastwards everything deteriorated. The further I rode out, the worse everything became. As I left Bloomsbury, which boasted cobblestone roads, the roads I now travelled on were unmade. Indeed, they were no more than passageways between buildings. The smells that assaulted me were indescribable. Raw sewage, garbage, dead dogs, cats, rats, so many rats I couldn't count them, were left to rot in the streets.'

Marion raised her eyebrows. 'Surely there was some sort of sanitation; people couldn't live in such filth.'

'Believe me, they did. There were sewers of a sort, hollowed out tree trunks near the surface to take rainwater to the Thames. I tell you, all sorts were thrown out of dwellings. Once I was almost showered with the contents of a chamber pot being emptied out of a window.'

Marion couldn't hide her grin as a giggle bubbled up in her throat.

'You can laugh,' Matthew grumbled, 'but when it rained, puddles of filth formed and made matters worse. As I rode on, the alleyways got narrower and narrower, gloomy and stinking to high heaven. Not only that, I learned that it was extremely dangerous after dark as these twisting thoroughfares were a boon to lurking footpads.

'The buildings were decaying terraced houses, leaning at all angles, and all without clean water or means of sewage disposal. I learned that each building was subdivided again and again in order to accommodate as many bodies in as little space as possible. Interspersed with these, were pigs and cows in some back yards and certain trades like tripe boiling, tallow melting, preparing putrid meats for animal feed, all added to the overall smell. Worst though, were the heaps of "night soil" gathered for collection overnight to spread on the fields. You will agree, I believe, that the conditions were appalling, lice and dirt everywhere. Consequently there was much disease, and death was common from infectious epidemics.'

Marion gave a sigh as she murmured, 'Those poor, poor people. No wonder they didn't live long in those days.'

'It was truly unbearable and I visited only three times, and I am ashamed to tell you so. My visits saved the London clergy making any similar journeys. I doubt they went very often, if at all.

'As I said, I made only three visits and it was after the third visit that I rode as fast as I could back to Bloomsbury and Bolton. I threw my cloak at Bolton, then as fast as I could I removed every stitch of clothing, convinced I was about to be eaten to death by fleas. Fortunately, he knew that after my earlier visits, I always demanded a hot bath and on this occasion he had one ready for me. I jumped into the warm water and scrubbed and scrubbed away at my skin.'

Matthew sighed before going on and then continued, 'With my head in my hands, I muttered to Bolton that I never wanted a day like this ever again. After wrapping me in towels, he said, "There's bacon and pease pudding for supper sir. Will I ask cook to serve?" He was trying to take my mind off the day's events, he knew my weakness for good food, but I wasn't interested.

"Later. A brandy first, and make it large, will you?" I replied. Bolton poured the drink and left me to my thoughts. Leaning back in my chair I closed my eyes and was disturbed by my feelings – feelings of shame, elation, disgust and a little pride. So Marion, this is what happened to cause me such distress on that day.

'There was quite a din in the church, but I was intent on preaching my sermon. As I was waiting I looked at the assembled crowd. There were men, who had obviously been drinking, staggering about at the back, shouting and jeering; one or more intent on a fight. There were women, all of whom were dressed in rags, some openly breastfeeding their babies, a practice unheard-of in society. There were also others, who quite clearly earned a crust or two with their bodies, boldly approaching any man, including myself a church dignitary, on that day. There were children of all ages with bare feet, obviously hungry, and with barely anything on their bodies to keep them warm. Everyone was standing and milling about. All furniture, I was told, had been stolen and burned last winter. There was a pulpit of sorts, which I understood was borrowed from another parish, and I stood on this, waiting.

'I was surprised and flattered at the number of people who had come to hear me, and when I queried this with the local preacher he said that there was a promise of gruel afterwards for those who could prove they had attended. In fact, he was collecting the marks of everyone who was present – a cross or similar beside their name.

'The preacher ineffectively tried to get some order and it wasn't until two rough looking fellows went among the crowd with sticks, that they didn't use I'm glad to say, that it was quiet enough for me to begin.

'I looked down on the restless crowd below me and at first I felt quite smug – smug because I had, and could, escape the sort of lives these people had. Then I had a fleeting feeling of shame at my selfishness along with a feeling that society, my class of people, had allowed such conditions. Lastly I felt impatient and irritated, not understanding why they were not attempting to improve their miserable existence.

'I coughed and someone yelled out, "Get on with it." I reddened and then began reading the Bible, and followed this up with saying that their life on earth was preparing them for life ever after, and that they were to resist every temptation to sin. You know the sort of thing. There was calling and laughter from the congregation again.

"We'd bloody starve if we didn't do a bit of thieving."

"God doesn't even know where we are."

"For Christ sake get on with yer gobbing, and let some of us at the gruel."

'All sorts of jibes like that rang out until one voice, a woman's voice, and I recognised the slyness in it, called out, "Can you say you're without sin yerself, sir?"

'I know that my face reddened again, a fact that didn't escape them as they jeered, pointed at me, laughed and shook their heads. I was rather rotund, and knew that I was gluttonous. I was lazy, and shamefully admitted to myself, that I was also unfaithful. I stood before those people and bowed my head, unable to say anything. It was when they began murmuring that I looked up, and began to feel more than a little uneasy. There was something familiar about the woman who had called out, and while listening to the crowd's mutterings, I looked at her more closely. A dirty, ragged individual, unkempt hair, barefooted, but with a proud carriage and a defiant look on her face. I was unable to place the woman who had made her way to the front. There was something I couldn't quite fathom about her. There she stood, swaggering and tossing her filthy hair away from her face. There's something about this woman, I fretted, but I don't know what is causing me such anxiety.

'The woman smiled knowingly at me, and I noticed she had good teeth, none missing, none of the blackened pegs like those about her. Still smiling, she turned to those assembled and lifted her outer garments, causing mayhem, and blew her nose on her ragged petticoat. The people laughed out loud and she gave a twirl, grinned at them and swirled her petticoats, showing a pretty pair of ankles. This of course, invited more laughter and cheers.

"Madam, this is a holy place of worship," I admonished. "I will ask you to leave if you persist in your present behaviour." I felt very smug saying this. I felt I had gained a point. It would have meant she would lose her scant meal.

'The wretched woman then said, "If you please, sir, I'm a mite hungry".' Matthew stopped talking when Marion gasped out with shock.

'Please tell me, please say it wasn't Magdalena.'

Matthew said softly, 'Of course not. So, then the wretched woman sighed and leaned forward, artfully displaying a very full bosom, causing me a small measure of er … excitement, shall I say.'

Marion gave a short chuckle. 'You're painting a very vivid picture. I would dearly love to have been there.'

'Well you weren't,' Matthew retorted. 'Anyway, the woman went on, "I have a trade but my lover keeps beating me, took his belt to me, bruised me well, he did." Looking straight at me, she whimpered with tears in her eyes, a put-on act, I warrant. "He beat me to a pulp, I could hardly stand and, what's more, he's done that to a good many others. One for sure he beat to death. So, my sin is my longing to kill the bastard."

'There was uproar in the room again and the preacher called for order. As solemnly as I could muster I told her that the penalty for murder merited the death sentence, and that she would be hanged by the neck if she carried out her idea.

'It was now that I was to experience a shock that was to alter my life. In a cultured voice she said, "If you please my lord …" I stared in amazement. I must have looked an idiot as my mouth dropped open. I recognised her immediately as Hannah Smithson Lacey.

'"If you please my lord, a pregnant woman cannot be hanged. That is the law is it not?" I felt myself becoming hot and spluttered, 'Are you pregnant?'

'She smiled. "You should know that, sir. Did we not share a bed night after night, not so long ago? Surely you remember?" Pandemonium erupted again. I told myself this couldn't be happening.

'I turned to Hannah and as coldly as I could muster I told her, "You are a common prostitute. Any of your, I couldn't for the life of me know what to call them ... your clients could have fathered the child."

'She smiled again. Still in her cultured voice she said softly, "But you were the last, sir. Only you for over three months, called me your darling little pigeon, so I know full well who the father is, and what's more, you had Bolton follow me. Made sure I was not enamoured with another." Then with a voice warm with promise that, oh, I knew so well, she softly said, "Remember my dearest, naughty, naughty boy?"

'There was jeering, cheering, the slapping of thighs and knowing nods from everyone in the church. At first, I was bewildered, and I was reminded of my visit to the appalling Bedlam Asylum such was the uproar. Knowing that a scandal was about to erupt around me, I waved my arms frantically for order, and shouted almost hysterically. "Let me away, get out of my way," and used my fists and elbows to clear a path to the exit.

'Yes, it's true, I was her lover. We were introduced at Lady Grayson's house party and, truth be told, Hannah was very lovely. At once I knew I could win her over. Oh, she flirted, eyes merry over the top of her fan and led me on, and like a fool I let it happen and enjoyed every minute in her company. I bought her gifts of jewels, hats – she loved hats – good food, stockings and anything at all she wanted. No doubt she sold them on. I really don't know. She would come to my rooms late in the evening, and stay until dawn. We drew the curtains around the four poster bed, dispensed with the warming pan, and she teased and tantalised me throughout the night. There was no doubt that she brightened my London visit. Why, I even got to the stage where I could hardly wait for her nightly visits.'

Marion held up her hand and said, 'Hang on a minute. Plump little pigeon! Funny sort of endearment.'

'Ah! Let me say she was well endowed in a certain area, full breasted, each like a fat, soft pigeon.'

Marion laughed until the tears ran down her face and Matthew laughed along with her.

'I knew nothing about her, where she came from, her family or what she did in the daytime. At first I didn't care, then I began to wonder, and that's why I had Bolton follow her. My goodness, she was careful, he had no idea of the activities she was up to. I thought she was a quality person as she seemed to be invited to most of the season's parties, the opera and racing events. She was always properly dressed for whatever occasion and able to converse intelligently, indeed every inch a lady. To this day, I don't know where she learned such airs and graces. I was such a fool. I was puzzled by her disappearance at the time and, despite Bolton searching for her, it was weeks before I admitted to myself that it was all over and to be truthful, although I missed her, I was more than a little relieved.' Matthew smiled.

'Well go on! What happened next?'

'Oh, the rest of my stay in London was frantic, as you can imagine. My thoughts were now for my wife. Although we had our differences she was a good woman, and didn't deserve to be hurt by my disgrace should it ever come to light. I got Bolton to discreetly arrange for Hannah to be placed with nuns in the north. I paid for her to have clean rooms and decent food until the child was born. It was her pregnancy of course, that made her lover react as he did – if he was her lover. Beating her was his revenge for her unfaithfulness I learned, but he must have been aware of her prostitution. Indeed, I suspect now that he might have been her pimp, and her pregnancy meant a loss of earnings for him. Consequently, no doubt, he would have punished her.

'It was Bolton who procured the baby boy, my son, for me. Bolton, through a chain of contacts, but I didn't enquire who was involved or how the child eventually came to me. All involved were amply rewarded from my deep purse, to ensure the child's parentage could never be traced back.'

'What happened to the girl, Hannah? Honestly, Matthew, taking a child away from its mother is every bit as wicked as all the other things you were guilty of.'

Matthew could see Marion was perturbed and answered, 'My thoughts were for the child. I've told you how unsavoury the area she was living in was. I could give the child a much better life and he was of my own flesh and blood. I had no reason to disbelieve her, you see. It was true, I had lain with her all that time.'

'I see, but what happened to her? You couldn't just abandon her, could you?'

'I left it to Bolton. He told me later that the nuns had arranged for her to go to Ireland, and work in a convent's laundry. She would be fed and kept warm and, frankly, I thought no more of her.

'Four years later I sat watching the little lad. We called him Michael, and I had all his linen monogrammed with the double M although at the time I didn't know why. It was also obvious that Bolton was fond of the child, teaching and coaxing his little master in all manner of riding skills. I knew that Bolton would always remain loyal, with promises of a permanent position and a generous pension when the time came, and my turning a blind eye to him helping himself to my snuff. The man seemed more than happy in his employment.

'My wife joined me in the stable yard. We both smiled indulgently at the boy's laughter. I had brought the baby to her saying only, "a foundling, mother an unmarried lady of note, a foolish indiscretion." She had immediately and lovingly taken the child from me, but didn't ask the question I guiltily fancied I could see lurking in her eyes.'

Marion sighed contentedly and said, 'Yes, good. A good story. You really should think about publishing all this. I could put you in touch with someone if you like.' Then she asked, 'and where did I, Magdalena, fit in?'

'Ah, you! A number of years before all this happened. I was in a carriage on my way to London. That was when I first saw you. I suspect you were no older than twelve or thirteen and you were barefoot, in a ragged skirt and as brown as a berry. The sun had just come out after a sudden heavy shower. I saw you and a very young boy splashing each other in a puddle, then you picked him up and swung him round and round and both of you were laughing. You were so happy and wholesome, I felt I wanted to stop and watch you. At the time I felt something in my heart stir, but thought no more of it. It was so brief a glimpse.'

He sighed softly. 'My wife engaged you as the child's nurse. You were a homely girl called Martha. I used to go into the nursery to look at Michael each evening, and you would be sewing the monogram on to his garments. In the summer months you were close to the window for the light, and struggling by candlelight in the winter months. I explained to you that the letter you were embroidering was also the initial of your name. You didn't understand, you stood up, looked at the floor and gave a little bob then said, "Yes sir." Those were the only words you ever spoke to me, although I greeted you, formerly I might add, each time I visited.

'Only once did I kiss Martha and she never knew about it. I'll tell you how it happened. Our little Michael was very unwell, indeed he had pneumonia and at the time we thought he might die.'

Marion's face showed concern.

Matthew hurried on saying, 'No, no he was fine in the end, but he was ill for a long time. The doctor came daily, warning us that things weren't good. I absolutely forbade him to bleed the child, he was weak enough in my opinion. My wife and you were inconsolable. I could ease my wife's fears a little with a few hopeful words of comfort, but never your distress. With all my heart I wanted to hold you in my arms as well, and whisper the same hopeful words. You were so young and inexperienced. Daily we found you in tears blaming yourself, but you were always so careful with Michael and his needs, that we assured you again and again that you were blameless.

'Night times were particularly fraught, and in order for you both to get some rest I volunteered to stay with the lad each night. On this particular night, you stayed up until gone midnight, sitting quietly beside the boy, wiping his brow, trying to feed him some warm broth and holding his hand. I saw how much you cared for him, and I loved you the more for that. I finally persuaded you to take to your own bed, a cot in an adjoining room. At first the child was restless, he was so hot and I sponged him down as I'd seen you do. Finally he settled and for a while I was able to doze in the uncomfortable armchair. It was around four o'clock when he whimpered again and I went across to him. At once I could see his temperature had gone down and, seeing me, he smiled briefly and promptly fell asleep again.

'I was overjoyed and wanted to let everyone know that at last there was an improvement. Common sense told me to let everyone sleep on, but I crept into your room thinking that worry might have robbed you of sleep, and I could tell you the good news. How I longed to wake you up to tell you, but then I saw your tearstained face. Instead of disturbing you, I brushed the tousled hair from your brow and bent down to lightly kiss it. Fortunately you didn't rouse.'

Marion frowned and asked, 'Why wasn't the child with you in your room? I mean, did all well-to-do families have nursemaids?'

Matthew nodded, 'It was all so different in those days. Quite often children rarely saw their parents until they were socially mannered, so to speak. We thought Martha would be good for the child, but my wife and I were determined to be with the child as much as possible.' He paused, 'It all worked out quite well. Each of us in our own way loved the little chap.'

'Too late you entered my life and I had to suffer your closeness for four years. One of the few times the Senate let me live on, seeing you almost daily, keeping my love for you a secret in my heart. I died four years on, glad of a son, but regretted breaking another of the terms and having lost you again.'

'So the Senate let you live on, partly in joy. At the same time because of your misdemeanour, they caused you much misery. Firstly, taunting you with the constant presence of Martha, and they kept you longer dreading your death. How this time, did they finish you off?'

'I was riding a horse instead of using the carriage in my haste to get home one moonless night. Relations with my wife had improved, and the thought of seeing the little lad and, of course, his nurse, all contributed to my haste to be home. I galloped straight into the overhanging branch of an oak tree. I'd intended to have it cut down, but forgot. I cracked my head open and fell to the ground. That was the end of that life.'

'I suppose you got the usual reception from the Senate.'

Matthew laughed, 'Of course.'

'Do you think the members of the Senate were able to go through their lives without breaking the rules?'

'I really don't know. I never asked, but I suspect not. They all seem to know how impossible it is to keep them. I suppose at some time, they too have been tested, and I'm their guinea pig to see if a blameless life can truly be achieved.'

'In that case, if you do succeed, not only will you get the girl of your dreams, but you could end up on the Senate yourself.'

Matthew was aghast. 'No thanks, not for me. I'd be quarrelling with them all day I'm sure.' He stood up and stretched. 'I'm off to the loo, won't be long.'

Marion watched him leave and panicked a little, feeling abandoned as she gazed at his back disappearing along the corridor. What further revelation would there be, she wondered?

Seven

'I'm not proud of myself you know, breaking the Ten Commandments,' Matthew said when he returned and sat down.

'Well, I suppose you're not, but, to be truthful, some are very difficult to keep, or to put it another way, easy to break,' Marion replied.

'You're so right. You can drift into trouble without realising it. Take the one that says, "Thou shalt have no other God before me." I just didn't realise it at the time and, boy were the Senate angry when I got back to them!'

'So, let's hear it then. We've at least another two and half hours before we reach London.'

Matthew got up from his seat opposite Marion and sat down beside her. The closeness and warmth of him sent her heart somersaulting, confusing her again. Think of Alex, she told herself as she edged away. 'Get started, go on.'

Matthew placed his elbows on his knees and cupped his head in one hand. He turned to look at her.

'Have I told you that I am falling in love with you all over again?' he murmured. There was no doubting his sincerity.

At first Marion was flustered, then laughed. 'I'm not listening. Just stop all of that nonsense. Remember you are telling me a story. No need to try to make it a reality.' She noticed that Matthew bit his lip then shrugged.

'It was a bit forward wasn't it? I mean, we have only just begun to get to know each other,' he smiled as he took her hand and added, 'Sorry,' as she pulled it away. He gave a sigh, 'I'd better begin then, shall I?'

Marion nodded.

'It was when gold was first discovered in Australia.'

Marion's eyes widened, 'Don't tell me you got rich! How wonderful!'

'Let me tell you, will you?'

'Go on then,'

'I was living in a small outback town in Australia when news came that gold had been found. I was a single chap living with my parents and tending sheep at the time. I decided to try my luck and, taking the family's only horse ...'

Marion opened her mouth to protest, but he said, 'Don't worry, we had donkeys and oxen as well. So off I went, all set to make my fortune. It took me a week to get to the area where the latest find was. The news of the gold had spread very quickly and many men set out to try their luck, even though the amount of gold found, turned out to be very small. As I was a loner on horseback, I was able to overtake others in wagons drawn by bullocks; wagons owned or borrowed by men of all trades. Others were walking with loaded wheelbarrows, and some were carrying all they could on their backs; all intent on making their fortune. Everything they needed had to be carried as there were no shops or dwellings on the way. There were no roads, just tracks to follow to the diggings, as the goldfields were called. There were bakers, farmers, builders, as well as a doctor, oh, countless others who had given up the safety of their own trade and homes in the hope of finding gold. Of course, some got rich from servicing the diggers' needs by putting a high price on the smallest commodity. Their presence on the gold fields meant that farming in particular began to suffer, causing hardship where communities had been abandoned.

'The government at the time was worried that the men might become lawless and violence would break out. It was decided that all gold prospectors must purchase a licence, believing that this would deter some. The licence fee for a claim of land to work, no more than about fifteen square yards, was thirty shillings a month. This was a huge amount of money for some, but somehow they all found the fee. The thirty shillings had to be paid even if no gold was found, but if gold was found the miner could keep it. To hold on to their claim the miner had to work on it every day except Sundays. A few men like myself found a little gold, but not enough to call ourselves rich.

'When I got to the site there were over three hundred men working already. I paid my dues and pitched my shelter. I can't call it a tent as it was merely a piece of canvas slung over some willow branches I'd cut down. After I had sorted out my equipment, I began work within the hour. I had been allocated a piece of land on the river's edge and within a few minutes I had a new neighbour. We hardly spoke to each other we were so intent on our panning.'

Matthew hesitated for a moment before he asked her, 'Do you know anything about panning for gold, Marion?'

'Only what I have seen at the cinema or on television.'

'I can tell you it wasn't a bit like anything you've seen. Let me give you a little bit of background. There are three ways of getting gold. One is to pan for gold, which is where I started. The gold lies just under the surface of the bed of streams or creeks and is heavier than sand. What you have to do is scoop up the water in a shallow pan. I have seen men use frying pans, saucepans, mixing bowls from the kitchen, anything to scoop with. You have to swirl the water, sand and dirt out of the pan carefully and if you're lucky, you might find a few flakes or specks of gold, sometimes no bigger than a grain of sand itself, left behind.

'I, along with thousands, truly thousands, of men and a few women, would stand in icy cold water for hours. Some men lost their feet, which rotted in the water. Hands would become numb, red and raw, and backs would ache as we constantly bent over. Some poor souls were infected by the water, which, as you can imagine became filthy. Very few people found gold, I mean a substantial find, enough to make a person rich beyond dreams. When any was found it was a spur for others.

'I found a little myself, just enough to pay for food. Food was limited to mutton, Australia with its multitude of sheep answered our hunger, and a damper, that is flour and water mixed to a paste, stuck onto a stick and toasted in the fire sufficed. We also drank gallons of tea. Occasionally I treated myself to a hot bath, where I laundered my clothes in the same water. With luck sometimes there were a few coins left for entertainment, usually a drink in the

beer tent with a girl singing, or a girl willing to share her bed.'
Marion opened her mouth to speak and he forestalled her, 'No, I
didn't! There were also some gambling tables and I resisted the
temptation, unlike one or two who eventually lost everything.

'One of the major difficulties was obviously the lack of clean
water. Diggers, as the miners were called, because of the nature of
their work, muddied the creeks, so cleanliness was very difficult.
Sewage, well we won't go into that, but needless to say, it was not
disposed of in a satisfactory way. Can you imagine the foul stench
of it all? Drinking water was carted in and was very expensive. In
spite of these hardships, the lure of gold was powerful and still
more miners continued to arrive. As the camp swelled with the
arrival of the men's families, diseases such as typhoid and dysen-
tery were common, and many died. In such a tight-knit communi-
ty, men, women and children died of the more common infectious
illnesses such as whooping cough, measles, diphtheria and scarlet
fever.

Marion interrupted, 'Sounds so much like the conditions in the
east end of London you told me about when you were a visiting
bishop.'

Matthew leaned forward. 'Conditions? Yes, for a while. The
biggest difference was that the Londoners were in despair, without
the means to improve their surroundings or lives, whereas the
Australians were full of hope, intent on getting rich and improving
their circumstances as they went along.'

'Yes, you're right, they had the land to spread out, but the
London dwellings were just replaced as they deteriorated, I suppose. There wasn't any room to expand was there?'

Matthew shook his head, 'No, just endless misery. So on with
my reminiscences.

'As the women joined their husbands with their children, conditions gradually began to improve. At first they lived in tents until
huts were built of wood and canvas, all dreadfully cramped. Although life was hard for the women, they were able to earn a few
pennies by washing and ironing, along with the making of jam and
soap, as well as some tailoring and repairing, even renovating
people's clothes. Some had brought along a cow or two so the
women made butter. This was a luxury and always sold quickly.

'Assayers set up makeshift offices and tested the quality and weight of gold and they also bought it from the diggers. Gradually traders set up stores. Hotels and boarding houses were built, mostly of wood and lined with calico – a cheap, unbleached cotton fabric. These were the people who benefited most in the gold rush days by selling food and equipment, or by offering bed and board and beer and bawdy dwellings.'

Marion slumped in her seat, said, 'We are so spoiled nowadays. I could never have endured those conditions. I like my shower every day and a clean bed at night. No, not for me, that sort of life.'

'But don't you see? It was an adventure, something entirely different from sheep farming, I can tell you. It was the same old routine every day and utterly boring. Shall I go on?'

'Of course, why not? I want to know if you got rich and where your girl comes in.'

Taking up his story again, Matthew said, 'By now the government was intent on keeping law and order on the site and their officers' accommodation was made of wood, as was the jail and quarters for the soldiers employed to keep order. Their presence didn't help the Chinese workers though. They worked so hard, harder than anyone else, but their rewards were the same as the rest of the diggers. Some of the prospectors thought they were faring better, finding more gold than themselves. Within a few months, weeks really, there was discontent among some of the men. They took it upon themselves to harass the Chinese, stealing or breaking their fragile wooden equipment, sly punches at lone workers, spitting, name calling and more than once, beating some poor fellow to within an inch of his life. All the racist taunts imaginable, made their life and law-abiding folks' lives a misery. Sad to say, the militia often turned a blind eye to such meanness.'

Marion held up her hand, and Matthew smiled. 'Yes?'

'Are you saying that no one intervened? Just let all this happen?'

'First of all the attacks were either in the dark or at night time. A gang would kidnap, I suppose you could say, a Chinese fellow and then set about him. No one saw what was happening. And, Marion, anyone who did witness such attacks, would hesitate to cross these wild, aggressive men as they knew they would soon pay for their interference, and probably the same sort of beatings would be meted out. No, it was wiser to keep what you knew to yourself.'

Marion frowned, and made a little humming noise through pressed lips. Matthew patted her arm. 'Shall I go on? I'm so afraid of boring you.'

Marion nodded. 'Yes, go on. I'm finding it difficult somehow to come to terms with the harshness of the time.'

'Well, that is how it was. Of course, with so many working the area, the gold ran out within a year or so and as soon as talk of a new site reached the field, miners left at top speed, including myself.'

Marion stretched and pulled her shoulders back.

'Oh sorry. Sorry, I didn't mean to go on so long. I hope you are not finding it all a bit tedious.'

Marion smiled, swept her foot around the floor to locate her shoes and, giving a little grunt, pushed her feet into them before saying, 'No, I'm loving the story.' She stood up. 'But please excuse me a moment, I really need to go to the toilet,' then burst out laughing when he said,

'Do you need a hand?'

'Not since I was three years old,' she retorted, and laughed again when he drew his shoulders up to his chin and scrunched up his face.

'Sorry, sorry,' he said. I only meant … with the train swaying along … I thought I could hold on to you along the corridor or something?'

'No, I'm fine.'

Nevertheless, he held her elbow until she reached the door and was able to support herself with the corridor rail. When she returned she dropped heavily into her seat.

'There's a trolley with refreshments on the way, and a cup of tea would be lovely,' she said.

Matthew nodded. The compartment door slid open.

'Tea, madam, sir?' a cheery voice asked. Matthew bought them each a cup of tea. The attendant added, 'How about a slice of Dundee cake? Made in Nottingham mind, but just as tasty. We also have some shortbread biscuits, they was made in Park Royal if I'm not mistaken.'

Both Marion and Matthew laughed at his selling technique and chose the Dundee cake. When he had gone and they bit into the cake, they looked at each other, and pulled a face at the sandy texture, and laughed together as they abandoned the dry cake. They settled themselves back into their seats and Matthew began his story again.

'Another method of extracting gold was called reef mining where gold is locked in the rock, usually quartz. This was found deep below ground and when the rock was dug out it was hoisted to the surface, then crushed to extract the gold. Chinese men were employed on a contract for this type of mining. It grew into a large business eventually until the gold ran out. This was later, of course, and I had no part in this type of mining. In any case I preferred to work on my own.' He was thoughtful for a moment, 'That was until I met Jake.'

'Jake?'

'Yes, Jake.' Matthew sighed, 'I met Jake when I was riding to yet another new area in Victoria where gold had been found. Jake was in no hurry, just sauntering along with his bullock and cart. He was always able to make me laugh with his laid back ways. Told me he was going to be rich, and send for his family, and never work again. "Not at the pace you're going," I told him. To cut a long story short, it was arranged that we shared the licence fee, and that I would go ahead and stake a claim. We trusted each other that much.' He sighed, 'There was a great deal of greed, crime and self-interest, not to mention racism at the time. Jake was from Ireland; came over as a young man and married a sheep farmer's daughter. He had a sizeable family and wanted independence; said sheep were smelly creatures.'

Marion smiled at him over her cup.

'So, when he finally reached camp, we began working together on what I had already started, digging into a small hill. I had decided that there were too many working the river. Also Jake was always mindful of disease and fearing for his family. He thought it a wise decision, especially when it rained heavily, causing the river to run fast.

'There were other diggers' claims scarring the hillside. Each had a makeshift hut or tent at the cave-like entrance to their workings. There were always risks that as each man hewed his way along his claim he would run into another fellow's. Quarrels and sometimes murder would occur as claims and counterclaims were made.

'With pickaxes and chisels Jake and I searched for lode, and we had some modest success. Within a few months, Jake sent for his wife and family, and they were accompanied by his wife's sister, Millie.'

Marion sat up suddenly.

'Me?' she asked. 'Is this where I come into your life ...?' she stopped before adding, 'Again?'

'That's right. Millie.' Matthew answered. 'She was eighteen years old and beautiful. Jake and his wife guarded her well. There were, naturally, many admirers and some, as you can guess, unsavoury characters who thought all single women and girls were available. Millie was never alone; her sister was always with her. When they were not doing the household chores, they took it upon themselves to teach the children of the miners. A hopeless task really. The boys in particular wanted only to be with their fathers or playing. They were wild, lacking discipline, so teaching was a hard task, but they persevered.'

Matthew gazed at Marion. 'You were so lovely then, and now. I fell in love immediately, but it was a long few months before Jake would let me near you, I mean Millie. One day, sitting on the muddy bank of the river, I found myself drawing the MM symbol with a stick in the mud. Jake saw it and laughed as he said, "Nowt will come of your dreaming lad, you can bet on it." I asked most evenings if I could walk with you and he just shrugged and said, "Maybe, one day. We'll see." And that's what happened. I asked one evening, expecting his usual answer, when he said, "Only along the river's edge and keep in my sight." After that we walked most evenings when the weather was fine.'

Matthew stopped for a moment and then said sadly, 'Marion, you will not like what I have to tell you next, but remember, I always have to pay with my life and with losing you.'

Marion was moved by both his wistfulness and sadness.

'It's all right, Matthew. You're talking of the past. It's all water under the bridge as far as I'm concerned. I'll not judge you.'

'Does that mean you believe me?'

She couldn't mistake the eagerness in his voice and cautiously told him, 'It all does seem so ... so plausible somehow. I just don't know what to believe. Do go on, Matthew. Tell me the worst.'

'Jake and I worked well together, each of us found small nuggets, mostly no bigger than, say, a cherry pip. These we put into a leather bag, and taken to the assayer when we had enough to sell. We shared the money we got for them equally. Most of Jake's share was spent on his family, food, school and medication, but I had fewer expenses and began to save my money. A temporary bank had been set up in the shanty town, and for a small fee my earnings were safe.' Matthew fidgeted in his seat for a moment and Marion suspected he was having trouble how to tell her what happened next.

Gently, she nudged him. 'Go on.'

'It was so easy to do, so easy. We dug deeper and deeper into the side of the hill, and had to purchase wooden poles to hold the roof up over our heads. We also had to buy oil lamps. We were so sure we were going to find a seam of gold. One day I found three tiny nuggets, and at the end of the day gave up only two, but Jake honestly put up the four he had dug out. I had kept one back. What sort of man did that make me? I'm ashamed to admit I cheated on my partner. Not once, but in the end many times, just a small piece each time, but it made a difference to my bank balance. Jake always had to spend his share immediately to keep his family fed and out of debt. My excuse was that I was in love and wanted to make a good safe home for Millie. I had no guilt about this cheating and, it was so easy.

'One day, it was a Saturday, Jake couldn't work, but sent a message saying his youngest had scarlet fever and their expected baby was on its way. I sent a message back saying I would work on and share whatever I found. I knew that would please him, put his mind at rest. I worked on for hours, and I was surprised when Jake's eldest ran into the workings, shouting. It was raining hard and he was soaked to the skin. He stood before me, shivering. "Dad says can you lend him two shillings for the doctor?" The sick child was getting worse and Jake's wife needed help. I sent the lad back to Jake and told him to say I'd be there right away. Only ...' Matthew paused again, shaking his head and obviously reluctant to go on.

Marion waited quietly.

Matthew had turned to face her. 'Only it was then I saw it. The biggest nugget of gold I had ever seen. I could not leave it there, and all thoughts and promises left me. I began at once to carefully hew around it, determined to get it out in one piece, the size of a walnut, but it was wedged in so firmly. On and on I toiled, and to my shame ignored another desperate shout from the lad imploring me to hurry. 'I'm coming, now,' I yelled back – but didn't.

'Perhaps it was two or more hours later, maybe more, when Jake joined me. There was torrential rain at the time and he too was soaked through. I could see he was dreadfully upset, his eyes red with weeping and his whole body sagging in defeat. He told me that his wife and baby had died. Then he asked what had kept me from giving him the money? I remember shamefully trying to bluff my way, saying time just flew. "Cost my wife and my wee son their lives," he said bitterly. Then very softly he said, "Goodbye Matthew. I thought you were my friend." I felt dreadful at that point; I would have been happy to give him the money. It wasn't the money that held me back, it was the promise of an easy life once the elusive nugget was in my hand. "For both of us," I told him, but he left me. He didn't shake my hand, just turned his back on me and walked away and never looked back.

'At first I was truly sorry. I had lost a good friend and the love of my life, you, Millie. Then the gleam of gold in the rock seemed to beckon again and to be honest, it was as if I didn't care anymore and I went back to digging. After a short while and without warning, the roof caved in. Sorry, yes, there was a warning. I toiled on even though I heard the poles creaking as they strained to hold up the roof, and I ignored it. The rain outside had caused a landslip and, I suppose, put more strain on the poles and I found myself buried alive. Debris all round and my arms, trunk and legs all pinned down by large rocks. I tried desperately to free myself but couldn't move. I was in complete darkness as the lamps too were buried. I waited and waited for rescue which never came. It happened in the late evening and I knew that the field would be practically empty as everyone would have gone for their supper. Sunday was the next day and no one was permitted to work the fields, it being the Lord's Day, and respected much more at the time. I also knew that Jake wouldn't be making enquiries of my whereabouts anymore and, no doubt, he made sure Millie couldn't. My injuries were worse than I thought and I knew I was getting weaker. I was aware that I was dying, an awful, lonely death. Justified, I thought to myself, for causing the death of others.

'It was just before the end when into my mind came the thought, "Thou shalt have no other gods before me." It was then I realised that the Senate were angry again.

'When I arrived before them, I faced a barrage of ridicule, and I believe one or two of them told Peter he was wasting his time on me. One said quietly in my ear that I would never achieve my goal, and another, who overheard him, nodded and said, "We shall make sure of that."

'So I'm convinced each of my lives is sabotaged by one or more of them. Peter urged me to try again, as if I had a choice. After all, he set the task and others, it seems, the rules.'

Eight

The train stopped at a station and Marion, standing at the window, crossed her fingers, hoping that no one would enter their compartment as it was almost like a haven now. She sat down and gave a thankful sigh when the train sluggishly began pulling away without anybody joining them. She turned to Matthew.

'I'm surprised no one ever comes into our compartment,' she said. 'I mean, it's Sunday afternoon and commuters usually travel back to London ready for work on Monday morning and there seem to be plenty of people about.'

Matthew gave a quiet cough and when she turned and looked at him she was amazed to see a flush on his face, at the same time as he gave her a lopsided grin.

'What?' she demanded. Matthew looked down at the floor then he lifted his head to face her.

'I, um … I, er, told the attendant that we didn't want to be disturbed. I slipped him twenty quid and he put a notice on the outside saying, "Do not disturb".'

Marion's eyes and mouth opened wide as she gasped, 'You what? That's going a bit far, Matthew. I mean, anyone might think we, we …'

'Well, we're not, are we?' he retorted, and added with a grin, 'Mind you I wouldn't mind …' then, as Marion folded her arms and scowled at him, said, 'Whoops! I thought you were going to stamp your foot again.'

There was firmness around Marion's mouth as she replied, 'I never stamp my feet. In fact I rarely lose my temper.' But the high colour in her cheeks belied what she said.

'Well I only meant that you stamp your foot metaphorically.' Sighing he said, 'I have so much to tell you and we have so little time and I didn't want any interruptions. I want you to know everything before we ...'

Sharply she interrupted, 'There is not, and never will be anything between us Matthew.'

Matthew was thoughtful for a moment, then murmured, 'We'll see.'

'I mean it. So tell me your stories if you wish. I won't pretend that I'm not enjoying them, because I am. So, Matthew, what's next? Come on, we've another six misdemeanours to get through before we reach London.'

Brightening up he said, 'Here is one of my lives I believe I can say I enjoyed. So settle yourself and I'll begin.'

Marion took her arm out of the sling. 'For a rest,' she told him and carefully eased the arm onto her lap with a satisfying sigh. 'There, that's better. Now I'm ready.'

'Can you imagine how a little chap of nine feels when, out of the blue, he, his siblings and mother are excluded from their village and friends? I couldn't understand it. We were a God-fearing family and attended church regularly, but backs were turned against us and my parent's friends would never answer us or at best gave a very rude answer. My father was very strict, reading the Bible daily and insisting we abided by its teachings. Easier to follow as a child I think. You know what I mean, don't tell lies, don't steal, go to church on Sundays, that sort of thing. Suddenly everything changed and it happened like this.'

Marion began to wriggle in her seat; she crossed her legs and leaned back. 'Sorry, just getting myself comfy,' she explained.

Matthew nodded approval. 'Right, are you ready now?' She bit her lower lip and slowly nodded as if she were a naughty child.

Matthew began again. 'Life was hard, really hard in the fifteen hundreds. There were increased taxes almost daily, mainly on wool exports. It was the biggest earner for the Crown at that time. Most of the land was given over to sheep-rearing for the wool which overseas markets were very keen to purchase. Fleece production became so important, that there was even a law stating that mutton or lamb could not be eaten except with the addition of a bitter herb. Well, poor people like us couldn't afford meat very often, if at all, so that didn't affect any of us in the village, but I did hear that the lord of the manor was quite indignant when his cook served his dinner with mint leaves. Someone though, had the bright idea of adding honey to the meal and to this day ...'

Marion interrupted, 'You're making that up! Mint sauce in those days, surely not?' As he opened his mouth to answer she said, 'I know, I know, you're going to say it's true because you were there.'

'I was, and I'm sure it's right because I also read it on the back of a beer mat in a pub recently so it must have some truth in it.' Matthew laughed at her exasperated expression. 'Shall I go on?' Marion nodded and he began. 'Where was I? Oh yes, taxes. Timber was also highly taxed; needed for shipbuilding as the country seemed to be constantly at war, first with France, then with Spain. Also taxed were bronze and iron as the country's weapons were made of these. Those big cannons you can see on the *Mary Rose* and on most ships right up to the nineteenth century are good examples.

'We lived in a small fishing village along the west coast in a cottage. In those days you could sail past the small inlet never knowing it was there. My mother loved the company of the other women when their men were at sea earning a living by fishing. There was singing and dancing when the men returned after a couple of days, especially if they had a good catch, but times got harder and harder. The women and their children, including mother and myself, often had to work in the fields behind the village to supplement our income, hoeing in the spring and summer months, and harvesting in the autumn. I was four years old and earning a living.'

Marion gasped in disbelief.

'Oh, come on, Matthew. That's going a bit far. Four years old indeed. I don't believe it for a second.'

'Well, I suggest you do some research, you'll be surprised. As I was saying, at four I was earning a few pennies a week as a bird scarer.'

'Sounds more like play to me.'

'Don't you believe it. If you wanted your pennies you had to work. Whatever anyone in the family earned went towards the common good. No one actually ever had their own pennies. Early in the day it was fun to chase the birds, all kids do it even now, but when it is nearly supper time you had to keep going no matter how weary you were. There was always someone keeping an eye on the workers, old and young alike. I fell asleep quite often and my mother would gently waken me, but my brothers would give me a slap so that I did my share of work. When I was a little older, around seven, I had to pick up stones to clear the land, and it seemed to me that the damn things grew, especially after rain.' They both giggled quietly, sharing the idea of such impossibility. 'Later still I joined my mother, who, on her own, tended sheep, hundreds and hundreds of them. In a way this suited us both once we had left the village.

'It was at about this time that my father decided to seek work elsewhere. He was so lucky, we thought, when he got a firm position and was provided with a horse, the equivalent of getting a job with a car these days I suppose. The only drawback was that his new employment took him away from home. He kept the details of his work to himself at first. On one of his visits home early in his new employment, he insisted that we move to a small but well kept cottage away from the village. It was then that the friends and village folk we'd known all our lives started to ignore us. No one spoke to my mother, and children were dragged away from my company.

'I couldn't understand it, so I asked my father what it was all about, why didn't the people like us anymore? He answered that mother preferred to be alone, that she didn't care for village tittle-tattle and that it didn't matter to her. As I said earlier, father was a God-fearing man, so although I thought his answer to be untrue, at the time I accepted it. This was difficult as mother had such a sunny nature, and loved nothing better than to gossip with the other women hour after hour, heaven only knows what about. I was forbidden to have anything to do with the boys or the men of the village under threat of a beating. I believe now he thought that our lives might be in danger from the angry village people or worse, strangers seeking revenge, but I'm only guessing.

'When I was about twelve and my father was away, I would wander down to the seashore of an evening. Often there were groups of men sitting on the ground, leaning in to each other as they mended their nets and talking in low voices. If I ventured near, they stopped, glared at me and told me to be on my way. Luckily, the boys of the village began to include me in their games of skimming stones, swimming races and telling each other ghostly stories as darkness came. Just once, one of the lads let something slip which I couldn't understand at the time, and said, "Your father is no friend of ours. Turned his back on us decent folks, shame he doesn't turn his eye my father says." I didn't know it then, but it seems my father was a government man. I was that proud of him when I first heard this, thinking he was really someone important. So he was in a way, I suppose, but an enemy of many at the time.'

Marion interrupted, 'A government man? What did that mean?'

'Basically, it meant he was a revenue man or, as some called him, a customs man.'

'I think I know where this is going. He shopped his neighbours, right?'

'No, I don't think he would have gone that far. He worked away from the village, patrolling the coastline a good twenty miles or so away, but the locals found out and turned against him and our family.'

'Great. So ...'

'So one evening when I ventured down to the seashore there was only one old fellow there and he called me over. Told me I was a clever little lad and would I go to the priest's house with a parcel? An adult outside the family had spoken to me! I was very excited and of course, I said I'd do his errand. Then he grabbed my ear, pinched it hard before he said, "You're to tell no one about this. Understand? Not your mother or father, definitely not your father or your brothers." He twisted my ear until I begged for mercy, promising him anything. Then he gave me a bundle wrapped in an old woollen cloth. Feeling through the cloth I felt a flagon. He shook me roughly and said I was to bring the purse the priest would give me back to him immediately. So I did as he bid. I ran like the wind in hopes of making a friend. When I returned he gave me a couple of herrings for my trouble, said I was a good lad and reminded me to say nothing, or else.'

'Herrings?'

'Yes, herrings. That was a sort of currency at the time in the village. I took them home to my mother who was very glad of them. When I handed them over to her she looked at me closely but, didn't ask questions. I'm sure she knew I wouldn't be able to answer truthfully, but we had a fine supper of herring dipped in oats and fried.

'After that evening, every time I went to the beach one or two of the men began to nod to me, and allowed me to stay close by them. The old man must have said something to them. It was a few months later when I realised what was going on. By chance I began to notice odd things like bales of fleece on the seashore. I mean, they could easily be ruined if a tide came over them or a high wind smothered them in fine sand. To me it seemed a risk with such a precious commodity, but everything was always gone by morning. Sometimes there were heavy wagons lumbering past our cottage on their way to the village late in the evening, but by daybreak when I had gone looking for them, they too had disappeared. It was smuggling, of course. Our little bay was ideal for such illicit trading. At the time I didn't realise the dangers of smuggling, fines, prison and, worst of all, deportation to the new world.

'One evening one of the men approached me. He was the father of my friend, Samuel. Seems Samuel had told him I could be trusted. I admit that I was a mite afraid of him as he could be very rough like all of the local men. He held my arm and shook me a little, and asked me if I could be trusted. I nodded two or three times. My teeth were chattering when he put his face close to mine and said if I ever breathed a word of what he was going to teach me, he would drown me.'

Marion gave a little gasp at this.

'Drown you? Surely not.'

'Yes, best way you see. People are always drowning at the coast aren't they? There was nothing surprising about the drowning of a careless boy in those days.'

'But wouldn't someone be suspicious? I mean, surely a boy would be missed? Your mother at least?'

'It happened quite frequently, quicksand, unexpected high tides, strong currents and boys, well boys always like to be adventurous don't they? In any case, if anyone was suspicious it was better not to voice it out loud. Smuggling was an unlawful business and had to be kept a secret '

'And you got drawn in, I suppose?'

'I was a lad. What do you expect? I was restless, ripe for excitement. Once my family were asleep, and only when father was away, of course, I would sneak off in the darkness to the seashore. Some nights there was a great deal of activity, men hauling barrels and crates up the beach and at first that was all I could see. Then one night Sam's father asked me to run back to his cottage for a lighted tallow candle. As usual, when I was asked to do anything, I had my ears boxed to remind me to keep silent. As you probably know, tallow is made from the fat of farm animals. The candles smelled dreadful and gave out a lot of smoke when burning. They were used to light homes and churches. I had to carry this back to him as quickly as possible in a wooden candle holder, which was quite a job because the sides of the lantern were not entirely closed in so that the light could shine out. I say shine, but it gave out only the briefest glow between the upright slats. I had to protect the flame with my hand to stop it being blown out from the draught of my running so fast. What didn't help was that the road was very uneven and in the dark I had to be careful not to stumble. I remember he just grunted when I got back, and sent me home. But ...' Matthew grinned, '... I only pretended to leave. Instead, I hid behind some rocks on the shore and watched as he entered a tiny cave under the cliff, followed by others carrying packages of varying sizes. I must have fallen asleep in the sand dunes after that.

When I woke up dawn was just breaking, the beach was empty of men and boats and I ...'

'You just had to go and look in the cave.'

Matthew laughed, 'Wouldn't you? Yes, I made sure that there was no one around to see me. Even so, I crept up quietly to the entrance in case someone was left on guard, then waited a few moments before I entered the cave. I could hardly believe my eyes.

'There were casks of wine, I couldn't read the labels, I think they were in French, as were the barrels of brandy. There were silk ribbons and fine lace spilling out from loose packages. There were also some unopened packages and I lifted one to smell it. At the time I didn't recognise the sweet, but pungent, aroma of its contents and learned later that it was tobacco. This was the newest hobby of the rich. It was considered to be beneficial to health and was especially valued for its calming effect. American Indians believed it would cure both mental and physical disorders. Europeans, on hearing of its curative powers, thought it a miracle herb. People suffering from toothache, earache, the common cold, aching joints or asthma smoked the tobacco, hoping for relief. Believe it or not, women in labour were encouraged to smoke it to ease their labour pains.'

Marion's eyes widened. 'Really?'

Matthew gave her a slow smile and shook his head. 'Beggars belief doesn't it?'

'It certainly does. Just think of everything being done now to discourage people from smoking. All the horrid illnesses it appears to be responsible for. Sir Walter Raleigh has a lot to answer for. Please go on, Matthew.'

'Ah, yes, the tobacco. As I breathed in deeply of its unusual odour, I was suddenly startled when someone grabbed me from behind. It was Sam's father, who had been keeping guard overnight, but had fallen asleep and I had disturbed him. I cannot tell you how afraid I was when he shook me until my teeth seemed to rattle in my head and yelled at the same time, "What you up to lad? Spying for your father?" I was trembling all over as I tried to tell him that no, my father was away and it was only curiosity that had me interested in the cave. "Curiosity?" he shouted, then boxed my ears, setting them ringing and bringing tears to my eyes. I suppose I was lucky he didn't beat me to a pulp with his fists.' As Matthew told his story he became more and more excited, talking fast and raising his voice. After a moment, in a softer tone, he went on.

'Then something strange happened. He sat down suddenly on an upturned, wicker lobster pot and put his head in his hands. I stood before him, still shaking, a little unsure and wondering what might happen next. I was just about to run for it when he told me quietly to stop jittering about, and sit on the sandy floor in front of him. Once I was seated he said, "If it gets out to anybody that I was asleep when on guard I will be banned from the village I warrant, just like your own folk. You could have been anyone, as it is you'll keep this quiet, boy. Agree?" I nodded before I asked very timidly, "Why does everyone work late at night and be so afraid of the government men?" The answer he gave made everything clear to me from that moment on.

'My friend's father, with his bright blue eyes in his tanned, lined face, looked at me keenly as he repeated, "Why? I'll tell you why, lad, so's you'll understand better. Firstly, who do you know around these parts who are rich, or let's say better off than your folk or mine, besides the priest and them at the manor? No one is there?" I shook my head. "We are all stuck in poverty. What doesn't help any of us is the taxation. We're taxed on stuff coming into the country and what we sends out. Things like wood we need desperately for new boats, and if farmers sell their fleeces they are taxed on any rewards they get. In fact you could say everything seems to be taxed, and taxed highly. Did you know animal feed is taxed and leather is taxed? That's why all the children are barefooted in summers and winters alike. You got shoes?" I shook my head. "See what I mean? Your father with a paying job too. It's just not fair on common folk like us. Another thing to remember is that for the last two years, and it looks likely again this year, we have had miserable harvests, so you can be sure flour will be scarce and expensive. If we can't fish in the winter when the weather's really bad, some of us will have a very hard time of it I can tell you. By doing this little bit of trading on the seashore, so to speak, we are improving our lot. Understand?"

"Yes," I whispered, and watched in amazement as he took out a clay pipe and filled it with tobacco from a small pouch in his pocket. I had never seen such a thing before. Next, out of his pocket came a flint stone and he struck it again and again until sparks set fire to a short stalk of hay in his other hand. He put this to the pipe clamped between his teeth and began to draw the smoke into his lungs. I suppose anyone in the village seen smoking by a stranger, not that we ever saw many new faces, would alert the authorities and questions might be asked. After he had finished, coughing and spluttering, he smiled at me as he told me that, besides all he'd already said, smuggling was an adventure for boys and grown ups alike. Life, he said, was very dull in the village and all the men enjoyed this huge secret. I was shocked to learn that some of the women were involved as well.

'I was cold and hungry by now, and he brought out a small flask and said to try it, it would warm me, and that was my first taste of brandy. He was right, after I'd finished choking on its assault on my throat, I felt its warmth seeping to every part of my body. From that moment on I had a taste for the stuff and it proved to be my downfall. He warned me not to tell anyone what he had told me or what I had seen, especially my father, as there were some in the village who were violent and greedy, and best to keep on good terms with them. They wouldn't hesitate to use force to keep up their trade. As he said this, I thought of my father and was anxious about him. I'd heard recently that a customs man had been stabbed with a dagger in his leg. "A warning," he'd been told. I knew it was true that there were brutish men around. To my surprise he then suggested that if I liked he could have a word with the others, and perhaps I'd be able to help them out sometimes. I didn't hesitate, of course I liked, and he laughed and told me to get myself off home and hold my tongue.'

Marion held up her hand and wiggled her fingers, then pointed and shook one at Matthew.

'Whoa. Okay, okay. Enough of the history for now, thank you. I want to know what you were up to and ...' she smiled a little flirtatiously at him, 'and where do I, or rather this girl you're so keen on, fit in?'

'I was just coming to that part. You realise, of course, as in my other lives, that the Senate has a hand in what happens next.'

'Are you sure? I mean ... Don't you rather bring trouble on yourself? Already in this life you're describing, you aren't completely blameless, are you?'

Marion could see in Matthew's eyes the depth of his feelings for her when he looked into her face, causing her briefly to wish she was in his arms. Quickly she dismissed this idea from her mind but softened her voice. 'Please go on Matthew,' she said and hesitated before adding, 'as long as it doesn't upset you too much.'

'Well at last you're acknowledging the history. I only wish that you could remember our past meetings for yourself, although at the moment I would settle for you believing what I tell you as true events.'

'Oh, give in, Matthew. Stop trying to convince me and get on with the story. We should be arriving soon and it will be too late to finish it.'

'At least another hour or so, I should think. I'll try to keep the history bits out but it might be difficult as, to be honest, it is all history of a sort isn't it?' Both of them stretched and Matthew stood up. When they had got comfortable and had settled down again he continued.

'It was Samuel's father who arranged for me to help at the local tavern on certain evenings, certain evenings where I would be useful elsewhere. By telling my mother I had an evening job collecting pots, spreading sawdust, any odd job that needed doing, I was able to be honestly out at night. By the time I was fifteen I was a fully fledged smuggler, one of the band. How I enjoyed the comradeship, the backslapping, jokes and tricks between us. I was accepted and no one ever mentioned my father. I was glad of this, as his son I would have been duty bound to defend him, thereby jeopardising my new found friendships.

'Our bay was so small that we were mostly left alone by the government men, as they thought it impossible for any large vessels to enter. From the shore we were able to see the top mast and sails of ships on the horizon long before they came fully into view. Many were legitimate, and we surmised they were on their way to and from Bristol, the biggest port in the area at that time. The ships we did business with would anchor way out to sea until nightfall, when they would sail in a little closer to the shore. We would then row out to them as silently as possible in our small fishing boats, we called them night boats. The night boats were filled to the gunnels with whatever goods we had – sometimes as ordered and at other times stuff to bargain with.

'I knew what was smuggled in as I told you earlier, but was often surprised at what was smuggled out. Mostly we had fleeces, plenty of farmers in the neighbourhood were willing to risk fines for a sizable profit. The carts that rumbled into the village at night and puzzled me earlier, contained iron, sometimes cannon. This shocked me at first, sending arms to the Spanish enemy, but, like the others, I thought of the payment I would get, so just accepted everything that went on. Another commodity was sacks of beans, these were to feed the enemy's horses.'

'Beans!' exclaimed Marion. 'Beans. I thought horses were fed hay.'

'Yes, beans. Seems it was horse feed at the time. Tons and tons went out from English fields. Our war horses too, were fed beans. I suppose, thinking about it, it would be easier to transport sacks of beans than sacks of hay. Another demand abroad was leather, in particular the soft leather of calves. Shall I go on?'

Marion smiled as she said, 'Well, you can hardly leave me here in suspense, can you? Of course, go on.'

'When we returned to the shore, many people had turned out to drag the laden boats up the beach. They appeared no matter what the weather, rain, hail, howling winds – winter and summer alike, blistering their hands on the ropes and slipping on the wet stones. As soon as the boats were secure they all quickly disappeared.

'The next job was to hide the contraband. You cannot imagine the odd hiding places. Goods were hidden in deep wells, the church tower, under the stone mausoleums that housed the bones of dead people of importance. We used the squire's barns, cellars in the tavern and under kitchen flagstones. I have even seen packets disappear quickly under women's skirts. Needless to say, strangers were not welcome in the village during these days, and I could see, now, why my family were treated so poorly.

'The rewards for smuggling were great for everyone, luxury goods could be bought so much cheaper as there was no tax on them. As you can guess, nearly all the gentry were involved. Know Kipling's poem, the "Smugglers' Song"?'

Marion said, 'The one that begins, "If you wake at midnight and hear a horse's feet …",' and together they chanted,

"Don't go drawing back the blind, or looking in the street,

Them that asks no questions isn't told a lie.

Watch the wall my darling, while the gentlemen go by."

'Oh, I absolutely loved that poem as a child. It gives such a clear picture of what was happening and rhymes so beautifully, don't you think?' said Marion.

'True. Well he got it right all those years later, still happening in his time.'

'And ours.'

'We were lucky that our own customs man was corrupt. As long as he was paid and had a share of whatever was landed, he chose to ignore what was happening. I believe he knew full well when something was on and stayed in his warm bed those nights, instead of catching us out and informing the authorities. To be fair, he was poorly paid for his duties, and generally speaking many custom officers were corrupt for that reason alone. That was father's undoing, although we managed well enough on his earnings. I understood from the villagers where he patrolled that he could not be bribed. Indeed, they were too afraid to approach him, he was quite an imposing figure on horseback and, of course, God-fearing and loyal to the crown. There were times when I thought he was in mortal danger from attacks from the likes of some I knew. As I said earlier, his visits home were few.

'Mother said nothing at all to me. She knew, I'm sure, what I was about, but gladly accepted some of the little treasures I was able to give her and was always thankful for any extra coins.'

'Now, Matthew, tell me about the girl. What was her name this time? What did she look like? Come on Matthew, how did you meet her and when? More importantly, did you love her and she you? Come on, tell all.' The anticipation on Marion's face delighted him and he half laughed.

'So, you believe in the girl,' he joked. 'Now all I've got to do is help you realise the truth.'

Marion laughed, 'Don't bet on it, my lad! Just tell me now about the girl.'

'I suppose I was about eighteen, maybe nineteen, and one night, as sometimes happened, the French sent their own small boat ashore. By the way, we didn't smuggle on a regular basis, every month or so, and once we went almost a year without contact. Anyway, on this particular night as I was helping to unload their cargo, I noticed a young fellow struggling with an overlarge packet and rushed to help. As I did so his cap fell into the water. I bent to retrieve it for him and when I glanced up in the moonlight I was shocked to see a girl grinning down at me, with black ringlets tumbling about her face. She said something French which set all of her companions laughing. I guessed it was probably about me and felt myself go crimson as I hurried away from her. She was so full of life, and I knew at once she was my soul mate. I found out her name was Marie and, yes, she was the prettiest maid I had ever seen, but she was not without fault.'

'What?' exclaimed Marion, 'Our precious heroine with faults? I can't believe it.'

'Surprises you doesn't it? Thought yourself perfect. Not really faults, just different. Believe me, Marie had the fiercest of tempers ever. I do believe she must have been spoilt by someone as a child, why else was she there? Pestered her guardian, I heard tell. She could hoist a bale onto her shoulders as well as any fit man, and she could swear like one too.

'I never saw her in any feminine robes, no swirling petticoats or a hint of lace or ribbons. The clothes she wore were sensible for the work she was doing, breeches and smocks, far too big, but they hid her body which, I thought, could only have been perfect. Marie was feisty, loud and laughed a lot. Her laughter was almost coarse, but I didn't care, I loved her wholeheartedly. I daresay it was obvious to all that I was smitten with her, and one night as I toiled alongside Samuel, his father said, "She's not for you, son." I didn't heed this at all, and decided to overcome my shyness and speak to her next time she came over.'

For a few moments Matthew was quiet and then, smiling across to Marion, he went on, 'I made sure I was working close to her on the next visit and the next. I had few French words, and she had fewer English ones so our conversations were, to say the least, difficult. I always felt she was secretly laughing at my awkwardness.

'One night both of us stretched out for the same large package and our hands touched. We both stopped, and looked at each other and I could see by her face that she had felt the same emotions as myself – a depth of feeling neither of us was aware of until that moment. It was all over in seconds and from then on there was a decided change in her attitude towards me. I saw only the gentler side of her and loved her the more for it.' Matthew was quiet for a moment.

'It was early in the evening, a summer's evening, when the French boat laden with contraband was spied on the horizon. There was excitement along with tension in the village. I swear any outsider would've known something was happening. I was beside myself with anxiety waiting to see if Marie was aboard. When the light was fading and the French craft drew nearer, I could see her pulling on the ropes to adjust the sails, as usual doing her fair share of the work. How glad I was to see her. I waited with bated breath to see if they were coming into harbour. Fortunately the tide was high enough for them to come almost to the beach. We waded out to greet them and at first I couldn't get near to Marie. I could see she, along with others, was being given orders that she seemed to be listening to intently, keeping her eyes on the leader. I must admit the intensity of her gaze gave me a twinge of jealousy, wondering if he was her beau, such was her concentration on him.

'Speculation was rife among our men on who she favoured most, some saying she was free with her favours for anyone who took her fancy. Some hinted darkly that she brought comfort, which was a veiled reference to bedroom pleasures, especially to those who had plenty of coins in their palms.

'We were never told of the personal lives of any of the French so it was all guesswork. These were harmless jests and they were soon forgotten by the fishermen turned smugglers I was with. I was seething inside, and couldn't bring myself to join in their banter; nor could I express my anger, as I am sure my interest in Marie would be frowned upon, even forbidden or, at best, I would be teased unmercifully. My jealousy was often aroused because Marie was given to flirting shamelessly among her own people, old and young alike. I thought of it as flirting but it was really no more than when I first saw her, laughing and joking; always in French.'

Marion was beginning to chuckle and burst out, 'I was a real shock to you then? It must have been my French blood or maybe I was frustrated with all that testosterone around. What do you think?'

Matthew grinned, 'I don't really know, but I do know that once we recognised our feelings for each other, I'm sure I was the only one she, you, ever thought of.'

'So go on, did you …?

Matthew, still grinning and chewing his bottom lip at the same time said, 'She must have been looking out for me as well. As soon as she had waded ashore, I watched as she scanned the English faces waiting in the semi-darkness. Then I saw her smile a secret half-smile to herself, and when she saw me smiling back she promptly turned her back on me. I was more than a little put out I can tell you.

'Work began at once unloading and exchanging goods. As we worked alongside the others, we didn't speak except to pass on instructions or messages, in a mixture of French and English, but we managed. This time I'd promised myself I would try to lure her away for a few minutes, just a few minutes for a kiss or two and to tell her how much I loved her. Our chance came when a wine cask broke open and the men from both countries laughed together as they took time out to sample its contents. I grabbed her hand and indicated the sand dunes. I ...'

Marion interrupted, 'The same ones I suppose where you fell asleep as a lad.'

Matthew nodded, 'The same. Marie laughed quietly and let me lead her away from the others. I'd planned all sorts for when we were at last alone.'

Marion's face was alight with anticipation and she said softly, 'So you seduced her?'

Matthew shook his head. 'Well not quite.'

Exasperated, Marion said, 'Oh no! Not the Senate interfering again.'

Matthew rubbed his chin thoughtfully. 'No, nothing like that at all. Oh, I'd planned a gentle seduction all right, but ...' He was obviously embarrassed.

'Go on,' Marion coaxed him, 'What happened? Did you get caught?'

'No way! All the sweet words and gentle caresses I'd imagined might happen between us were, how shall I put it ...?' For a few seconds he was thoughtful, '... were amateurish. I tell you, Marion, I was shocked, astounded and, to be honest, more than delighted. I could hardly believe it, she was the one who was the more experienced, set the pace and ...' embarrassed at the memory, 'I must say, was extremely generous in her amours.'

Marion screwed up her face, calling out loudly, 'Wow, wow, too much information. Stop right there.'

Indignantly Matthew said, 'Well, you did ask.' Both began laughing.

Matthew pulled back his shoulders and stretched before going on. 'It was not to be, of course. I never saw Marie again. The Senate had again allowed me that brief time with my beloved but it was time for the reckoning.'

'Oh, not again.' Marion said. 'They are a mean-spirited lot, aren't they? Surely they could have allowed you a little more happiness. I'm beginning to dislike them intensely. Did they kill you off after your ... your moments of passion?'

'No, and I was thankful for that. No, they had more in store for me. Remember I told you that brandy was my undoing?' She nodded. 'The gang were paid with coppers or, more often, something from the goods secreted away. Often I took part of my payment in liquor, mainly brandy, sometimes wine. I hid it away in the small copse at the back of my home. Once, just once, I took a length of fine lace for my mother and she was entranced with its intricate weave. Often I would see it pinned in her hair or in a bow around her throat, but, needless to say, she hid it from my father.

'I spent a great deal of time on the beach waiting and hoping that a boat would come with you aboard. In the sand, I daily etched out the MM, sometimes yards long, others times tiny like the little secret in my heart. One evening, feeling downhearted, I went to the woods to drink my favourite tipple, brandy. It was the first time I had ever got really drunk, and I truly wasn't aware of it happening. Unfortunately father had returned early from one of his shifts.' Matthew sighed, 'They were usually about six weeks long, and we weren't expecting him. I staggered into the house and there he was. As bad luck would have it, mother had fastened the lace strip to her gown.'

Marion's eyes widened, 'Oh, good Lord! You were both in deep, deep trouble now.'

'You can bet on it. Father was incensed and questioned both of us relentlessly. How? Where? When? Oh, how we lied when he shouted at us that first evening! Mother said that as most of the family were married or had left home, there were sometimes a few coppers left over, so she had been able to buy the lace from a travelling pedlar. "It was so pretty," she told father, "I couldn't resist the smallest of the pieces he had." I think father chose to believe her. Pedlars had such a poor reputation, selling inferior or stolen goods. It was quite possible for such a trader to have illicit French lace amongst his wares. Rarely did the rogue visit the same place twice, so there was no way my father could check her story anyway. Matthew paused then added, 'By the way, a group of pedlars at that time were called "an impertinence of pedlars" which seems to me, to be very apt.

'Father was much more severe with me, and I could tell he suspected me of being involved with the dubious men of the village. Every day he was at home he questioned and questioned me, but couldn't beat any information out of me, try as he might. Mother denied knowing anything as well. How could she? All I ever told her was that I was working at the tavern when I left her some evenings. Father even went to the tavern to confirm this, and when the lads told me later we were able to laugh at how he had been hoodwinked. Apparently he'd asked why I wasn't working every evening. The innkeeper had told him that with taxes so high men weren't supping so much ale and he was only able to pay me for my services occasionally. When father left for his duties a week later, I could see he wasn't happy He had hardly spoken to me except to question me, and tell me of the perils of drinking, that my next place would be in hell and, unlike his usual self, he was churlish to mother.

'The night father left us, a boat appeared on the horizon and there was a buzz of excitement about the village. Once it was dark we made our way down to the beach. One of the men flashed his lantern, a sort of early Morse code. He put his hand in front of the candle to hide its glow and then took it away to let it shine seawards. This let them know that it was safe to come closer. They answered with a brief, weak flash of their own lantern and soon afterwards the French boat was being hauled onto the beach.

'It was a small boat and not many men were required to unload it. I was disappointed that Marie was not on board. As we began with utmost speed, and as quietly as possible to unload barrels and packages, we suddenly heard a loud voice calling out for us to stop what we were about. Some men made a run for it, and the French, who were desperately pulling their boat towards the open sea, fortunately escaped. The customs men opened fire on them with their matchlock pistols, and thankfully their shots were wild. I was chased by a man on horseback and I ran for my life, but I was captured. Three of my companions were also caught. We ended up in the pit of Exeter Guildhall which served as a prison at the time. The pit was the bare cellar beneath the newly built Guildhall, and we four were kept there with others to await the Lent quarter sessions.

'I was imprisoned for two months until the trial. As we waited we went over the fateful evening again and again. At one time they tried to blame my father, but there had been no time for him to have alerted anyone. He had left only two or three hours or so before we were caught. We were all quiet workers. Even the ponies' feet had been wrapped in old rags so that their trotting couldn't be heard on the cobblestones, so we couldn't understand how we had given ourselves away.'

'Ponies? Why ponies? I thought it was all manpower to shift things?' Marion queried.

'That night the magistrate was waiting for letters and the squire's lady was expecting a bale of silk. The squire lent us the ponies as we were to deliver their packages as quickly as possible.'

'Oh, I see. I suppose you got paid extra for that?'

'No, all part of the service. One of our group was the look-out man, he was supposed to have warned us, but his signal to alert us of danger never came. He told us that he was shocked when, from nowhere, a gloved hand came over his mouth and he was unable to give the warning whistle. Someone, we all agreed, had betrayed us.

'At the trial all four of us were found guilty, well we would be, we were caught breaking the law. We were each to pay a fine of twenty-five pounds, impossible for all of us. We had to stay in prison until it was paid, all of us had little hope that someone might pay up to release us.

'One of the men I was with was taken away and given his freedom. I later learned that he had implicated the priest, squire, magistrate and a Lord, stating that they had received stolen goods. These people in turn were fined, which was no problem for them and they never saw the inside of the prison. There was never any question of them helping us.

'I had two visitors whilst I was incarcerated; firstly my father. I had hoped that in his love for me he would pay the debt, though I doubted he had that sort of wealth. I shall never forget his words. He said I had lied and cheated all against the faith; that what I had done was treasonable against the Queen and I was lucky to have escaped being deported to the new world and, even worse, the death penalty. Next he said that I had dishonoured him and his family name. I was no longer a son of his, and I was to change my name so I could not be associated with him. Finally he told me never to return to my home or the village. He left me in tears. I was but twenty-one.'

Marion broke in. 'Well, he was right I suppose. You were guilty of all he said, but it's a hard father who can turn his back on his child.'

'I know, and I felt so abandoned, which was his intention.'

'So who was your second visitor? I hope they had some money for your release.'

'No. My second visitor was my mother. It seems she had walked the best part of the way, although one or two people had given her a lift on a cart. When I saw how tired, thin and unwell she was, I was ashamed that I had caused her such distress. It was at about this time that I began to suffer from gaol fever or typhus as it is now called. Not surprising, as the prison was overcrowded, dark and filthy with no sanitation, and our constant companions were cockroaches and lice. My mother could see I was shaking with fever and had a rash, a sure sign of the illness. A good number of prisoners died from this disease long before they ever saw the magistrate. When mother saw the state I was in she wept and put her arms around me, whispering all the time, "My son, my son." I wept alongside her until she left for the long, lonely journey home. Not once did she reproach me. Shortly afterwards I succumbed to the fatal illness and found myself in the presence of the unsympathetic Senate again. Needless to say they were not surprised to see me.'

When he had stopped speaking he realised that Marion was rummaging in her bag and was surprised when she fished out a tissue and wiped her eyes.

'That was so sad Matthew,' she sniffed. 'I really felt for your mother and I could tell you had a measure of remorse. Honour thy father and thy mother was the one you broke that time wasn't it?' She gave a last dab at her eyes carefully so that her mascara wouldn't smudge, pushed the tissue up her sleeve and asked, 'Tell me Matthew, every time you start a new life, do you get the same parents or new ones?'

Matthew gave a half smile. 'I never get the same ones twice, always new ones and always honest people. I think the Senate hoped they would have a good influence on me, and so they did until circumstances altered everything and I blame the Senate for that.'

'How can you? You're responsible for your actions.' She laughed, 'Hey, I'm getting carried away here, thinking all of this really happened.'

Matthew shook his head in despair.

For a few minutes neither spoke, each lost in their own thoughts. Marion gazed out of the window and noticed the shadows getting longer. Turning back to Matthew to ask a question, she was surprised to see that his eyes were closed.

Marion sat and enjoyed looking at him. His long legs were stretched out, his hands resting lightly on his thighs and an almost imperceptible smile lingering on his face, a face she would dearly like to caress. In her heart she admitted it was crazy to have these feelings for a virtual stranger, but somehow it didn't feel as if he were a stranger. What is happening, she wondered? Perhaps all he is saying is true, that we are soul mates and that he has to redeem himself. I just don't know. The more practical side of her insisted that, yes, indeed he was a brilliant story teller, but how stupid to even think any of it was true. As he stirred, then settled himself more comfortably, her heart wanted to believe, but knew that his striving for her love was impossible.

Nine

Matthew woke with a start five minutes later, sat up straight, rubbed his eyes and grinned at her. 'Just resting me eyes. Gazing at you has almost worn them out.'

'I'm thinking it's more likely your tongue that needs a rest.' Preening herself a little Marion said, 'I trust you like what you see, worth the effort?'

'I do believe you're flirting with me.'

At once, Marion felt guilty, admitting to herself, yes she had flirted a little and was over-quick with her reply. 'Never. Get that idea out of your head now, at once.' She watched the bewilderment on his face at her quick, sharp tone. 'Sorry,' she said, 'I was only fishing for compliments really.'

'No, don't be. Don't be sorry,' he said. 'It's my fault really. I was, I suppose, making a clumsy pass. I should be saying sorry to you.' There was a broad grin on his face as he added, 'Mind you ...' and laughed out loud as she wagged her finger at him and said,

'Don't you dare say anything more.' Marion leaned back in her seat before saying, 'Matthew, once you know you have broken a commandment, are you scared? I mean, you know that you must

return to the Senate and that means you have to die, doesn't it?'
She sat quietly and waited.

After a thoughtful few moments he answered. 'I'm not scared
of dying, but it is the how and when. I mean, will I have an early
death? It usually is. Not like some folk who have been told by their
doctors they have only so long to live. I wouldn't like that at all,
but I do know that sooner or later I will die. On a few occasions,
for instance, when I was the bishop, it was a number of years
before anything happened; other times death is almost instantane-
ous.' He paused for a moment. 'The how is a different matter. My
imagination ruins the time I have left. I think the worst death was
in the gold mine. It was dark, I was in pain and so lonely.'

Marion gave him a sympathetic look as she said, 'It must have
been awful for you.'

Matthew leaned towards her. There was urgency in his voice as
he said, 'There is something I need to tell you, something that
always bothers me. The Senate always forgive, that is Peter always
does. I do think most of them know how remorseful I am, and are
willing to give me another chance. Yes, to be fair, they always send
me back whole, every fault pardoned. This one broken commandment is the one that haunts me every time I return, and remember
the awfulness of it. One, I promise myself, I will never, never
repeat.'

The compartment door slid open and stopped him speaking
further. It was the steward with the tea trolley.

'Well, folks,' he said, 'enjoy your cake? Not so bad was it?' As
he picked up the empty crockery he saw the remains of the abandoned cake in the saucers. Grinning at them he said, 'Oh, not to
your liking after all, was it? Must say it's not me favourite either,'
and laughed at his confession. As he left the compartment he
turned back and said, 'Not long now to Kings Cross, thank Gawd.
Finished for the day then I have. Good evening to you both.' He
closed the door behind him as they murmured, 'Good evening'
back.

Alone again, Marion turned to Matthew who had leaned over,
dropped his head down and his hands were spread on his thighs.
When he lifted his head there was almost a look of guilt, followed
by a look of suffering on his face.

'You know, Matthew, you really don't have to put yourself
through all this. You behave as if you really lived all the stories

you're telling me. Tell yourself it's fiction, for that is what it is, and you won't feel so bad.' She hesitated adding, 'You really don't have to tell me, you know.'

In a pleading, anguished tone he answered, 'I must. I was there. I did all that I tell you. You should know how I was. There should be no secrets between us. I want ...,' he twisted away from her then turned back saying, 'I don't know what I want. To be free of this particular guilt mostly, I think.'

Marion watched as he tried to put his thoughts into words. 'It's not important, Matthew.'

'I want you to know. I want you to know that I believe all the past events and suffering have been worthwhile. I have found you Marion and I want to be with you always. This is what I've been striving for – to be with you forever.'

Marion turned away from him, unsure of her own feelings as a voice within her wailed, 'That's what I want too,' but another inner voice cautioned, 'Be careful. Say nothing.'

'Matthew, it isn't going to happen. I ...' He put up his hand to stop her saying anything further.

'Wait. Let me tell you of my nightmare time, the time I committed murder.'

Turning back to him she said softly, 'How long have we known each other, Matthew? No more than twenty-four hours. Long enough for me to be sure that you would not, indeed could not, murder another soul.'

'I did and it happened like this.'

Shaking her head and giving a soft sigh, she said, 'I'll stop you if I think you're getting yourself too upset. Alright?'

He nodded and began, and smiled as he remembered. 'We were betrothed, engaged to be married at Christmas time.'

'Who, Matthew? Who were you engaged to?'

'You, as I said, but you were called Mary then.'

'And when was this?'

'Mid sixteen hundreds, in the middle of what is now called the Civil War.'

'Never got my head round that period of history.'

'No, it was a difficult time. As I said, we were to be married. Our fathers' land was next to each other. I was the second son of a farmer, a wealthy farmer I suppose you could say. At one time I believe I was destined for the church, instead my father made me the farm manager. I never got my hands dirty doing things like mucking out the sheds, haymaking or ploughing, the everyday jobs, but I was expected to manage the workers, pay them and, believe it or not, monitor their behaviour. One or two, family men, were heavy drinkers chancing their jobs and homes, and I do believe I helped curb their irresponsible behaviour. Father wouldn't tolerate any bad language either. Truth to tell, they were all good workers, so I only reminded them to behave and never had to dismiss anyone. It was possible my father knew, he was soft like me and didn't fancy telling them to go. I was also responsible for the upkeep of the outbuildings, barns and suchlike. No daily chores for me then, so I had plenty of time for hunting, fishing, well, all things wealthy people did at that time.'

Marion interrupted. 'I suppose you were on a horse, otherwise you would have been worn out if it was a sizable farm.'

'Yes, you're right, but it wasn't as big as your father's land, his was almost as far as the eye could see. I think at times my father was quite envious, but at others I heard him say that if he had as much land as that, he would never have time for merrymaking.'

'So how did you meet Mary? Was she pretty? Hopefully clever, not cloying, I hate women like that. You know the type, expecting the man to be responsible for everything while they cling possessively to him.'

Matthew spluttered, unable to keep back his laughter. 'You! Clingy, never. Determination was your second name. Why, I do believe now I recall, that you deliberately set out to snare me!'

Marion picked up the newspaper and swiped him on the chest. As the paper found its mark he pretended it hurt and doubled up.

'Hey, steady on.' He mumbled, 'I see you haven't changed much from that time.'

'You deserved that. Continue.'

'Yes, you asked how we met. Being deep in the Devon countryside, there was little in the way of entertainment, but there were endless parties and that was where we officially met.'

'Officially met? Was there an unofficial way of meeting then?'

'I get your point. What I meant was that as our two lands adjoined, and, as children, we played together so we were not strangers to each other. As adults, of course, things changed, chaperones and courtship, that sort of thing. Girls' reputations had to be preserved for their eventual marriage. So, after being tutored at home until I was seven, I went away to be educated. Firstly, to a grammar school, and later on to university, where I learned Latin and complicated maths. More importantly there was some military training should I ever be called to serve in the royal household.'

'Did you?'

'Wait. You shall see.'

'And did Mary get any education?'

'A little. At first your mother taught you your letters, and then you went to a school in town to learn about music and needlework, accomplishments that were considered more suitable for girls. It was thought academic subjects were not necessary. There were no grammar schools for girls.'

Marion grunted and tutted. 'Typical!'

'Of the times, yes I agree, but life in the grammar school was no fun. You wouldn't have liked it at all.'

'I have yet to hear of a boarding school that was fun. It was a boarding school, wasn't it?'

'Yes. We began our lessons after prayers at around six thirty in the morning. In the winter it was unbearably cold. I was so miserable when I first went there. We had short breaks for our meals and then worked on until about five thirty. Absolutely no slacking, ever. If anyone fell behind in the lessons and didn't keep up, then he was punished.'

'Did you ever get punished?'

'No way! What? Have my breeches taken down and my bare buttocks exposed so the master could beat me with twigs! Often he asked the other boys to hold down the boy to be chastised.'

Marion laughed. 'Bare bum, you say. Umm ...' and Matthew laughed along with her.

'Anyway, the party where we met, which was to celebrate the completion of a newly built manor house, was a grand affair. I'd just had my twentieth birthday and I wore a shirt of the best linen with ruffles, a silk jacket, knee length breeches, white stockings and boots. It was quite an elegant turnout, though I say so myself. My hair was dark with natural curly ringlets in this life. A good number of the gentry wore flowing wigs and my hair was the envy of many. I also had the beginnings of a beard to match. I was quite tall, and knew that the eyes of the matrons and their daughters were on me, and I believe I charmed them all. I suppose I was considered a good catch.'

Marion pulled a face at him. 'Please, please don't tell me Mary threw herself at you!'

'No, my dear. You, she, was a bit huffy, ignored me. Of course that got me interested in her straight away.'

'So, tell me, what was she wearing?'

'A gown of silk. That's too easy. Let me try to explain. Mary wore a clean linen shift and something like a petticoat – my mother told me that – and over it she wore two long dresses.'

'Two!'

'It was the fashion. The dresses were in two parts, rather like a suit. A long-sleeved bodice – a blouse I believe you would call it – that came down over the stomach and a matching skirt. The top skirt was hitched up at the waist so that the under skirt could be seen. All were in silk and beautifully embroidered with silver thread; your father must have spent a small fortune on the outfit.' Matthew stopped and stretched his arms above his head.

'Oh dear, run out of story now, have you?'

'No. No. Just stretching out a bit. A long journey, isn't it?'

Marion agreed. 'I know just how you feel. I'm a bit stiff myself.'

Turning back to her, he said.' I'll carry on, shall I?'

Marion smiled encouragingly. 'Carry on.'

'At the start of the party everyone was milling around, then the men retired to side rooms where games and gambling took place. There were card games, chess, cribbage and dice. I enjoyed a game of chess with my brother, but all around us we could hear heavy bets being placed. It was difficult for us to concentrate as often there were groans of disappointment or loud shouts of laughter as someone won another's fortune, which set us wondering who.'

'Did your father or Mary's gamble?'

'I suspect as much, but it wasn't my place to ask those sorts of questions.'

'And the women? What did they do?'

'The women sat together in groups. and moved from one person to another catching up, I believe, on each other's families. Isn't there a newspaper that records, "Hatches, Matches and Dispatches"? Well, I reckon it was something like that. Some had come great distances and probably had not seen each other for months or even years.'

'Gossip. Nothing like a good old gossip. There was plenty at Aunt Amy's I can tell you, but go on.'

'It wasn't long before we heard the musicians tuning their instruments in the great hall. Every gentleman of note was expected to know how to dance, the most popular being the measures. Dance masters were employed by many of the gentry to ensure perfection, not a step to be out of place. So the dancing began. At first I watched the dancers, smiling and chattering to their partners as they moved, and then I saw you. You were so regal, graceful, dipping and turning so smoothly into squares or circles demanded in the measures, I knew at once who you were – my reason for being granted life and I made it my business to capture you for the next dance and the next. Of course, you were unable to reject me outright, it would have been extremely bad manners. It was wonderful as you walked with stately grace and curtseyed beside me in each of the dances. During the first two dances you refused to speak or even look at me directly, but gradually you began to accept me and when the time came for supper, you allowed me to escort you to the dining hall.'

'On your arm. I hope, like a proper lady,' Marion said.

'Like a proper lady, perfect. When we entered the hall we were amazed at the spread of food provided. I cannot begin to tell you of everything there was to eat. There were hot meat pies of lamb, beef and venison, as well as fruit pies filled with spices, raspberries and currants. Ox tongue cooked in nutmeg or, if you preferred, herring with scrambled eggs. Guests were amazed to see pineapples and bananas, for some it was the first time they had ever seen such fruit. Only a truly wealthy family could afford such luxuries. Forks had been introduced from Italy earlier in the century, and the host had provided every guest with one. To finish the meal there was syllabub or cheesecake, all accompanied with either mead or spiced wine.'

Matthew gave a half smile as he looked at Marion across the compartment and said wistfully, 'It was a magical time. So our courtship began. Within a few months I asked your father for your hand in marriage. I was so nervous and when I summoned up the courage, well you won't believe what he said, he roared out laughing and said, "Take the wench." As soon as he saw the dismay on my face, he slapped my back and shook my hand, then demanded that I take great care of you.'

Marion chuckled 'That's just the sort of thing my father would say now.'

'Anyway, arrangements were made for us to marry at Christmas. Both families had agreed to share the cost and build us a house at the joint boundary. Two or three times a week you would ride from your home and I from mine and we would meet at the site.' Matthew sighed, 'We thought the house would never be ready.'

'But in time it was?'

'Yes. You were determined to have it to your liking. Almost every week there was to be an alteration, you wanted oak doors at the entrance and mullioned windows everywhere. When I said the cold would seep in during the winter months you said you preferred to have light, plenty of light. Nothing gloomy in our house, you said, and promptly ordered brocade drapes to cover the windows in wintertime. As for the kitchen! A flagstone floor and the largest brick-built fireplace ever. On order, were carved chairs and, without any show of modesty, you ordered a four-poster bed. I was a bit annoyed when you said you'd also ordered some warming pans. I had to hold my tongue on that score as you were still a maiden, if you get my meaning.'

Solemnly, Marion nodded, holding back her mirth. 'Perhaps she thought you might not ...'

Matthew stared at her, said nothing at all, winked and continued.

'There were endless changes it seemed to me. You were determined it would be as modern and practical as possible.'

'And why not? So important to get it right at the start of any marriage, I think.'

'I suppose you're right, but to answer your question. Yes, in time it did indeed get built, but not for us, never for us.'

Marion felt disappointed and her heart grew heavy. From what she had learned from Matthew so far, he never won his true love. What surprised her more, was that she was now beginning to identify with each of the women he professed to be seeking. Were they all the same one, as Matthew insisted she asked herself, and am I really she?

'So, what happened?' she asked.

'It was obvious to all that there was unrest in the country. We'd heard about the Parliamentarian and Royalist skirmishes around the country over the last couple of years. It wasn't until an agent of

Prince Rupert came to our part of Devon, seeking support for the King from the men-folk of the area, that we finally became involved. Along with others I joined the King's army, now swollen with men from Cornwall.'

'Ah, so all that military training at the university wasn't in vain then?'

'No, it proved to be more than useful. We had our successes and failures, but I thought every battle was a private hell for each individual. It is hard to say who fared best. On both sides there were the cavalry who wore a form of protective armour, back and chest padding usually stuffed with straw that was difficult to penetrate with lances and suchlike. Long boots that covered the thighs were essential as a sword thrust finding the main artery was lethal. Some had steel helmets and the whole ensemble was very heavy and uncomfortable, especially during the summer months. And, I might add, feathers were not worn in battle, they were part of the finery worn by gentlemen in happier times, especially if they were to have their portrait painted. It wasn't unusual for a cavalry man to lose and change horses more than once in a long battle. Cavalry men would carry and fire pistols into the enemy ranks at the start of a battle and then wheel their mounts round and charge with drawn swords.

'There were also some siege guns, usually used just before the main battle started. They were cumbersome and fired cannon balls, but it took time to load them, no more than eight or ten an hour. Once they had fired the guns were usually left in place until after the battle. There were also lighter guns on wheels that were loaded with shrapnel, anything metal that could be found, and were greatly feared as they inflicted the most hideous of wounds.

'Most times there were dragoons, noted for their sniping accuracy in firing flintlock muskets at the fleeing enemy but, if needed, they formed up with the pikemen. Once the initial charges had been made, the pikemen were centred in the middle of the army and used their pikes, some as long as sixteen feet, all with a steel tip. It was strictly forbidden, but most of the men cut their pikes or poles down by two or three feet, as they were difficult to wield in battle and cumbersome to march with. In the main the pikes were used to push the enemy back.

'After one such battle, it now being harvest time, many common folk slipped away back to their homes and farms. The saving of their produce was far more important than the war if their families were to survive the long winter months.

'With reduced numbers on our side, we lost most battles. Did I say I was a Royalist? I could no longer bear the noise of clashing arms, gunfire; the cries of the injured men and the shrieks of the fallen horses. Men who went on fighting in close combat were exhausted, including me. Often it was impossible to see who was friend or who was foe in the gunpowder smoke. After yet another defeat I, along with others, was forced to go into hiding.

'The Parliamentarians were ruthless in their search for us. They hunted us down relentlessly. At night it was easier to move around the countryside. Carefully, oh so carefully, I slowly made my way over the moors. I ate what I could find in the moonlight, mainly berries. I was heading towards Exeter, where some of the inhabitants were sympathetic to the King's cause. I had made plans to escape with other men of importance, before my last battle should we fare badly. A boat was constantly to be at the ready to take anyone to Holland who was fleeing from the Parliamentarians. When I finally arrived at the appointed rendezvous I was too late. The boat had left two days earlier.'

Marion moved her injured arm cautiously and began to try to put it back in the sling. When she winced, Matthew jumped to his feet and said, 'Here let me help you,' and gently guided the sling over her arm.

She smiled her thanks to him. 'Are you going on or do you want a rest?'

'You're enjoying this, aren't you?'

'Matthew, I'm more than intrigued. I need to know how you break your truce with the Senate each time. I'm looking forward to you getting the better of them.'

'It might just happen in this lifetime, we'll see, but not in the one I'm telling you about. So, Marion, there I was stranded at Exeter. Not a safe place to be. One could never tell whose side anyone was on. It was so dangerous for anyone to associate with Royalist military personnel. I decided to cut back across the moors and make my way to Colyton, where the villagers were known to favour the King.

On the way across the bleak moors, godforsaken and unfriendly even in summertime, I was nearly caught. Around midnight when a small number of the enemy were changing camps I nearly walked into their midst. Fortunately their chattering alerted me, and I jumped off the beaten track just in time, landed among brambles and nettles, but that was better than the alternative. I didn't fancy being a prisoner. All I wanted was to see the king reinstated and to go home to my wedding.

'The journey would take me within a few miles of our homes and our new house. By now I hadn't seen my family for over four months and I was desperate to see you. Of course, there was no way I could really risk seeking any of you. I'm sure, because of the number of searching troops about, that I was on the wanted list. I could not seek help from any of your family or mine or our retainers. The men working on the farm might attempt to aid me, but that would have meant imprisonment for them also, possibly worse. They would be accused of treason against the state. Certainly, they would have been heavily fined and possibly all our homes would have been sequestered. Another form of reprisal was to burn down an offender's property.'

'For helping their own relatives? That was very harsh. Surely they were family men too?'

Matthew shrugged. 'That's how it was at the time. I daresay the Royalists meted out similar reprisals – not that I was party to any of them.

'Two days it took me to reach the hills overlooking the acres of land my father owned. As I gazed down on the flat land below I was consumed with homesickness. I could see the place was overrun with Cromwell's men. I knew then it would be impossible for me to make any contact whatsoever with my loved ones. In the hills, so familiar to me, I knew of a good hiding place. Not exactly a cave, but there was a large overhanging slab of rock, really large and the ground beneath it sloped back into the hillside and was dry. In front, the grass was worn away, the result of a sheep run, so footsteps would not be seen, but I had to be careful not to disturb stones to prevent them rattling down the hillside. Much relieved and looking forward to a few hours sleep, I quietly entered the little hidden haven.

'I nearly jumped out of my skin and yelled out loud when I almost fell onto a body – a body that groaned as I bumped into it. Someone had already taken refuge there, and he told me later he had found it by chance. Robin, a lad of fourteen, and recently married he told me. Robin came from Colyton, the village I intended to reach. He was just a child really, and now and again I heard him call out for his mother in his dreams. A twisted ankle had prevented him going any further. He certainly wasn't able to move very much. The ankle might even have been broken as there were times when I had to cover his mouth to stop him shouting out with the pain.

We were there for close on fifteen days, waiting for the army to move on. We were trapped. We had little to eat and hunger haunted us day and night. I was hungry before I even reached the overhanging rock. I would go out foraging in the dark for fallen apples and sometimes a few plums, not enough for two, but we shared. Once I was lucky enough to catch a rabbit. I flung myself down on the creature, broke its neck and we ate it raw.'

At that Marion shuddered, then frowned. 'I don't know what is worse, killing a living creature or eating meat raw!'

'When you are really hungry to the point of almost starving, you'll do anything for food.'

Marion nodded slowly. 'I suppose so. I've interrupted you again haven't I? Do go on please.'

'Robin told me that most of the people of Colyton were Royalist supporters, and were known to be able to secure a safe route to the fishing village of Seaton. Seaton boatmen were friendly, and often risked their lives to help those fleeing to Holland. That was our plan. By now, thankfully, Robin could take a few painful steps, and we hoped, that in a day or two he would be strong enough to start out on our journey once the camps broke up.

'One night I ventured as far as our unfinished house about two miles away, hoping that one of the workers might have left some food behind, very unlikely, and if he had, probably the birds or mice would have made short work of it. Nevertheless, I set out and on reaching the house, now nearly complete, I became at once both excited and sorrowful. Excited because seeing it held such promise, and sorrowful as I knew it would be a long time before these troubles were over. I could have wept at the futility of it all, the war, the politics, just about everything at that moment. I found a partly eaten pasty, half eaten by someone and a rat, I think, had nibbled at it. I could have eaten it there and then, but instead decided to share it with Robin. Carefully I carved our initials on Mary's precious oak door, M and M intertwined and heart shaped at the bottom, before going back to our hiding place.

'I returned to the house the following night but there was nothing there, the same the following night. On the third night I found a large wedge of cheese wrapped in a piece of clean linen, at least half a pound in weight. It could only have been Mary, she must have guessed I was close by. I wondered how she managed to leave such a generous feast. She would've walked the three miles from her home as all the horses had been taken from the farms for war service. I was overwhelmed with joy to think she knew I was near, and had probably told our families. I can imagine the relief they felt knowing I was still alive. How, I wondered, did she pass all the militia to-ing and fro-ing about the countryside?'

Marion threw back her head and laughed. 'Oh come on Matthew,' she said, 'Easy, like all women would do for their loved ones, flirted, distracted the male. Not hard to do, especially if she was as pretty and as determined as you said, and no doubt a charming diversion for the soldiers.'

'I didn't want to think along those lines at the time, thank you, but I suppose you're right. When I got back to Robin we cut the cheese into three to make it last in case I was unable to go out if the weather was bad or if I was not lucky enough to find something to eat on my nightly excursions, which I didn't, by the way, find anything.

'On the third night, leaving my small share of cheese for when I returned, I ventured out again for food and found nothing. That night the weather changed. After so many days of dry weather it began to rain; hard, driving, cold rain that seemed to penetrate my bones. The thought of that little piece of cheese, such a prize for me, that my dearest had faced danger to leave for me, kept my spirits up for a while. I smiled to myself as I thought of our wedding day to come once this dreadful war was over. I'd never leave her again, I promised myself. Of course I knew that the square of cheese, no bigger than a matchbox, was not enough to fill me, but it would perhaps ease the hunger pains in my stomach for an hour or two. On and on I walked, very aware of the possibility of meeting a foot soldier, and knowing I was not strong enough to defeat him in a face to face confrontation. I was cold, very wet, hungry and tired when I got back just as day was breaking. I sank to the floor and pulled out my dagger to spear my piece of cheese. At first I was puzzled when I couldn't see it, and began to get anxious when I couldn't find it.'

Marion, now completely absorbed by Matthew's story asked, 'Where was it?'

'I'd left it safe on a flat stone.' Matthew bit his lip and hesitated, 'I cannot tell you how angry I was when I asked Robin if he knew where it was. As I looked at his face, I realised he had stolen my little share and eaten it. "I was sure you'd find something tonight," he whimpered as he curled himself away from me. I had never experienced such anger as I felt at that moment. All thoughts of hope for an ending to our misery along with all thoughts of chivalry left me.

'There was a roaring in my head, my heart beat fast and everything seemed a blur. You've heard of the 'red mist before the eyes'? Well that's how it was. The dagger was still in my hand ...' Matthew stopped speaking, and Marion watched as he slumped down in the seat and put his head in his shaking hands. When he lifted his head to look into her face she could see his misery.

'Matthew, don't. Please don't say anything more. Please,' she begged softly.

He took her hand and this time she didn't take it away, knowing he intended to go on, and that he needed courage to do so. He breathed deeply and swallowed and the heaviness in his voice, when he began to speak again, made her long to take away his pain.

'Marion, all the forgiveness the Senate gave is all very well, but how do I forgive myself?'

'I don't know, except that the remorse and sorrow you are suffering now should be enough.'

'It isn't,' he said bitterly. 'I had the dagger in my hand and without hesitation in the dim light I thrust it into Robin – not once, but again and again.'

Marion watched as Matthew shuddered and seemed to relive the awful moment. 'He didn't die straight away, but lived a little longer, not making a sound. Just before the end he whispered he was sorry, that he deserved my wrath and I was not to blame. He forgave me, Marion. I had taken his life and he blamed himself. I held his lifeless body in my arms for most of the day. I was weeping as I did so.

'It was late afternoon when I decided to make my move. I didn't care whether or not I would get to Seaton. I cared about nothing. That's not true. I cared greatly that I would not see Mary again. I knew the Senate would take me back at any time now that

I had failed yet again. As I walked wearily across the meadow I was halted by a militia man. I made a feeble attempt to run and he fired his pistol. His lead ball hit my leg and I fell. Another fellow stood over me and fired directly into my heart. I was grateful for that. I knew no more of that life.'

Marion longed to ease his pain, tell him all this would pass. 'What I don't understand is why the Senate didn't allow the murder of Magdalena's father to count. To let you murder a second time was so unfair.' Seeing the look of dejection on his face, she crossed to his side and put her arm around his shoulders and she felt him relax against her.

'I don't know what is happening between us, Matthew. I long to believe all that you tell me but I cannot see how it can be so. All I know is that I can't bear to see you suffering such distress. I tell myself it's self-inflicted yet know in my heart that it is very uncharitable of me. I only know that I see you are tormented by these events, whether they are imaginary or real to you. You will be ill if you keep on like this.' As an afterthought she asked, 'Tell me Matthew, when you return is your memory with you from birth?'

Matthew smiled. 'Thankfully, no. The Senate, as you can tell for yourself, can be really mean at times, but it isn't until you, that is Magdalena, comes into my life. Once she appears, then the memories flood in mercilessly.'

'Well that shows a bit of compassion, I suppose.' Pulling herself up straighter in her seat she suddenly said quite briskly, 'I'd love to confront the Senate. I'd make sure they would know how angry I feel about their treatment of you. Yes, Matthew, I would even stamp my foot.'

Matthew gave a fleeting smile. 'Yes, I bet you would,' he said.

Marion continued. 'How dare they let you suffer centuries, yes centuries,' she repeated as Matthew tried to correct her. 'Let them see how cruel they've been to you. Setting you up, deliberately placing you in circumstances where to break one of the commandments is the only answer. Well, perhaps not all of the situations, but it's just not fair. It's time you won your lady, Matthew. Next time, tell them so.' She was breathless when she finished, and was quiet for a moment before adding, 'Better still, insist on seeing the top man. What did they call him?' She pulled her bottom lip between her teeth and frowned a little, trying to remember. 'Yes, that's it, The Higher Authority! You tell them that. Next time you find yourself in front of them demand to see him and don't back down, don't be put off by any of their tactics. They were very anxious that he didn't find out that their first destiny for you didn't work out, weren't they? You give them a scare next time.'

With a half smile Matthew answered. 'If only it were that simple but thanks for the advice. I'll think about it.' He leaned against the backrest, folded his arms and asked in a soft voice, 'So now you know what I did and why I felt so wretched telling you. Can you forgive me?'

'I do forgive you, although there is no need. It was a number of life-times ago,' she paused before saying, 'Matthew, I'm finding it more and more difficult not to believe your stories. I've tried to resist, wanting them not to be true, that you were indeed making up tales to entertain me, but ...'

At once Matthew's face brightened, 'At last,' he said.

'Don't get carried away. I said there was a "but". I know I would be deeply hurt if I discovered you were kidding me all the time.'

'Never. I would never lie to you or want to give you pain. Have I not made it clear that I love you? All I ever wanted was for you to have a happy life, and me to be a part of it no matter how small.' As an afterthought he added, 'Your complete rejection of me would be unbearable, but even so, as long as you live you will know deep in your heart that I love you.'

'You mean Magdalena.'

Smiling, he said. 'Yes, Magdalena.' He reached for his jacket and as he put his hand in its pocket said, 'I think it's time we had a little treat,' and with a flourish produced a hip flask. He poured a measure of brandy into the screw top, not much bigger than a thimble and handed it to her. 'Here's to truth,' he said as he raised the flask to his lips and she answered as she held out the stopper for a refill.

'And to your true love.'

Ten

Matthew shook the empty flask hoping there was a little left, replaced the screw cap and placed it on the seat beside him. The brandy, although each of them had less than a pub measure, relaxed the air of sadness they had been experiencing. Marion fumbled in her bag and brought out her make-up kit and tipped its contents onto the seat beside her. Among the items were tweezers, a nail file and a couple of odd earrings. Matthew picked up the tweezers, squeezed two or three times and feigning surprise, asked, 'What on earth do you use these for?'

Marion raised her eyebrows and gave him a quizzical look. 'Come on, Matthew. Haven't you got any sisters? They must have used them on their eyebrows now and again. Confess, you knew that didn't you?'

He laughed and said, 'No, they didn't. If they did I didn't see them.' He looked down at her smooth legs, then in mock horror pointed to them and looked up into her face, 'Please,' he begged, 'Please don't tell me that you actually use the tweezers on your legs. I mean ...'

At first Marion was amazed and she looked back at him and he grinned at her.

'Oh you! You're teasing me again. Shut up,' and handing him a powder compact, she instructed him to open it and hold its tiny mirror in front of her. When he did as she asked, he watched as she ran a comb through her hair, which sprang back into natural waves, and then powder her nose. Glancing at him she saw on his face a look of both amusement and indulgence.

'What? What are you grinning at?' she snapped, 'We're nearly there and I don't want to look like a worn out hag.'

Matthew laughed out loud, then leaning closely in towards her and through half-shut eyes exclaimed, 'You! A hag! Never. You are more beautiful than ... Oh, I don't know.' He closed his eyes for a second, then exclaimed, 'Mia Farrow or Kim Basinger or

Princess Diana; even Elizabeth Taylor in her younger days.' Gazing into her eyes, he added softly, 'Truly more beautiful than any of them.' He put his forefinger on his chin and murmured, 'Is that a spot …?'

Marion pushed him away and half laughing said, 'Spoken just like a man! Of course they're beautiful women, they probably have the best cosmetics money can buy straight from Paris. I get mine in the High Street. They also have advisors and beauticians who know exactly how to hide any blemishes or sudden spots. They probably don't know one end of a lipstick from the other. Mirror please.'

He resumed his position holding the mirror up for her. While she gazed intently into the mirror, moving her head from side to side and touching her face gently with a finger, she said, 'I can't see any spots.'

'Oh yes, just there,' he said, pointing to her chin. Marion looked frantically in the mirror, then realised he was teasing again and glared at him.

'Honestly, to me you are lovelier than any of them. I mean it Marion, you always will be more beautiful than any other woman to me.'

She picked up her lipstick, and was about to apply it, when the train gave a little jerk and Matthew's arm moved slightly.

'Keep still, you idiot, I can't see what I'm doing. I'll have lipstick up my nose if I'm not careful. Hold the glass up a bit.' He lifted it higher. 'No, down a little,' then as he complied she said, 'that's better.' She lifted her head and smiled at him. 'Anyway, thanks for the compliments. Trust me, they do help a girl, especially when she can only use one hand.'

It was as she was putting her cosmetics away that the train slowed and then shuddered to a stop.

'Now what?' she said as she raised her eyebrows and collected the scattered contents of her make-up bag.

Matthew shrugged his shoulders. 'Just hope it's not for long.'

Both sat waiting patiently, but it was five minutes later when the guard knocked on the door and opened it at the same time. Standing at the threshold he said, 'Sorry, sir, madam. A bit of a problem with the signals ahead. Maintenance, nearly always carried out on a Sunday. Always on a Sunday, I should say. Fewer people travelling they say, so not too many passengers inconvenienced. Shouldn't be longer than another ten minutes or so before we're on the move again.' He sniffed, 'That's what the driver reckons anyway. Me? I'll believe it when it happens.'

Matthew nodded. 'That's fine. Thanks for letting us know.'

As the guard closed the door, Marion sighed, 'Don't go pinning your hopes on that bit of information. Ten minutes? He doesn't believe it for a start. Bet it'll be more like forty if I know anything.'

'Well, I hope you're wrong. We won't get into Kings Cross before half past eight at this rate.'

As he said it, Marion felt a sudden feeling of panic; eight forty, nine o'clock at the very latest would be the last time she would see him. An aching sadness crept into her heart as she realised this. The ache was real. Somehow, she realised, Matthew had become important, no, more than that, she thought, he had become very dear to her. Sharply, she told herself, I have got to put a stop to all of this. She hesitated in her thoughts searching for the right words, this closeness, she decided. When we arrive, I'll call a cab, tell him quickly and make my escape immediately by jumping into the taxi straight away. Pulling herself out of her lowering spirits she said, 'Listen Matthew, last time I heard something about a signal delay, I was on a tube train. Fortunately not underground. My friend and I were in the last but one carriage when over the tannoy, in the train, not the one on the station, someone said, "Sorry for the delay. We have a signal failure ahead. We should be on our way shortly." My friend, Judith, and I were reading, and I looked up from my newspaper to glance out of the window. I couldn't believe my eyes. There were police officers everywhere, at least thirty or more. I could see every one of them had an intent expression on their face as they slowly moved towards the train. The police were on both platforms, in the adjoining car park on one side behind the platform, and in the gardens behind a fence on the other. A couple of officers entered our carriage. I nudged Judith, and when she had seen what was happening, she turned to me with such a look of shock, and promptly asked one of the officers what was going on. He didn't answer, but stood guard at the open doors, holding his baton ready for whatever was coming.

'We watched absolutely spellbound as about six officers poured into the carriage next to ours. Judith and I watched through the glass in the doorways between the carriages. They didn't hesitate, but rushed towards a seated man. There was a bit of a scuffle, no more than three or four minutes at the most. We heard some grunting and a voice shout out something like, "You're hurting me." After that we saw the police drag a big man, I mean big, at least sixteen, maybe eighteen stone and over six foot tall. Anyway, between them they dragged him by his legs out of the compartment and spread-eagled him on the station platform and handcuffed him.

'Afterwards I heard one of the policemen, he must have been a senior officer of some sort, his head tucked down to his radio, saying things like, "We couldn't risk the lives of the fifty odd people in the carriage. He's got a gun. Couldn't be sure if it was loaded or not. God only knows what he intended. Anything could have happened. That's enough to justify this manpower. We're getting him cuffed now and taking him to the station." All very dramatic at the time. We never found out what it was all about, nothing in the papers or on the television news. So you see, they use "signal failure" for all sorts of reasons they don't want the public to know about.' She paused for a moment. 'It was pretty obvious to all on that occasion what was happening.'

'Were you a bit scared?'

'Not really. It was all over in minutes, and to be honest, any danger had passed. We were really not too close to what was happening. I mean, if the man had fired his gun before the police had got hold of him then, yes, I dare say I'd have been scared. Just seeing a gun or hearing the noise of a shot alone would do that. I'm not too fond of guns myself. Not that I have ever had anything to do with them. It's odd though; we searched and searched the national and local newspapers to see if there was any report of the incident, but nothing.' She stretched up her arms and then looked out of the window. 'At least we're not stuck in a tunnel,' she said.

'True enough, though there's not much going on outside, is there, not even a cow grazing? Quite a good view really. I quite like country scenes, I find them restful.'

'We are quite close to a village over there, Matthew. You can just see the cross on top of the church. See?' He nodded. 'Isn't that another of the rules laid down, do not make a copy of anything on earth or in the sea and worship it? What does your Senate say about that I wonder?'

'It's very strange. You see, I don't really know what they think.'

'What do you mean?'

'Well, I did overhear them discussing it more than once. Seems they don't all agree'

'So, did these virtuous men actually quarrel?'

'No, of course not. They just had a number of in-depth discussions.' He went on, 'One or two thought that the instruction, "No other God before me", and, "you shall not worship a graven image", are the same thing. Others disagreed, saying that a graven image had to be made in the likeness of something. For instance, angels or any creature on earth or in water and then worshipped instead of the Higher One.'

'So there's no definite ruling? Just as well, nearly all the world's religions have some sort of artefact to turn to.'

'Makes no difference to the Senate. They say that although the main religions have different ceremonies and ways of worshipping nevertheless they all share certain beliefs.'

Half teasing him, Marion said, 'I bet you can you say what they are, can't you?'

'Only what I've learned from the Senate,' he replied. 'I'm no scholar of the scriptures myself.'

'So, what are they?'

'Firstly, they all believe in the power of God and that there is life after death. All use stories to tell the scriptures and all recognise that there are guiding rules, commandments if you like, for every person to follow.'

'Ah, so now we are back to the commandments.'

Matthew looked at his watch then leaned out of window. Turning back to her said, 'I can see the signal is still red ahead, but nothing else seems to be happening. I do wish they'd get a move on.'

'Told you not to expect to move in ten minutes.'

'It's already been ten. What are they playing at?' he grumbled.

Marion told him to sit down, and as he settled himself back into his seat, she said, 'Be patient. It could be an hour. Listen, when I was talking about artefacts, statues, whatever, some churches have images in wood or stone, of what they think the Virgin Mary or saints might look like.'

Patiently he said, 'That's the whole point, don't you see? You must have seen for yourself, people on their knees in front of these images and actually praying to them, sometimes even kissing them. That's what makes God angry, according to some members of the Senate. They say praise and praying should be to Him alone. Worship of any image is false worship; not only in the Christian faith but in other religions also.' Matthew turned to her and said, 'Listen, the debate, indeed debates, that went on between the members of the Senate came about because, to some of them, I was guilty of worshipping a false god.'

'Which God, and did you?'

'What, worship him?'

'Yes,'

'Depends how you look at it.'

'So go on, tell me.'

'It was in the fifteenth century and during that lifetime I was a samurai.'

'A Japanese warrior?'

'Well, to say a warrior, that is the common assumption, but between wars, and there were many between the regions at that time, samurais followed an ordinary life as farmers, artisans and so on. As in Europe, there was a hierarchy of order and wealth. The samurai code meant respect for those above and those below themselves, and they had to always set an example of chivalry. Samurai eventually became known as martial gentlemen. Loyalty to their immediate superiors was paramount, who in turn were loyal to the higher lords, right up to the ruling emperor. We were encouraged to take care of our weapons, mostly curved swords, and work hard at our martial skills. We also had to read and write, mostly for knowledge, and be able to trust one another.'

'Were you good at all of these – I suppose you'd call them rules?'

'Yes, they were rules, but unwritten rules passed on from generation to generation; rules of ancient guidance for living a good life. And yes, I was good at keeping them.'

'So tell me, what happened to make the Senate uneasy?'

'Without hesitation, I went into battle with my master, known as a daimyo, a high ranking warlord who was named Harunaga. We were trained not to fear death, indeed to welcome it so, believe it or not, when Harunaga was killed it was a joy to all his samurai warriors – we became warriors each time we were called to battle.'

Marion held up her hand to stop him. 'Just a moment, a joy? At the death of someone you respected? I don't understand.'

'It meant that he was not defeated in battle, which was considered a disgrace; in other words, he had an honourable death. If he had lost the battle in order to pass over into death, he would have had to perform seppuku, a sort of hara-kiri. This was a self-inflicted and a painful death which we were all expected to witness. That would have been harder to bear for all of his followers.' Matthew paused and was thoughtful for a moment. 'Although I said we were joyful at his death, I was in fact distraught,' he said. 'He was my mentor, a generous, kind, but firm father figure.'

'Were you tempted to commit … what did you call it, seppuku?'

'Not really. I consoled myself by visiting Harunaga's shrine every day. This had been designed by a first-class architect, and had an arch and rockery and a wooden image of a man. Firstly I would burn incense to cleanse the area and chase away evil spirits, and I offered food and a little saki, before kneeling in prayer for his soul hour after hour.'

'For the rest of your life? Surely not?'

'Yes and no. Yes, until I was called to battle yet again. I could not disobey my new daimyo, Harunaga's nephew. It was in this battle that I lost my life, honourably I might add.'

'And that is when you arrived back with the Senate who were undecided about your worshipping at Harunaga's shrine?'

'That's it exactly, and I do believe they are still undecided.'

Marion looked at Matthew through half-closed eyes, sucked her lower lip and said, 'I've got to ask. Where does the girl come into this story? I mean, the whole way of life of a samurai is very male orientated isn't it?'

'I know what you're thinking. Naturally, family traditions had to follow on and, of course, they married. As for the girl, she was Harunaga's daughter. I saw her almost daily after her father's death; she too took offerings to his shrine. Mimi she was named and of course, because of the class situation, there was no way I could ever speak to her, let alone love and marry her. Mimi would have to marry someone with the equivalent or higher rank of her father. I could have married a commoner, who would have made me comfortable with her dowry. But it was Mimi I loved.'

Marion quietly said, 'Mimi, I like that. Was she aware of you at all?'

'I think so, as I sometimes caught her looking at me over her fan.' Matthew brightened for a moment, 'But I did draw out the MM design on washi. Didn't look quite the same in Japanese but the initials were clear enough. I let it flutter towards her and I know she saw it and I like to believe she understood the significance of it, because she gave a very slight nod of her head.'

'And what is washi, please?'

'Washi? A type of paper. Some believe it to be made of rice and therefore edible, but it was a form of paper made from all sorts of products. It was made mainly from the stalks and husks of rice and other produce and not edible at all. Of course there is edible rice paper made from the kernels of rice. Still used today I believe.' Matthew rolled his head around his shoulders and said, 'I'm getting stiff,' then stood up and stretched.

'Yes, but going back to artefacts we were talking about earlier, what about the rosary? Surely that's not included?' Marion asked.

Having loosened himself up a little, he sat down and answered, 'I can only tell you what the Senate's views are. It's all too much for me to understand.'

'So what do they say about the rosary?'

'Some members of the Senate are very concerned that there are people who rely heavily on their prayer beads. They pray to Mary rather than to God. Others believe fingering the beads as they pray are asking Mary to intercede on their behalf, and yet some say the recitation of the rosary brings comfort.'

'What about statues of saints? Surely saints are ordained, created, whatever to protect everyone. I mean, each trade adopts a patron saint and offer prayers to him or her. Saint Cecelia, for instance, for musicians, I believe. Then there's Saint Christopher? We all know he is the saint that travellers turn to when seeking a safe journey.'

'It's the same. In some churches – remember in Christianity there are many branches – it is permitted to do so. Others insist that all prayers should be directed straight to God.'

Marion sat for a moment. 'But the most fantastic art, be it sculpture or paintings, depicts Christianity. Some are in cathedrals, churches and the like.'

Matthew nodded, 'I know and many in the Senate agree that they were necessary in the past to teach the illiterate about the scriptures. For example, a baby in a manger with farm animals and angels overhead and haloes galore, tells the congregation that it is the story of Christmas.'

'True, so they were acceptable then. What about the great number of religious pictures now in galleries all over the world? People appreciate and enjoy the beauty of someone else's gift. They're not worshipping anything, just thankful there are such treasures.'

'So true, Marion. In fact ...'

Oh good, thought Marion. I think he is going to tell me of another one of his adventures.

Eleven

Matthew was surprised to see the look of anticipation on Marion's face. 'What?' he asked her.

'You're going to tell me another of your tales, aren't you?'

'Well ...' he began, 'What we've been talking about reminds me of something. It was just after I left university. I went on a holiday to Italy, one of those touring package ones. It was called something like "Visit the Treasures of Italy" and I thought that would be interesting. I went with my sister Rachel, she was into art and suchlike. It was very hot. We went everywhere in an air-conditioned coach. What caught my eye were the fields and fields of sunflowers, but in a way they were disappointing as the heads were far smaller than I thought they'd be.'

'That's something I've promised myself, to go and see the sunflower fields. I believe there are many fields of them in France. So where did you get to in Italy?'

'We went to Verona. If you had been with me, I'd have tried to get you on to the famous balcony, and on bended knee, I would have proposed to you.'

'Behave, Matthew.'

'Right,' he said smartly, and in a gentler tone, 'but wouldn't that have been romantic!'

Marion, feeling herself getting embarrassed, urged him to, 'Get on with it.'

'We visited Rome, naturally. Thankfully we had an escorted tour booked. The queue to get into Saint Peter's was unbelievable; snaked for over half a mile I reckon, and it was only eight thirty in the morning.' Sighing he went on, 'Oh, but so worth a visit. Firstly we had to cross the huge Piazza San Pietro.'

Marion raised her eyebrows questioningly.

'St Peter's Square,' he answered, 'with two beautiful fountains. Did you know there are a hundred and forty statues of saints positioned on the top of the facade?'

Marion shook her head.

'Then we went into the basilica itself. Paintings, statues and tombs along each side of the aisle as you enter. Everyone was excited and the crowds, you could hardly move, were chattering and pointing. Every now and then a Brother, as they were called, asked for silence to respect the holy place, and things would quieten down for a short while. Too much to tell you now. Perhaps we could go one day?'

She gave a gentle smile as she slowly shook her head. 'Go on, where else did you go?'

'Hold on a moment,' he said as he reached inside his jacket for his wallet, then let out a sigh of relief as he located his ticket. 'Got your ticket safe somewhere?' he asked.

Giving him a look of disdain she answered, 'Of course.'

'Of course,' he mimicked, thinking he had looked a little foolish in her eyes when he panicked over his own. 'So, the tour,' he continued, 'We went to Pisa and saw the tower, and Venice, where we had a gondola trip along the canals. A very special experience, best shared with a loved one I think.'

Matthew looked straight into her eyes and neither spoke, both gauging the other's thoughts, until he took a deep breath and went on, 'There were closely packed dwellings along the banks with flower pots bursting in a riot of colour perched on the steps and along the pathways. Occasionally the gondoliers passing by would break into song, which echoed back across the water.'

'Sounds lovely. Did your sister enjoy the trip?'

'On the canal? Yes, I saw her blush when our gondolier began singing to her. You know the sort of thing, big, brown mournful eyes and deep, deep sighs.'

Marion chuckled. 'I know exactly what you mean.'

'But I spoilt it for her afterwards when I told her he did it so she would give him a big tip! That brought her back to earth.'

'Honestly, call yourself a romantic. How could you do that to her?'

'Ah, well, you don't know me well enough yet, do you? Anyway, she's my sister and used to my teasing.'

Marion saw his face cloud over as he said, 'The rest of the holiday wasn't so wonderful. We were there when the earthquake happened. There'd been slight tremors for a few hours, and our guide said it was nothing to worry about. The coach made a winding journey up the hillside to reach our overnight hotel in Assisi. It was during the early morning that a serious earthquake shook the town. We shared a room to save money, and were woken up hearing things rattling and saw that everything in the room was trembling. At first we thought that a large aeroplane, although there was no airfield close by, was about to land as there was an incredible noise. The building felt as if it too was moving. We could hear people calling and rushing about outside our room. We quickly dressed and joined others outside the hotel. There was no panic, but it was scary. The big tremor was over, although shock waves continued for some time, so there was a constant danger of falling debris. It was all over in a few minutes, but the devastation was dreadful.

Matthew took a deep breath, 'Lovely old stone buildings, homes, offices, cafes all reduced to heaps of rubble. Cars were buried and lanes and alleyways blocked. White faced people stood in shocked groups, sobbing. Rachel and I clung together, grateful to be alive.

'There were of course, casualties. The Basilica of St Francis of Assisi didn't escape. I was told later that the most valuable work of art, the cycle of frescoes showing scenes from the Gospels, Mary and Saint Peter had been destroyed. These dated back to the thirteenth century. Fortunately our hotel seemed to have escaped with little damage, and after an hour or two we were able to return to our room. At least, Rachel did. I made my way to the Basilica to see if I could help, but it was all under control with small bulldozers and men beginning to clear the rubble.

'I was told that already a team of experts, art restorers and technical experts from all religions were assessing the damage. Altogether there were about forty people in there. I had just decided to find Rachel and see if we could summon up a coffee from somewhere, when around half past eleven another quake, bigger than the previous one, struck. It was quite unexpected and, sad to say, two of the experts and a couple of friars in the vaults died when the walls collapsed on them. More frescos were damaged. All repaired, I'm told, within two years or so.

'More buildings and homes had been destroyed, and I found myself along with local men and women, frantically clawing at the rubble to rescue those trapped beneath. We worked for hours. Dust was everywhere and until we were given some flimsy masks, it got into our mouths and nostrils. It seems the dust cloud could be seen for miles around. The locals shared their food and drinks with me and others of our party. The locals seemed constantly wanting to show their gratitude, thanking us over and over again for our help. Our pace slowed as we got nearer to where someone thought there might be a relative or friend. When we brought out a body, be it a child or adult, there was much weeping, almost a united mourning, all heads bowed in prayer and sorrow. Rosary beads were constantly being fingered and, yes, they brought comfort to the owner. Rachel, fortunately she already knew the rudiments of first aid, helped with the injured before ambulances took them away.

It was about four in the afternoon when she came looking for me. I had sweated profusely and dust clung to my damp, torn clothes. This was the same for everyone. I was thirsty, my nails worn down to the quick, and my hands were bleeding when she found me. The first thing she said was, "The tour manager has arranged for us to fly home at eight this evening. The services are here now and he says we might be in the way." She took me back to the hotel where I had a wash and changed into some more respectable clothes while she packed my bag.

'We had a light complimentary meal from the proprietor before meeting up with the rest of the coach party. As we left we saw that an emergency unit had arrived in the main square and had begun to erect tents for the homeless in a nearby sports ground, and this pleased us. It was a glad and sorry trip home; glad to be going home and I was sorry that I could do no more to help those who in so short a time had lost so much and had become my friends.'

'But you'd done as much as you possibly could, Matthew. What a dreadful ending to your holiday.' For a moment or two there was silence in the compartment, until Marion said, 'Going back to where all this discussion started, what about other faiths, Judaism or Islam, for example? Are they as demanding?'

Matthew shrugged his shoulders. 'I told you, I know as much about graven images as you do. I do know that both religions, Christianity and Judaism follow the teachings of the Old Testament. Having said that, it is thought that the leaders of Judaism absolutely prohibit such images, but there are instances where they are used for religious reasons. There are angels on the Ark of the Covenant, for instance, not worshipped, but as described in the Bible.' Matthew paused. 'I hope I'm getting all this right. I've never seen it for myself, but I've read somewhere that nowadays some synagogues have pictures of mythical creatures along with pictures of lions, fish, elephants and other animals, birds and plants painted on the walls. These, it is thought by some in the Senate, are symbolic of God's creation and acceptable.'

Marion interrupted, 'So is it the same for the Muslims?'

'It would seem so. They also strictly forbid the worship of any form of idols but decorate their mosque walls with scripts from the Koran, mosaics, floral designs and geometric shapes. As you know, the mosques are greatly admired for their colourful tiles. Blue is a favourite colour. The tiles featured on the domes of minarets are mostly a deep cobalt blue or turquoise, turquoise meaning "colour of the Turks". The tiles, if you didn't know, are positioned on the dome to reflect the desert sun.' He stopped for a moment, then added, 'Like Christianity there are divisions in their faith. Some mosques do depict paintings of the living and dead and creatures are portrayed in their temples and homes. Other branches of Islam forbid even photographs of loved ones.' They were both silent for a few minutes, lost in their own thoughts.

Marion muttered, 'There is so much I don't understand, but the commandment goes on to say that he is a jealous God. She paused. 'I wonder, is he afraid of losing his power, that even a painting could actually take his place?'

Matthew smiled. 'You and me both, we may never know. I doubt even the Pope can analyse it all, but no, I think God's position is safe enough.'

Marion said, 'But He threatens to punish four generations with an infliction. Perhaps that's why people have hereditary illness. What do you think?'

'No, I think you're going a bit too far there,' Matthew answered.

She sat thinking quietly for a moment. 'What about holy relics and things like that? Some sensible grown-ups put their faith in such things.'

'I know what you mean. What people believe to be supposed relics like the bones, rags or hair from holy men and women of the past,' Matthew said.

'Yes, that's right. Even, I've heard, the nails from the cross. Apparently if the person who is sick or distressed kisses the box such relics are in and leaves a gift no matter how small, they can expect to be cured.'

'Intelligent people question this. Some, including members of the Senate, emphatically state that all such relics, in whatever faith, are foolish.'

'But people pay for the privilege. Some are desperate,' said Marion

Matthew nodded. 'So who are we to question them?'

'If it brings them a measure of comfort, why not?' she answered with a shrug.

Matthew reached over for her bag. 'I'm getting hungry. Got any sandwiches left in here?' he asked as he began to open it.

'Hey, stop that. That's my bag. Give it back. I'll look in it myself, thank you.'

Grinning, he handed it back to her.

'There's a couple of biscuits. Will that do?'

'Is that all? I thought your aunt packed you a good supply.'

'And you've eaten most of it. There's a ham one left, but better not as it's been around for a few hours now.'

'Biscuits will have to do then,' he answered as he stretched out his hand to take them from her. 'Do you want one?' She shook her head. 'Good, I'll demolish both of them.'

Watching him munching the first biscuit, nibbling around the edge of the second, she was overwhelmed with the conflicting emotions he aroused in her again. Once we get to Kings Cross, I've got to tell him, she told herself and despaired at the thought of having to hurt him.

Matthew looked up and rubbed his hand across his mouth. 'What? Why are you looking at me like that? Crumbs around my mouth?' and he wiped his mouth again.

Smiling at him, she said, 'No, nothing like that. I was just wondering how lucky charms figure in religion?'

'The Senate gives them no credence either.'

'Oh, I don't know?' Marion said. 'I mean, I can remember my father telling me that my grandfather always had a florin, you remember them, a two shilling coin, proper money, dad used to say, and granddad said his was a lucky coin. It was customary for him to pay an agent for the football pools a two shillings stake every Wednesday. Paydays, cash in hand, were every Thursday, so one Wednesday, being short of his stake money, Thursday was too late as the money and coupon had to be posted in time for Saturday morning, he parted with the florin. My father said grand-dad moaned for hours that his luck would change now his special coin had gone.'

'Just a coincidence, Marion. Destiny is what it's all about and can't be altered. Look what happened to me. As far as I know I'm the only one who ever did alter fate. Whatever happens in a lifetime is already mapped out before we get here. That is the main task of the Senate, to plan out a life for everyone.' He gave her a slow, gentle smile as he asked, 'So, did his luck alter?'

'Well, yes it did, as a matter of fact. That's the funny thing,' and she gave a quiet chuckle. 'It seems the next day, his wife, my grandmother, went to a whist drive and won!'

'So, it was her luck really, but still, all in the family.'

'That's not all by a long way. Next day on his way to work he found a ten bob note. Ten shillings! A fortune in those days, dad said.'

'All coincidence, honestly.'

'Or maybe destiny? You won't believe what's coming next. Saturday afternoon granddad was glued to the radio. Everyone had to be quiet while he marked off his coupon. Dad said everyone jumped out of their skins when granddad whooped, danced around the kitchen and grabbed grandma and kissed her over and over again. The pools had come up trumps. "Four hundred pounds plus a bit more" he was yelling, enough in those days to buy a house.'

'Seems to me,' Matthew said, 'you can believe in them if you like, your grandfather did, but I don't think his lucky florin had anything to do with it. Just proves my point – it was all intended to happen.'

For a moment or two he was quiet, before saying, 'Some of the Senate and myself, think that people who carry such charms, be they a rabbit's foot, medals, stones or, as in your grandfather's case, a coin, believing that such a token will either bring them good luck or ward off danger, are putting their faith in impossible things.'

Marion frowned, looked away from him, then turned back and her face lit up as she said, 'Yesterday we were at Rosemary's wedding ceremony in a church, with all the blessings and, everything following the tradition of most brides, she had a number of lucky charms to guarantee happiness. For instance, she carried a horseshoe. I mean, it's like ensuring luck, isn't it?'

Matthew grinned as he said, 'If people only knew how the Senate laugh when they hear or see people putting their faith in such things.'

'Well, I can see why the carrying of a horseshoe could be lucky.'

Matthew groaned as he said, 'Go on then.'

'You're scoffing at all of this, aren't you?'

She noticed he smiled as he said, 'I'm listening.'

'I looked it up for Rosemary before the wedding as she said she definitely wanted a horseshoe. It seems most people believe that as a horseshoe is made of iron so the union of the two concerned will be as strong as iron. And …'

Matthew burst out laughing again.

'And,' Marion went on, ignoring his amused reaction, 'as they, the horseshoes, are fired for strength, it is said that the couple's passion will be as strong and long lasting.'

Trying to keep a straight face, Matthew asked, 'So, what about all the other wedding superstitions? All to do with good and bad luck as well, I suppose? What's that little rhyme brides cling to? Starts like, "Something old, something …"?'

Marion continued it for him, 'Something blue, something borrowed something new, and a silver sixpence in your shoe.'

'I suppose you know what that's all about. Did Rosemary stick to them?'

'Yes, she did. She wasn't going to take any chances, not that I think she has anything to worry about. They're daft about each other.'

'You couldn't miss it could you, how much they love each other? So why "something old"?' Come on, what's the significance of that one?'

Marion grinned. 'I can explain. The "something old" should always be given by a happily married woman in the hope that her happiness in marriage would be passed on to the new bride.'

'Something new?' he queried.

'Easy. New marriage, so "something new" ensures the couple's happiness and prosperous future. The "something borrowed" should be something of value lent by the bride's family. The bride has to return whatever it is to ensure good luck.'

'Now tell me why "something blue"?'

'The custom of wearing "something blue" by the bride represents her faithfulness.'

Matthew nodded as he mocked, 'Very important. Tell me, did Rosemary have a silver sixpence in her shoe?'

Marion giggled, 'I don't think so. She didn't limp down the aisle, did she?'

Matthew looked squarely into her face as he said, 'I'll tell you something for nothing. Rosemary's luck began when she met Dominic. He's a good man and long may their happiness last.'

'I second that.' As she tilted her head to one side, she asked slyly, 'Matthew, do you have a lucky charm?'

Again he laughed out loud saying, 'Marion! What would be the point? Nothing can ever change my destiny, nor can anyone else's, except perhaps by the Higher Authority's intervention, and that's not likely to happen.'

Sharply she turned to him and said, 'Like I said earlier, all the more reason for you to seek him out next time you're before the Senate. See if things can be changed.'

Matthew closed his eyes before saying softly, 'So, you understand everything now. You know and want us to be together, right?'

Turning away from him to hide her consternation, she ignored what he had hinted at, and answered, 'I want your suffering to end, Matthew. That's all. It is time you found some peace in your life.'

'I ...' the train gave a jolt, both fell gently back in their seats as the train slowly gathered speed. 'At last, we're on our way,' he said as he gave out a relieved sigh.

'How long do you think? About twenty minutes?'

He nodded.

'Can I ask you something, Matthew?' He raised his eyebrows and nodded again.

'In the Senate's plan of destiny for you, have they ever made you a hero? I mean a real hero. Have you ever rescued someone from a fire or saved someone from drowning. Anything brave or really dangerous like that, for instance?'

'Sadly, no. I suppose it might be construed as redemption or something and that wouldn't suit them at all. I'm just an ordinary person in every life. I had parents, brothers and sisters, went to school and earned a living somehow. Like any other person growing up. The same sort of early life nearly everyone experiences. Just a normal life every time until I meet up with you.'

'But if I remember rightly, you saved your sister from a hanging, and your first love, Magdalena?' He nodded. 'You saved her from what was sure to be an unhappy future. You also helped to rescue people when the earthquake happened, which was a brave thing to do, knowing another 'quake might happen at any time. I'd have thought that would have been in your favour.'

'Seems not,' he replied. He stood up and said, 'I'll gather up our bits and pieces, shall I, so we're ready to go straight away when we arrive, okay?' Matthew collected up the newspapers and food wrappings and Marion opened her holdall for him to place them in. Picking up his flask, he shook it. He turned down his mouth in mock disappointment at it being empty and he put it in his pocket. They sat down opposite each other, waiting for the journey to end. Matthew stroked his jaw and smiled at her.

'What?' she said, meeting his gaze.

'Nothing in particular, just looking at you.'

'No, you're not. You're staring at me.'

'I'm trying to get a mental photograph of you. When I'm away I'll be able to picture you in my mind and that will make our separation bearable.'

To her mind, if he were able to do that, the hurt she must inflict on him soon, would keep coming back to haunt him. She looked at her watch, another five minutes and they would arrive, five, maybe ten minutes before she must tell him the truth, then it would all be over.

'Well, just stop it. It won't work. If you don't stop now, I'll start pulling faces so your images will be all over the place. And stop laughing at me,' she added as he began to chuckle.

'Whoa there, lady. Are you about to stamp your feet?'

Marion screwed her face up, stuck her tongue out at him and said, 'I never stamp my feet.'

Twelve

The train slowed down as it approached King's Cross station. There was a hissing of air as the brakes were applied and finally it was stationary. As the train neared the station, Marion's agitation had grown. She kept raising her knee and slipping her heel out of her shoe over and over again. She scratched under the plaster on her arm, and turned her head from side to side to look at the tall buildings they were passing. On one side the sun, now lowering in the sky, gave a camera flash through the gaps between the buildings, whilst on the other side the windows reflected the dwindling rays of sunshine.

Marion was experiencing a kaleidoscope of emotions knowing that, shortly, she would have to tell Matthew everything. The stories Matthew had told her had moved her immensely. His suffering, determination and disappointment when each time he had failed had not discouraged him from his quest to find Magdalena. Marion was well aware of his excitement and anticipation, thinking that she was the girl he was seeking and they were to be together forever. Believing that at last he had lived a blameless life, he hoped the Senate would relent, and he would finally be with his loved one. Common sense niggled at her. It was all make-believe on his part, she tried to tell herself. Yet she was still unsure, as it sounded so plausible, and he was so open, almost naïve, and desperate to make her believe him.

Now she was apprehensive. She dreaded giving him the news, knowing that his distress and pain would be unbearable to witness, and she was fearful of the repercussions that might follow. Looking at him she knew, dare she admit it to herself, that she loved him. But what sort of love she asked herself. Not the love between a parent and offspring, or of the love between brother and sister. Certainly not the sort of love between two passionate people. At the thought of lovemaking with Matthew she allowed herself the ghost of a smile, but to be honest that wasn't in her mind at all. It was a special love, she thought, between good friends, but somehow she felt it was more than that. She only knew in her heart that leaving him and never seeing him again, was going to be hard.

Matthew stood up and put out his hand to pull her to her feet, 'Come on. Cheer up, we're here at last.'

As she heard the concern in his voice, she realised that she must be looking tired and downcast.

Looking out of the window he turned back to her and said, 'I think it best we wait a few minutes, let the crowd thin out a bit. They're all rushing and jostling as if there's no tomorrow. We'll hang on so no one can jog your arm. I wouldn't want that to happen.' He looked at her drawn face and realised she was exhausted. 'How are you feeling?' he asked.

'I'm fine, Matthew. It's been such a long journey, hasn't it? I dare say I'm a bit tired.'

'You're sure? Pain getting you down a bit?'

She shook her head. 'Yes, I'm fine, thanks. Do you think we can go now?'

He looked out of the window, and nodded. 'Yes, I think we can make a move. The crowd has thinned out a bit.' He said, 'Leave that,' as she reached for her case. 'I'll see to it. Just carry your bag and we'll be fine.'

As they stood on the platform he looked around and said, 'There's a bit of luck.' He strode off and hailed a passing porter driving an empty electric trolley. Marion watched the exchange between the two, a mini pantomime. The porter began shaking his head, trying to move on, and shook his head again as Matthew placed himself in front of the trolley and put a restraining hand on the man. Finally Matthew pointed to the cases at her feet. As she watched, the porter began to smile and nod as Matthew passed over some paper money, and in no time at all their cases were piled onto the trolley and taken to the ticket barrier.

Matthew took her bag from her and, with his other hand under her elbow, guided her along at a fast trot. Her high heels made a staccato echo on the concrete as they tried to keep up with their luggage. Once they were reunited with it, the porter gave an old fashioned touch to his cap, muttered, 'Thank you, sir. Much obliged,' and drove away.

Marion and Matthew stood for a few moments looking at each other, each reluctant to say goodbye. Unable to bear the suspense any longer, she began looking around for a taxi and, seeing the queue of cabs waiting, put up her hand to hail one. At the same time she reached out for her case. She was desperate to put into practice her cowardly resolve of leaping into a taxi to make her escape as soon as she told him the truth.

'Matthew there's something I've ...'

'Hold on a minute,' he interrupted, 'I've just had an idea. Why don't you have dinner with me now? I know of a little Italian place not far from here. The owner is a friend. Well, I like to think he is as I'm probably his best regular customer. The most fantastic Italian food I've ever tasted. What do you say?' When he saw her beginning to shake her head and look around for a free taxi, he begged, 'Oh, come on. It's only ten to eight. I promise I'll put you in a taxi at ten.'

'No, Matthew. I can't. I need to tell you ...'

'Tell me over dinner then. Surely it can wait? We can put our cases in a locked luggage compartment over there so we don't have to ...' He stopped in amazement as Marion, stamped her foot in exasperation and said his name crossly.

'Matthew.'

He watched as she put her hand over her mouth and let out a sigh. 'What is it, what's wrong?'

Looking straight into his eyes she said softly, 'Matthew.' She hesitated for a split second. 'I'm married.' At last she had spoken the words that she had been dreading. To both of them it seemed as if the world stood still and there was a wall of silence around them. As he looked at her he saw her sadness. As she looked at him she saw disbelief, then dismay on his face. She wanted desperately to fold her arms around him, to hug and comfort him and to take away his pain.

Handing her the holdall he had been carrying, he strode away, his hands curled into fists, and she could see how angry he was. He whirled round and came back to her and almost wailing, asked, 'Why didn't you tell me?' He dropped his shoulders and shook his head as he repeated in anguish, 'Why didn't you tell me?'

Closing her eyes for a split second and then looking up at him she whispered, 'I tried. I tried a number of times, Matthew, but there was always an interruption, mostly you, but Aunt Amy as well and when my little niece wanted a push on the swings. You even asked who Alex was that time, remember?'

Matthew clapped his hand to his forehead and groaned, 'Yes, I did. I remember that and I meant to ask you again. Sorry,' and he began pacing, two or three steps away from her, then turned back and repeated the movements again and again. Marion's injured arm began to ache and so, in order to cradle it for a little comfort, she put the holdall on the ground. Finally Matthew stopped prowling and stood beside her.

'Oh, God,' he breathed quietly as he looked at her nursing her arm, 'that's it, isn't it? The bastards have tricked me again.' He pointed as he said triumphantly, 'Your arm.'

'My arm? What do you mean?'

'I mean that because your left arm and hand are hidden by plaster and a sling your wedding ring is conveniently hidden. Don't you see? They, the Senate, planned it all.' His face was red with anger and lifting and, shaking his fist into the air, he shouted at the top of his voice, 'You won't win. I'll not let you.'

Marion put her hand on his arm to restrain him and pleaded, 'Please, Matthew. Please stop. I'm so sorry, truly so sorry. I never meant things to get this far. At first I was convinced you were a storyteller of sorts. I couldn't believe you, then gradually a number of things seemed so ...' she hesitated, '... so possible. I began to have doubts and found myself believing that I did, indeed, play a part in your past lives.' She stopped speaking for a moment before adding, 'That doesn't mean that, like you, I remember any of the past, just that at times in my own life, this life, I felt there was something missing, I didn't feel whole somehow, and now ...'

Clutching her hand between his and still agitated, he answered, 'It's not your fault. Stop saying sorry.' Then, raising his voice again, he shouted, 'It's those holier than thou bastards.' Pulling away from her, he repeated at the top of his voice, 'Bastards! Bastards! All of you.'

Passers-by began to glance in their direction and glide way. He glared at them.

One traveller lifted his head with an amused smile, and mouthed to Marion, 'You okay?' She smiled weakly and nodded back.

'Matthew, let me go now. I'll get a taxi. Try to forget me. Who knows what destiny holds for you?'

There was no mistaking the hopelessness in Matthew's voice. 'They know.'

'I might not be the girl you're seeking. There are ...'

She stopped when Matthew looked at her.

'How can you say that? You've just told me that you felt you were part of my life. You know and I know that you are the girl of my destiny.' They stood in awkward silence until he said, 'Tell you what, let's have some dinner anyway. You can tell me all about Alex and I promise to have you in a cab by ten o'clock. What do you say?'

Marion thought for a few moments, and silently tried to justify saying 'yes'. She was hungry, she was going home to an empty house and she would have a few more precious minutes in his company. As she nodded her head in agreement, Matthew produced coins for the lockers, picked up their luggage and swiftly stowed it away. As he handed over her locker key he said with a ghost of a smile, 'In case you're wanting to beat a hasty retreat.'

Gently he took her hand and they linked fingers as they walked through the exit, and on to the small Italian restaurant nearby. Marion was immediately entranced as they entered. An enticing smell of herbs wafted from the kitchen and she noticed strings of onions and garlic bulbs were hung over the bar. It was clean, and the low lighting giving just enough light to see the food one was eating and, although it was very busy, a subdued quietness in the room with music playing softly in the background, added to the ambience. Murals of country scenes with blue skies and pictures of various Italian cities, which Marion instantly recognised, covered the walls.

The proprietor embraced Matthew and shook his hand, then turned to Marion and, with a wide smile, gave a small bow. Waving his arms around, shouting out instructions in his native language and flourishing his white serving cloth, he escorted them to a secluded table at the back of the premises. Looking at the menu, Marion quickly gave up as the choice was extensive, and she really wasn't sure what she wanted.

Turning to Matthew she said, 'You order something, will you? Something light will do fine.'

'A glass of wine first, I think, and then we'll order.' Beckoning the waiter over he ordered a bottle of Prosecco.

'Certainly, sir. A light sparkling wine to freshen the palate, sir. A good choice, if I may say so,' volunteered the waiter, his eyes resting briefly on Marion. After he had poured each of them a glass and left, they raised their glasses, and not being sure what to toast, smiled instead. The wine was cold and refreshing.

After looking down the menu for a few moments, Matthew said, 'I think some bruschetta to start with, don't you? With fresh sliced tomato. What do you say?'

'Sorry to be ignorant, but tell me what it is first.'

Matthew laughed and Marion was glad to see him do so. It was as if, for a moment, he had forgotten.

'Bruschetta is toasted bread lightly covered with hot olive oil with a topping of your choice. I thought tomatoes would be fine for us.'

'Sounds just right to me. Go ahead then, order it. The lovely smells in here are tempting my appetite a bit.' She took another sip of the wine, 'Or the wine maybe.'

Matthew looked at the menu again and then asked, 'How do you fancy an omelette? Cooked the Italian way, of course.'

'An omelette. That shouldn't be too heavy. I think I could manage one. Yes, I'll settle for that.'

'Right, I'll order the lobster, mushroom and leek frittata with some fresh vegetables. That should do us nicely.' He called the waiter over and placed their order, adding, 'We're not in any hurry.' Lifting his glass he took a sip and, looking at her over its rim, said, 'Now Marion, tell me about this husband of yours. He must be someone really special.'

Smiling, almost to herself, she replied, 'He is. Where to start? I love him, of course. He is all I ever wanted.'

'And he loves you? Well that wouldn't be hard to do.'

Marion's voice held a warning as she said, 'Matthew. I will only tell you about him if you promise firstly not to interrupt or, and I know you will, not to try to compare yourself to him. Promise?'

'Okay, okay. I promise.'

The waiter approached with their starters. When she took up her knife, Matthew drew her plate to his side saying 'Do you mind?' as he cut her food into bite size pieces and passed the plate back. Taking his first mouthful he said, 'This is wonderful, I'm starving,' and took another bite before saying, 'So how old is he and what does he do? And more to the point, why wasn't he at the wedding with you?'

Marion wiped her mouth with her napkin and swallowed. 'You're right, this is lovely. I like the herbs they've added as well. To answer your question, Alex will be thirty-one next month and is a tiny bit shorter than you, and you could say he is solidly built, very muscular.'

She had popped another piece of bruschetta into her mouth when Matthew, pretending to flex his arm muscles exclaimed, 'Are you suggesting I'm flabby, woman?'

Marion giggled, and realised he might be accepting the turn of events and doing his best to recover his spirits, although she did wonder if it was bravado for her benefit. What will he be like when we part, she wondered?

'If you are, you should be ashamed,' she scolded.

'Feel that, judge for yourself,' he said as he flexed his biceps again.

Marion ignored his invitation and took another piece of bruschetta, and he sighed when she didn't do as he requested.

'Oh, go on then, tell me more about Alex.'

'Well, I won't pretend we are Mr and Mrs Perfect, although at times I feel we are, or that it was a match made in heaven or that we are soul mates ...'

'No, because you and ...'

'Don't interrupt,' she almost snapped at him and then added softly, 'You promised.'

'Sorry. Please continue. I'll try not to distract you again, I promise.'

Marion pushed her food around the plate with her fork, before saying, 'For me, Alex is someone special, someone to share my ups and downs. He makes me laugh at myself.'

'So where did you meet him?'

'We met about four years ago at one of his friend's birthday party.' Marion smiled to herself at the memory. 'I was with a friend, just a friend, Philip who, once we were there, promptly went chasing after someone he fancied. Oh, I didn't mind at all, that's the sort of friendship we had, but it did mean for a short while I was alone, and that's when Alex came on the scene.' She pushed her plate away from her and said, 'I can't manage any more of this,' and laughed as Matthew helped himself to what she had left.

He wiped his mouth, gave a satisfied sigh, and leaned back in his chair. 'And? What happened next?'

The waiter, hovering nearby, came across and topped up their glasses, readjusted their cutlery and took their empty plates away.

'Come on, tell me.'

'I hadn't really noticed Alex until he came across and sat beside me. He said, "Good, he's left you all alone. I hoped I'd get a chance to talk to you." Then without as much as a by your leave, he cheekily said, "Come on, let me take you for a proper dinner. I hate all this finger buffet stuff." At the same time he pulled me up to my feet, and, still hanging on to me, located my coat and ... and that was that. We became a couple.'

'You must have known almost at once then, that he was the one. I mean, you didn't protest, did you? Just went off with him. Did you fall in love straight away or what?'

'Not straight away. I was more than happy though when he said he wanted to see me again. In a short time a strong bond seemed to tie us together. He had a way of looking at me, always looking out for me, everything around us seemed so bright, so alive. For me it was a unique feeling, one I'd never experienced before, and I realised I was in love with him. We were, are, always happy to be together.'

Some fleeting expression on his face caused her to give a gasp, 'Oh Matthew, I'm so sorry. All this must be like a knife in a wound to you. I'll stop now. I can't bear to upset you further.'

'Don't be silly,' he said as he stretched his hand across the table and rested it on her arm. 'Well, yes, of course it hurts, but in a way I'm happy because you're happy. Does that make sense? Tell me now, why wasn't he at the wedding with you?'

'I would dearly love to be with him all the time. Some hopes though.'

'What does that mean?'

'His work takes him away for weeks, sometimes months, at a time.'

The waiter, a young nephew of the proprietor and dressed in the uniform of the establishment, red toreador jacket and almost too tight black trousers, returned with the second course and fussed around them, Marion in particular. With deliberate slowness he put the side dishes of vegetables and serving spoons at just the right angle and placed a clean table napkin on Marion's lap. It seemed to Matthew that he was doing all this in order to be close to Marion, silently urging her to notice him, and Matthew was glad to see she drew away from the unwanted attention. The waiter's chances are nil, he thought, like my own. Matthew and Marion gave each other an amused smile, fully aware of the waiter's antics. Once he had left them, after wishing them, 'Buon appetito,' with his dark eyes resting on Marion, Matthew offered to cut her food again, but she declined, saying that she could easily cut the frittata with the side of her fork. Both helped themselves from the selection of vegetables drenched in butter. For a short while both stopped talking and tucked into their meal.

Having cleared his plate, Matthew put his elbows on the table, cupped his chin in his hands, and was the first to speak. 'So what sort of work does your man do to keep you apart? A week is a long time, let alone months.'

Quickly swallowing what was in her mouth, and dabbing at her butter coated lips with her serviette, she said, 'You always ask me questions when my mouth is full.' She went on, 'He works on oil rigs.'

Matthew's eyes widened in surprise and said, 'Surely not a roughneck? I mean ...'

'I know exactly what a roughneck is and, snob that you are, no he is not.'

Slightly embarrassed, Matthew said, 'Well, I know roughnecks have to have some experience before handling the drills and suchlike. I just thought ...'

'You thought wrong then. Alex, is an engineer, he has a good Engineering Science degree from Oxford.' She took another mouthful and chewed thoughtfully. 'He tells me, though, that he loves getting his hands dirty and doesn't mind lending a hand at anything that needs doing. He enjoys every moment of being part of a crew, and, of course, the money's good.'

'Mixes well with people, then?'

'Yes, he does. You'd like him Matthew, honestly.'

Matthew raised his eyebrows, amused at her assumption.

'You would, I know you would.'

'It's unlikely that I'll ever meet him but the only reason to like him, as far as I can see, is that I need to know and be sure, that he takes great care of you.'

'Well, of course he does,' she snapped. She picked up her glass and took two or three sips before saying, 'I've met some of his fellow workers, roustabouts, roughnecks, engineers in all sorts of trades and the management personnel. All speak very highly of him. Seems that not only is he reliable but he is also the crew's all round entertainer. They call out their favourite songs for him to sing as he has a good voice and usually knows those they ask for, though I know his favourite types of songs are country and western. What he is really best at is impersonating others especially members of the crew and their seniors, who all take it in good spirits. You should hear him taking off the comedians on television, got their voices and movements down to a "t". For instance, Alex tells me the crew really love it when he does his Tommy Cooper routine and tries to do tricks and they go wrong. Believe me he's no magician, so it's all real mistakes he's making, and all the time he's telling one line, clean jokes, nothing too risqué, or so he tells me.

'How do you know all this? Does he tell you?' Matthew asked looking at her in surprise. Laughing, she said, 'Of course he does and at every family gathering, especially at Christmas, he goes into a new routine. I think he wants to try out his new material before risking it in front of his mates.'

Matthew rubbed his chin and said, 'So, if he had been at the wedding he might have ...?'

'I don't think so. It was Rosemary's special day, and I don't think Aunty Amy would have approved, not that she minds at other times.'

'Is he on land or offshore? I think I'd prefer land myself, if there were an accident at least one might be able to run away, but at sea ... that's altogether different.'

'At present Alex is stationed off the coast of Ireland, but he has been all over the world. Today he finishes his two weeks tour, two weeks on duty then two weeks off. Tomorrow he'll be home and I'll be so glad to see him, and know he is safe, as he often tells me how dangerous the work can get.'

'So I've heard. Rigs are such confined spaces which make it difficult for the workers to escape or be rescued should a gas or oil leakage cause an explosion. Not suffered anything like that himself has he?'

Marion shook her head. 'No, but I fear for him when I read of some of the disasters. He frightens me sometimes as he laughs when he relates some accident or other. Once he told me that some of the men he was working with had to be rescued by helicopter when several of the anchors holding the rig to the sea bed had broken loose. It was the sort of rig that is moved from place to place. As there was a storm threatening, some men, including Alex, although I suspect he volunteered, had to stay behind to stabilise the rig with the remaining anchors and engines. I don't know what engines he was talking about or what they actually did, but the men had to stop the rig from drifting. Of course they got the situation fixed even though the rig had apparently drifted nearly a hundred feet, which surprised them. Alex said that winds of up to seventy-odd miles an hour, and waves up to forty feet, hampered them greatly. But even as he was telling me, he was reliving all the excitement again, I could tell.' She took a deep breath and went on.

'Anyway, during the next two weeks he's been enrolled for a three day safety training programme. He says he has to attend them as part of his contract and, of course, hopefully he will know the right thing to do should anything happen.' Lowering her voice, she said, 'I try not to let him know how anxious I feel when he is away, because he is always telling me that working offshore with only the sea around, although unnerving, is a challenge and a bit of an adventure. He told me it is awesome to see storms brewing. Nature at its best, he says, and exciting, but that's so typical of him. Any sign of danger and he seems to enjoy it all the more.'

Both had finished eating, although Matthew made it his business to clear the leftover vegetables. The waiter, ever anxious to please, quickly took the empty plates and dishes away and murmured, 'Desserts?'

Matthew nodded and was handed a new menu. He enjoyed the discomfort of the waiter who quickly went away, knowing he had made a mistake, when Matthew promptly handed the menu over to Marion. Matthew grinned, and asked Marion, 'Anything there you'd like?'

Laughing, she scanned the tempting choices, before saying, 'Everything! But to be honest, I couldn't eat another thing. You?'

'I'm very fond of tiramisu, but, like you, I've had enough, so I'll give it a miss tonight. How about a coffee?' Marion nodded, and he called the waiter over to give their order.

'We'll finish the wine first,' he told the waiter, 'so in about ten minutes would you please bring the coffee? Thank you.'

Within half an hour they had finished and the bill had been paid. As they left, there were dramatic farewells by the excitable proprietor urging them to visit again soon.

They sauntered back to the station and collected their luggage and then Matthew hailed a taxi.

'Where to, guv?' The driver asked.

Matthew turned to Marion, telling her to give the driver her address. He opened the door for her to step inside, followed her and sat alongside her. The journey took no longer than fifteen minutes. Neither spoke, each lost in thoughts of what was to come, but it was Marion who sought out his hand, twining her fingers through his and appreciating the warm feeling the contact gave her. The taxi pulled up outside her house, and neither of them moved, but looked at each other, dreading the goodbyes that had to be said. Matthew was the first to move. Picking up Marion's case he turned to the driver and asked if he could wait for a few minutes. Marion slid along the seat and stepped out onto the pavement and, without haste, led the way to her front door. As they reached it the security light came on, illuminating the anxiety on their faces. Matthew put down the suitcase and put his hands in his pockets.

Silently they stood together until he said, 'Well, Marion, here we are. There are all sorts of things going through my head at the moment. I feel cheated, of course, and disappointed that you are not free to be with me. At the same time I wouldn't have missed these last two days with you for anything. They have been wonderful, just being with you, being able to talk and knowing that you understand my, once again, doomed need to find you, my destiny.'

'And mine too. I'm going to miss you. I'll never forget you, Matthew.'

Matthew smiled down at her upturned face, and her heart beat wildly, and she dropped her head so that he wouldn't see her dismay. The taxi driver gave a short honk of the horn. They both looked round at the sound as if they had forgotten he was waiting. Matthew took her door key, unlocked the door and put her case into the unlit hallway.

There was bleakness in his tone as he said, 'This really is our goodbye. We shall never see each other again, not in this life. Find a corner in your heart for me.'

Marion heard him choke back his despair as he continued, 'I love you, Marion, I love you dearly. I always have and always will.' Putting his hand under her chin, he lifted up her face, hesitated for a fraction of a second, then gently, so gently, kissed her. Marion felt tears pricking beneath her closed eyelids, and a lump in her throat stopped her answering. Releasing her abruptly Matthew began walking down the path away from her. He turned, rushed back to her and seized her hand. Turning it over he kissed her palm, then folded her fingers over it. 'For you to remember me by,' he murmured in a broken whisper.

'Matthew, I ...' Putting his fingers to his lips he shushed her and walked away quickly, but not before she had seen the tears wet on his cheeks.

Marion turned away, closed the front door, kicked off her shoes and made her way to the sitting room. She looked out of the window and saw the tail lights of the taxi in the distance. The room was in darkness. She didn't turn on the light, but sat down abruptly in an armchair, and let her own tears escape.

Thirteen

The headlights of a passing car cast its soft glow around the quiet room like a large torch beam, and then left Marion in darkness again. Giving a little sob and wiping her eyes she stood up, edged her way around the room, switched on the light and drew the curtains together. Almost at once her spirits lifted. She was home, home with all that made this house her very own. She wandered around, touched a black cat ornament Alex had bought. She ran her hand over the polished table, frowned at the flowers wilting in a vase of murky water and wondered why she hadn't attended to them before leaving. On the wall one picture frame seemed a little crooked, and she eased it back into place. She turned around and saw an untidy collection of magazines and a book on the sofa. Picking up the book she began reading the open page, remembered the story, and promised herself she would read it later in bed. She put the book on the coffee table and gazed around the room. She smiled and was overwhelmed as she saw their wedding photograph. They'd had an enlargement made of that particular shot, just the two of them. Alex, handsome and striking a pose in his tails and top hat, and her at his side, her dress billowing slightly. She smiled as she remembered he had whispered, 'Hurry up, will you? I'm busting for a pee.'

Marion, still smiling at the memory, gently ran her finger down Alex's cheek and whispered, 'Hello, darling, I'm home,' and felt tears pricking behind her eyelids again. As she turned slowly around, she lovingly took in every detail of the room, then said out loud, 'There truly is no place like home.'

Intent on getting herself a warm drink from the kitchen before making her way to bed, she had to go into the hall. Beside the abandoned suitcase lay a pile of letters, but her eye caught the red winking light of the answering machine. She pressed the button as she picked up the telephone. An impersonal voice told her there were four new messages and one saved message. The first message was from Aunt Amy who hoped she had arrived home safely, hoped that the journey had not been too tiring, and to ring back in the morning after a good night's sleep. She was relieved and happy to hear the voice on the next message. It was Alex.

'Hi precious. Only another twenty-three hours and I'll be with you. Can hardly wait, got lots to tell you. Did you enjoy the wedding? Sorry I couldn't be there but you know I would if I could. Sorry I haven't phoned earlier, all sorts of delays, God knows why. Love you lots. Sleep well my darling and tons of kisses until tomorrow.'

There was a lump in her throat and the threat of more tears as she whispered back, 'Love you too,' at the same time telling herself that all these emotions were getting her down because she was so tired, but knowing at the back of her mind that she was still thinking of Matthew.

The next message was from her secretary, telling her that there was a board meeting on Monday, and the chairman had asked could Marion be there at eleven for a couple of hours? The last message was from her dentist's receptionist to remind her to make an appointment for a check-up.

Wearily she looked at the suitcase, and decided that some time tomorrow she would sort it out. She picked up the heap of mail and made her way to the kitchen equipped with almost every labour-saving appliance, some white and some of stainless steel. The fridge and freezer were humming efficiently and everything was clean and perfect. It was a struggle to make herself a mug of coffee with one hand, and she was glad to sit down to drink it while opening the mail. Not for the first time, she wondered how on earth the postman managed to carry the post from house to house as the weight of what she had just carried was considerable.

There were a number of catalogues, women's fashion mostly, household gadgets and linen, a couple of gardening ones and the monthly issue of Sea and Flight for Alex. Smiling, she also noticed that he had ordered a copy of *The Comedians' Magazine*. There was a free local paper which was immediately thrust into the wastepaper bin. This was joined by the varied and colourful leaflets advertising Indian, Italian, pizzas and other delicacies – ready cooked for speedy home delivery.

As she thumbed through the letters she saw the familiar envelope containing her bank statement, and the rest appeared to be either charity begging letters, which sometimes made her feel

uncomfortably guilty as really, she felt, it was impossible to contribute to everyone. They too were added to the waste pile. A letter
from her sister, Sarah, in Australia, made her smile as she opened
it. She read about the antics of Sarah's three sons, all under ten,
how Spring in the southern hemisphere was encouraging the
flowers and finally, saving the best bit of news for last, Sarah wrote
that the family would be visiting in time for Christmas. Almost at
once, Marion began making plans in her mind. Pantomimes for
sure, and visits to Hamley's toy shop were top of her list. She
realised that she was being ridiculous, as it was still only late
August and there was plenty of time to make plans.

She placed her empty mug in the sink, filled it with water and
turned off the light. She made her way upstairs to the bathroom
where she cleaned her teeth and rinsed her face, too weary to do
much else. She opened the bedroom window and breathed in the
fresh air, surprised that she hadn't noticed how stuffy it was in the
house. It took her twice as long as usual to undress, and get into
bed which was frustrating. The coolness of the cotton sheets and
pillows was welcome on her hot tired body and she stretched out
blissfully, longing for sleep.

Although feeling drowsy, sleep eluded her, for as soon as she
closed her eyes a thousand thoughts rushed into her mind. There
was no doubting her love for Alex, they had shared so much
together. It was true he was away a great deal and she'd heard
often enough the saying, 'absence makes the heart grow fonder'
but her love for him was steadfast, whether he was at her side or
far away. If he should find someone else she would be bereft, she
told herself, and because her love for him was so strong, she would
let him go. But would she? Or would she do her utmost to keep
him? Forgive him? Do anything to have him close? There was no
doubt that he loved her. Hadn't he said so this very evening on the
telephone? But what if ...? Tomorrow she would show him how
much she loved him. With that thought uppermost in her mind,
she tried to settle down to sleep again, but found herself tossing and
turning, crumpling the sheets and making herself uncomfortable.

Marion knew full well what was really troubling her and sighed.
Matthew, without a doubt. Matthew, who had spent all day trying
to convince her they were soul mates from almost the beginning of
time. He had insisted that they had a shared destiny designed by
the Senate. A destiny that he had, he confessed, foolishly changed

and thereby caused their separation. He had found her in his many lives, convinced that she was his one true love, and next time their love would be eternal. But could she believe him?

Alex is my soul mate, she said to herself softly. We share so much, partners in everything; he was her lover, helpmate and friend. Life with him was so satisfying, but an inner voice told her, yes in this life. Could she believe Matthew? Was she the soul-mate that he had lost? In another time would they be together? Was it her fault that he had, today, broken another commandment? He had to, she told herself as she was already married. Did the Senate deliberately arrange their meeting after her marriage to ensure Matthew's failure? Round and round the thoughts kept troubling her until at last she finally fell asleep.

The persistent ring of the telephone roused her, she stretched out her hand and picked it up and said sleepily, 'What?' not knowing who it was and wishing they hadn't disturbed her.

'I miss you,' he said. 'Have I woken you up?'

Marion was thrilled at the sound of Matthew's voice, and almost ashamed of her reaction, but smiled nevertheless.

'Are you there?' he asked. 'Answer me. I'll go if you want, but just let me hear your voice once again.'

Marion switched on the bedside light and sat up.

'Hold on a moment while I get comfortable,' she answered and heard him chuckle at the other end of the line. After adjusting her pillows, she leaned back into them.

'How did you get my number?' she asked. 'I never gave it to you, I know that for sure and, yes, you did wake me up.' She heard him give a little embarrassed laugh.

'You know how devious I can be, don't you?' he answered. 'Remember when you tipped out your make-up bag on the seat? I forget what you were looking for, but there was an odd earring and, well … Well I don't suppose you have missed it yet, but I er – borrowed it shall we say? It is just a small memento of you to tuck into my breast pocket, and to cherish when I go to Africa. I hope you don't mind too much.'

'So what's that got to do with my number?'

'I phoned your Aunt Amy, told her I had found your earring and that I would like you to know it was safe.'

'Oh, it must be the pearl one, I lost its partner ages ago. You can keep it, hope it brings you luck.' She heard the mock chiding in his voice as he said,

'I thought I made it clear that charms and so on were not for me?' There was a pause and she heard a soft sigh as he said, 'So, Marion, how are you feeling now? I don't mean your arm. I mean, I know I've rocked your boat, perhaps caused you distress, and wondered if you have settled in your mind, and can go on loving Alex? Will you tell him, by the way, about me crashing into your lives?' There was a long silence before he cautiously asked, 'Marion?'

She could almost see him in her mind, the head turned to one side and the anxiety on his face.

'Yes, Matthew, I'm still here and yes, of course, I'm going to tell Alex about you, and your lives as you told them to me. And yes, I do and always will love Alex.'

'Will you tell him I want only your happiness, that we shall never see each other again?' There was a hesitation before he added, 'Will you tell him that I love you?'

'Please, Matthew, please stop saying you love me. There is no way I'm going to tell Alex anything that might make him anxious. I shall pick my time and words very carefully, but be sure he will know about you.'

'Thank you, I feel I owe him that much.'

Marion slipped down the pillows a little and pulled the sheet up to her chin, then gave a laugh when hearing him say, 'When we were in the station and you told me you were married, well just before you actually said so, you stamped your foot. I knew you would. From the beginning I thought you looked like a foot stamper!'

Smiling to herself she replied, 'Well, you wouldn't shut up, would you? I couldn't get a word in edgeways.'

'Ah, yes, I remember you wanted to clear off quickly, and I wanted to be with you for as long as possible. Why was that? Why did you want to disappear so fast?' There was no immediate answer and the silence lengthened. 'Hello, you there?'

A subdued voice answered, 'Yes, Matthew, I'm still here. The only answer I can give you, and it is the truth, is that you were so happy, so upbeat and sure about everything. I was about to destroy it all for you. I didn't want to hang around and see you suffer.' She paused, before adding, 'But I did in the end, didn't I? See your disappointment, your sadness, your anger and, to be honest, it distressed me as much as you.'

'Does that mean ...?'

'It means, Matthew, that I care, I care about you very much, and you know as well as I do, there can be nothing more.'

'I know. I know that, of course, but you will always be in my thoughts in this life, and the next and the next and the next.' When he heard her quietly laughing he said, 'Stop laughing. Oh I know it still doesn't seem possible to you, but you'll see one day.'

Softly she said, 'Good night and goodbye, Matthew. I'm going to sleep now.' Both were reluctant to put the phone down.

The silence continued, then Matthew, desperate to hold her attention and to keep in contact as long as possible, said brightly, 'Before I go, did you know that I broke another one of the Commandments today?'

There was obvious surprise in her voice as she asked, 'Really? As well as "Thou shalt not covet thy neighbour's wife"?'

'Yes, another one besides that one.'

'Which one was that?'

'The one that says, "Remember the Sabbath day, to keep it holy".'

'Oh come on! That hardly applies nowadays, nearly everyone breaks that one, I'm sure. In this modern world there is so much to do and to be honest, so much to see before one gets too old. Surely it isn't so relevant today as it was in the past when life was so much slower?'

Matthew laughed quietly, 'Well, I suppose you're right, given the hustle and bustle we experience today. As you so rightly pointed out, not so long ago it was quite different. Are you settling down to sleep now or shall I tell you how I broke that particular one?'

'I can't miss that, can I? After all I have heard about the others. By the way, when you've broken all of the commandments, does that mean you're back to square one or will the Senate call it a day and let your original destiny happen?'

'I don't really know. I would like my true destiny to take over so that we will eventually be together, but it's up to them. I don't expect they were overjoyed when I yelled at them in the station.'

'Hmm. That was really something to see,' she laughed, 'I thought you were going to stamp your foot!'

'Me! Stamp my foot. That's a girl thing.'

Marion started to protest but he interrupted her,

'Shall I tell the story or not?'

'Oh, go on then. I'll never sleep if you don't. I'd just keep wondering how you had upset the Senate again, wouldn't I?'

'Right, you probably know that different cultures, or societies whatever, believe that Saturday is the Sabbath, but no matter which day, Saturday or Sunday, the same restrictions applied. For instance, certainly no work was to be done, no lighting of fires or travelling. There was to be no pleasure-seeking like singing, or hunting and definitely no alcohol. Marketing or business deals were not allowed either.

'It so happened when I was a young lad in 1903 I lived in a remote Welsh village. Not a village really, as there were less than ten or so homes. I was the eldest of four brothers, just into my teens. Every Sunday everyone was expected to attend the tiny chapel without fail. We had what you would call a "fire and brimstone" preacher who knew everyone and their business. Every Sunday this preacher would raise his voice, getting louder and louder and thump on the pulpit with his fist or crook. I think he thought the crook made him a shepherd of our souls. He would point at someone, anyone, who in turn would be terrified wondering what transgression they had committed. He threatened to cast each and every one of us into Hell. This preacher kept telling us of the everlasting fire, that it would be our task to tend it. and that it would be unbearably hot and was our punishment for sinning. What scared some folk most was that he always said death was the punishment for breaking the commandments, and he insisted God would close Heaven's doors to us.' Matthew paused and when he went on, Marion sensed the pity in his voice as he said, 'Some of those trusting people didn't realise that their sins were so trivial it didn't justify the preacher's wrath. "On God's behalf", he used to thunder.

'My father used to say that the preacher had to shout and bang about to keep everyone awake. When I and my brothers went to bed, we could hear our parents in the next room talking about the sermon. It wasn't long before we were all giggling when we heard father shouting and ranting just like the preacher and my mother laughing fit to bust.

'One day there was great excitement amongst the neighbours. It seems that a circus was to visit the town some ten miles away. Of course there was little hope of anyone visiting it. Money was scarce, almost non-existent for most families, including ours. Everyone made a living by growing as much food as possible, and keeping a goat or a sheep. Bartering between the neighbours was common.

'I decided to seek out the circus to see if there was any employment to be had, however temporary. Naturally, I also anticipated the thrill of seeing the circus at first hand. The circus was to arrive on Monday morning, so I thought if I set out early on Sunday morning, I would be there as it arrived, and stand a good chance of getting work of some sort. I didn't care how menial it was, but I dearly wanted to take home a few coins for my family.

'I left before anyone was awake, and hoped mother would forgive me for taking a crust of bread from the pantry. Ten miles, mostly over the mountain tops, is a long hike. The mist obscured the view so that more than once I had a fright when a sheep ambled onto the path ahead, it looked so ghostly. The path was stony, wet and treacherous and more than once I slipped. The couple of streams I had to cross were icy, but I was glad to have a drink. Anyway, I finally arrived late on Sunday evening. I was very tired but made myself as comfortable as possible at the edge of the field where the circus was to be set up.

'I woke up to such a bustle of activity, people talking, laughing, grumbling and scolding. All busy preparing for the events to come over the next week. I was told later that the circus folk observed the Sabbath, but once the midnight hour had passed they began their journey to the next venue. I approached a fellow who looked as if he was in charge, and asked if there were any jobs I could do. Not wanting to be bothered by me, he pointed to a man struggling with a line of horses. I knew little about such creatures, but such was my determination that I went across to him. It turned out he was glad of my help. It was: fetch this, get this and hold this, tie this, on and on, all jobs I could manage. Joe Manukyan he called himself and I stayed with him mostly. He saw to it that I had somewhere to sleep, and something to eat. There were other chores about the site I volunteered for, and was usually rewarded with a farthing or two.

'Besides the circus there were all sorts of sideshows and exhibitions and I was sworn to secrecy once I found out how the people were duped. There were peep shows, and magic booths, and freak shows as well as a menagerie. Not on a grand scale, but it did boast a lion. During the circus performance people were spellbound by the bravery of the lion tamer. They were amazed when it obeyed instructions at the sound of a whip cracked by the trainer. There were a couple of snakes and, as they are not my favourite creatures, I was thankful that they were well fed which kept them sleepy. There were also some domestic animals, like dogs and rabbits. The children that came to the circus seemed to enjoy them most.' Matthew paused for a moment before saying, 'Oh, there were clowns and conjurers too. I learned a lot of tricks from them and was able to entertain my family and neighbours when I got home.'

Matthew was thoughtful for a moment before saying, 'Here's one my brothers loved. I used to tell them I had eleven fingers and, of course, they didn't believe me. To prove it this is what I did. You can try it if you like. With one hand count the fingers on the other, five right? Then you start at six with the other hand and get to ten. Of course you do, but to prove that I had eleven, on one hand I counted backwards from ten, so ten, nine, eight, seven, six, then I held up the other hand and said, "and five more makes eleven." A good one that, don't you agree? You try it.' There was no sound at the other end of the line, so he asked, 'Are you awake Marion?' and laughed when he heard an exaggerated snore answer him.

'I suppose you're waiting to see where the girl comes in, aren't you?'

'Naturally, every story hinges on your meeting with her doesn't it?'

He laughed. 'Majida, she was called. She was a slim, dark haired girl a few years older than me, and the daughter of my benefactor, the horse trainer. I was a bit shocked to see she wore trousers, but quickly understood that this was for her modesty. Majida followed the conjurers' and clowns' acts, and did trick riding on her father's horses round and round the ring. I thought some of the feats she did were very dangerous, like standing up on the galloping horse's bare back, sometimes on one leg, arms outstretched, hanging down the side of the horse as it raced on or jumping from one moving horse to another. Each trick brought gasps from the crowds. She was so tiny I wondered how she was able to control such a beast. I was just a boy at that time, but I fell in love with her, although at the time I didn't know that was what I was feeling. I found a lump of chalk and, without knowing its meaning, I began drawing out the MM symbol again and again, mostly on the sides of the wagons which served as sleeping quarters for the circus folk.

'The week came to an end and our paths had rarely crossed. By now I had a good number of coins to which her father generously added a florin. It was late on Saturday night, and I was determined to be home early the next day. It was then that Majida spoke to me for the first time. She was petting and grooming her horse.

"Here," she said in broken English and smiled as she handed me a small linen poke, a little sack with drawstrings, with the letters MM embroidered on it, her initials of course, "Put your money in here. You don't seem to have any pockets." I know I blushed and wondered if she had any idea of how I felt about her. I stammered my thanks and goodbyes and then set out for home.

'It was on my way home that all my past life memories were renewed. At first I didn't understand – remember I was not yet fourteen.'

Marion interrupted him, 'I've said it again and again, the Senate were so unfair to you. How could you possibly understand love at that age?'

'I can tell you I grew up fast that night. I sat on a boulder halfway down the mountainside and let everything flood back. I wept as even then I knew the futility of it all. I was convinced at the time that the preacher would know of my feelings for Majida and would no doubt broadcast this, along with my folly of not keeping the Sabbath, from his pulpit, then cast me out of the village.'

Marion sympathised. 'You were a poor little boy. Such a fear to go home to, all that suffering, just because you travelled on a Sunday.'

'Two Sundays,' he replied. 'But things looked up once daybreak came, and in the distance I could see my home. No smoke from the chimney though, a dead giveaway if someone in the house had been working. You just didn't invite the preacher's wrath, or as he put it – "God's wrath." Matthew chuckled as he said, 'What would people do today with all those prohibitions, I wonder?'

'Ignore them, which is what most are doing anyway,' she retorted.

'So you see I'd broken another of the commandments.'

'You're not stopping there, are you? Come on, I want to know what happened next.'

'You sure? I've been nattering away for ages. Aren't you tired?'

'Yes I am tired, but I want to know what happened in the end.'

'Right. I lifted the latch and entered the cottage. Everyone was seated around the table eating bread and dripping – no cooking for mother. When they saw me the children shouted out, they were so pleased to see me. My father stood up and came across to me. I was sure he was going to clout me, so I forestalled him by handing over the linen bag filled with my earnings. The look of disbelief, then joy, on his face was worth every hour I had worked.

My mother took my face into her hands, and was concerned to see the dried streaks that my tears had left. She asked what had happened. How could I tell her? In any case her answer would have been that I had had a bad dream, a nightmare. If I told my father he would have said I was being fanciful, so I held my tongue unable to tell either of them. I remained silent, just saying to everyone who asked, that I had been working with the circus folk, that it had been a long way to travel and I was tired.

'There was no escaping chapel and, as I had forecast, the preacher roared out to all assembled that I was one of God's fallen, I was a sinner and he, on God's behalf, would punish me. The preacher, if he had his way, would have had me burned at the stake, he was that far behind the times or at the very least banished me. He had in mind to put me in the ancient stocks, a punishment banned for some fifty years or so, but my father protested. The preacher then decided I was to be with him, on my knees, every evening for two hours praying and begging for forgiveness until the following Sunday.'

'And did you? I have a feeling that you didn't.'

'You're right. I defied him and, what's more, my father sided with me. Neither of us ever attended chapel again. Mother did and took the rest of the family. She told us she said plenty of prayers so that ours would not be missed.'

Very quietly Marion asked, 'How did the Senate get you back to them, Matthew? Surely they must have let you live on as you were so young.'

Resignedly, he answered, 'Not them. I suppose in a way they were intent on giving me as many chances as possible. A few weeks after my return we, my father and I, were still being shunned by our neighbours on the preacher's say so, such was their fear of his condemnation. On this particular day I was out looking for our lost goat. I spotted her high up on a ledge and climbed up to get her. Really there was no need as goats are very agile, and eventually she would have made her own way down. Mother wanted her milk to make cheese that day, so up I climbed and ...'

'I can guess the rest. You missed your footing and fell, and the Senate had you back in their clutches again.'

'Yes, that's exactly what happened. I dare say the preacher was jubilant, his prophesy of death for sinners had come true. No doubt the villagers were awed by his prediction. As usual, I was mocked by some of the Senate members, but others openly said that this time the test had been unfair, that I was too young. But it wasn't long before I was sent back to try again.'

For a short while nothing was said, then Marion, after looking at her bedside clock said, 'Do you know it's nearly one o'clock? I think we'd better say goodnight now, don't you?'

'You're right. I'm leaving for Amsterdam tomorrow afternoon to meet up with some colleagues, then on Wednesday we are flying to Nigeria. I haven't even started packing. Are you going into your office tomorrow?'

'Only for an hour or two in the morning as the boss has summoned me. Some minor crisis or other, I expect. I shall be home in time for Alex.'

'Good. So you'll have a few days off to be with him?'

'Yes, but on Thursday he is going on the course I told you about and I'll go into work then. Goodnight Matthew, I mean it this time.'

'Good night cariadon.'

'What does that mean?'

'Look it up. I'll give you a clue. It comes from where I've been telling you about, my days in Wales.' Then he added very softly, 'Forever, Marion, forever.'

Still holding the phone by her ear, she was surprised and a little dismayed when she could only hear the dialling tone.

Fourteen

When she arrived at the office before eleven, Marion was able to catch up on the office gossip and politics. Asked about her cousin's wedding, she happily told her colleagues of the event, how lovely Rosemary looked, the bridesmaids and their dresses, the flowers and the reception, everything she could remember. She didn't mention Matthew. Jeanette, her best friend, looked at her keenly with a questioning expression.

'What?' asked Marion, turning away from her, 'Why are you looking at me like that?'

Jeanette placed herself in front of her, and gave her a little poke in the chest. 'You're up to something. You're glowing, you look happy. Something's happened, I can tell.'

Marion felt herself going hot and hoped Jeanette didn't notice. Matthew, she acknowledged to herself, was the reason for the quiet happiness she was experiencing. Yes, they had parted, for good, she reminded herself. The raw pain squeezed her heart and trying to ignore it she turned to her friend.

'Rubbish,' she blustered. 'The something you're on about is my Alex is coming home today, and of course I'm happy. Wouldn't you be?'

'You bet I would if your Alex was coming home to me,' Jeanette laughed.

Marion joined in with her laughter. 'Hands off, madam. Mind you, if I ever do get fed up with him ...'

Jeanette raised her eyebrows and gazed at her intently again. 'Hmm, Alex you say, but I rather think it's more than that.' Then excitedly added, 'You're not, you know, preggers are you?' She hugged herself with glee. 'You are, I can tell. How wonderful.' She hesitated, 'When's it due, Marion? Come on, tell me!'

Marion opened her eyes wide in surprise and shock, then quickly said, 'Shut up, will you?'

There was awe in Jeanette's voice as she whispered, 'You are.'

Marion didn't answer, and pretended to repair her make-up, unable to look at her friend. There was no way she was telling anyone about Matthew. The wonderful, turbulent weekend was still in her mind. Fortunately she was summoned to the meeting and left Jeanette convinced she knew Marion's secret.

The meeting was a waste of time, and revolved around an author who, as the chairperson put it, had an ego as big as Mount Everest. Marion thought the problem could easily have been sorted without her. On her way home she purchased a few groceries, but nothing for their evening meal, certain that Alex would insist that they go out for dinner. Calling in at the dental surgery she made an appointment to see the dentist the following week. On the way home she treated herself to a light lunch.

Once she was home again, she began changing to get ready to meet Alex. She put on his favourite blue knee-length dress, made up her face carefully and let her hair hang loose as she was unable to do much else with it. Alex's flight was due to arrive at Heathrow at around four thirty, and she planned to take a taxi and meet him. Choosing clip earrings, which were the easiest to put on, she was interrupted by the telephone ringing.

At its sound her heart turned over. At the same time she felt guilty even though she knew it couldn't possibly be Matthew as she knew that he was now out of her life forever. She picked up the phone.

'Hello,' she said cautiously and was delighted to hear a dear, familiar voice after all.

'Is that my beautiful wife?'

There was a smile in her voice as she replied, 'Yes, but only if that is my handsome husband Alex asking.'

He chuckled at her quick answer. 'Well love, do you want the good news or the bad news first?'

Her heart sank at these words as she needed to see him, hold him and feel safe in his arms. 'You choose,' she said and there was no mistaking the disappointment in her voice.

'Now don't get in a tizzy, old girl. Ready?' He heard her sigh resignedly, and he continued, 'The good news is I am on my way home. I've made a few decisions and, I … Well, you will soon know all about it.' He heard another sigh, this time one of relief. 'The bad news, and it isn't that bad really, there seems to be a minor strike or something, by the luggage loaders, so everything and everyone is delayed. I'm stuck in Belfast for least another six hours or so.'

'Oh, please don't say that Alex. I so want to see you.' She paused, 'So what time do you expect to be home then?'

He could tell she was disappointed and said, 'Sorry old girl I'm missing you too. Early tomorrow morning I think, I hope. Around two o'clock I reckon. I'll get a cab home and as soon as I arrive I'll bring you a cup of tea in bed, then I'll climb in beside you and ...'

'Not going to waste any time then?' she interrupted and smiled as she heard him chuckle again.

'Got to go now, love you, bye.'

Marion said her goodbyes to the dialling tone.

It was gone eleven o'clock the next day when Alex finally arrived home. Marion was concerned at how tired he was, and made him a cup of coffee, after which he decided to go to bed. He kissed her lightly on her forehead as he made his way to the stairs.

'Catch up later, babe,' he murmured.

It was nearly five o'clock before she heard him showering and in another half an hour he came downstairs and folded her in his arms. The smell of his familiar aftershave was comforting, as were his tender kisses, and she knew without a doubt that she loved him.

'Sorry, love, sorry to have kept you waiting.' Still holding on to her he stood back as he said, 'Let's have a look at you then.' Drawing her close to him again, he whispered, 'You'll do,' and together they laughed as she gave him a gentle slap with her good hand. 'How's the arm coming along? Nearly better?'

She nodded as she answered, 'Another couple of days, I think, and then I can discard the sling and have a lighter support.'

She didn't protest as Alex suddenly grabbed her good hand and pulled her towards the door, saying, 'Come on, let's find somewhere to eat. I'm starving.'

They slept in late on Wednesday, and Alex cooked a breakfast of scrambled eggs on toast. As they were drinking their coffee and just as Alex had taken a mouthful to drink Marion casually said, 'I've met someone.'

He choked and spluttered coffee down his clean shirt. Very carefully, he put his mug down, looking at her at the same time.

'You what!' he exclaimed.

At once Marion knew he had mistaken what she had said, or rather she realised that she hadn't made it clear. Quietly, she said, 'Oh, Alex. As if I would,' and was glad to see him relax a little.

'Well, it was a bit of a shock coming out like that. So what does, "I've met someone" mean? You'd better explain.' He looked down at his stained shirt, shook his head in disbelief then looked at her. 'I'll change in a minute. He lifted the coffee pot to refill his mug and asked, 'Want some?'

Marion shook her head. 'His name is Matthew.' Alex just kept looking at her, waiting. 'Matthew Hope, Dominic's cousin. He was at the wedding and we travelled home together. But, Alex, he was so interesting, full of fanciful stories.' How disloyal, she thought to herself, how dismissive of Matthew's courage and agony.

'What sort of stories? Real stories or as mother used to say, – are you telling me stories – when she thought someone was telling lies?'

'Mostly historic stories, making himself the hero of each, but honestly they were so entertaining.' Her inner voice whispered, 'Sorry, Matthew.'

'Go on then, tell me some of them. We've plenty of time.'

At the end of her abbreviated account of the tales she had been told, Alex leaned forward on his elbows and said, 'That chap ought to get that lot down on paper and have them published. They're bloody marvellous.'

'I suggested that, but he said he hadn't the time.' What she hadn't told Alex was the role of the Senate, that Matthew was being tested or that Matthew loved her.

Slowly, with his head lowered, Alex said softly, 'You know for a moment, just a moment, I really thought you'd found someone else and you were going to tell me you were leaving. I can't begin to tell you how devastated I felt.'

Tears pricked her eyes, and she leaned forward to touch his hand and said, 'I'm so sorry. I should have worded it differently. As if I would do that to you. I love you Alex, you're the only one for me. You should know that by now.'

Leaning back and folding his arms across his chest and grinning at her, he said, 'Well, if he didn't fall for you there's something wrong with the guy.'

Marion laughed as she airily replied, 'Oh, he did. Told me a thousand times he loved me.' There, she told her inner voice, I've told him. What she couldn't tell him, was her feelings for Matthew. How could she when she couldn't understand them herself?

Later that morning they decided to have a picnic somewhere by the Thames. It was mid-week and they thought Windsor would be ideal, but the place seemed to have been invaded by hordes of visitors. They felt lucky when, hand in hand, they strolled along the river bank and found a quiet picnic spot a little distance out of the bustling crowd. After their meal and as they were lying down on the ground gazing up at the sky, Marion suddenly sat up.

'Alex.'

'Hmm. What?' He murmured drowsily pulling her down beside him again.

'You said you had something to tell me when you were on the phone, something you were quite excited about.'

He turned on his side and leaning on one elbow he rested his chin in his hand. There was a measure of excitement in his voice.

'I did. I have. It's so ...' he searched for the right word. '... so, well you could say, challenging.'

'So, tell me.'

Marion reached out for the wine bottle. 'There's a little left in here. Want some?' He held out his glass and she shared what was left between them.

'Listen, Marion, I'm more than flattered really.' He took a deep breath, 'I've been asked to arrange the Christmas entertainment on the rig. They, the bosses, suggested something like an Old Time Music Hall. They think I'd be a good Master of Ceremonies. There aren't many willing to perform, of course, so I could ... well, I intend to crack jokes, one-liners I think, and I can sing one or two numbers and do some new impersonations. What do you think?'

'What sort of jokes?'

'Mostly in-house types probably, but some from the past.' He gave her a smile, a smile that she knew well, a smile that seemed to suggest something else was coming. He took her hand. 'So ...' he began,

'I knew it. You're going to ask me to do something impossible aren't you?'

'No, but it will be easier for you to do, being in the business so to speak.'

'Come on then, what is it?'

He breathed in softly. 'Would it be very difficult for you to check on the copyrights of comedians' material? You know jokes, mannerisms and things like that. I don't want to get into any litigation with accusations of plagiarism or theft or anything.'

Marion sat quietly for a moment before answering.

'Please,' he added.

'I'll do my best, but you'll have to give me an exact list of what you are going to use so I can research each thoroughly,' she said finally.

'Thanks, darling, I knew you'd help. You realise, of course, that I'll be trying out all of my stuff on you for the next few days?'

Marion gave a groan and begged to be spared the ordeal of what she was sure were going to be lame gags.

'Don't be mean. Bet I make you laugh, well ...' and seeing the scepticism on her face he added, '... well sometimes maybe. Here's one; a fellow asks a stranger, "Are your relatives in business?" "Yes," he replies, "in the iron and steel business." "Oh, indeed," says the other, very impressed, "Yes, me mother irons and me father steals".'

Despite herself, Marion giggled, 'Honestly, Alex, that is so corny. Where did you get it from?'

'I reckon the guys will love it. It will get them booing and heckling, which will all add to the atmosphere and fun of the show. I got it from the Internet and here's another – want to hear it?'

She rolled her eyes with exaggerated patience and teased, 'Go on then.'

'I know a man who eats nothing but Chinese food. His mate asks, "Why is that?" And he answers, "because he's a Chinaman".' Marion gave out a long groan.

'Here's one for you,' she said. 'Knock, knock.'

Quickly Alex asked, 'Who's there?'

'Nuff.'

'Nuff who?'

'Nuff of your ridiculous jokes.'

Alex put on a mock sad face. 'Really?'

Marion laughed, 'Well don't overdo it.'

For the rest of the day, Alex kept her laughing with his attempts at being a comedian. At bedtime he said, 'Just one more, okay?' She raised her eyebrows but nodded at the same time.

'A couple in their eighties were watching the six o'clock news while eating their dinner. The newsreader was telling a story of how in a leafy suburb someone had frequent male visitors to her home. The neighbours were indignant when they realised the woman was running a brothel. The newsreader went on to ask, "What would you say if a brothel opened next door to you?" and the old man, without blinking an eye or stopping eating, said, "Bloody handy".'

Marion couldn't hold back her giggles. When she had quietened down she said thoughtfully, 'I wonder if you could use this?' and told him how to prove he had eleven fingers. Marion had surprised herself, she thought that Matthew was safely at the back of her mind and now she had reawakened her awareness of him. Matthew wasn't out of her life, she was certain of that, no matter how she tried to make it so. Alex was cleaning his teeth and she was in the bedroom when she called out to him, 'What are you thinking of singing?' She waited as he swilled his mouth and sauntered back into the room.

'Not really sure yet. Got any ideas?' he asked.

'There are a few ideas mulling around in my head that I thought might be useful,' and she could tell by his face as he looked at her that he was pleased she was after all interested in his determination to put on a good show.

'Really. Such as?' he asked.

'What I've always enjoyed are monologues. Like those that Stanley Holloway used to recite. Things like, "Albert and the Lion", I think it was called, and "Sam, Sam, pick up tha musket". There's plenty more to choose from. You should be able to mimic his voice, there's lots of old recordings somewhere.'

'Hey, I like that idea.' He was quiet for a moment. 'I really like it. Yes, I think I'll definitely give that a go. Have you got anything else lurking in your clever little mind?'

'What about a singsong at the end?'

'I'd thought of that, but need something a little different. Not sure what though.'

'How about using some of the popular tunes and writing your own words. You could do something about life on the rig, or the bosses or the food – all of them, in fact.'

Alex was fidgeting with excitement and then, hugging her fiercely, said, 'You're brilliant. Thanks a million, my lovely girl. Already my head's buzzing with ideas. It's going to be quite a show, I'm thinking.'

Running her finger down Alex's chest and looking up into his eyes, she said, 'You'll do fine. You will make a very good Master of Ceremonies and everyone will love you, I'm sure of it, and, what's more, I'm going to be so proud of you.'

Fifteen

Alex was cheerful and full of enthusiasm the next morning when he said goodbye to Marion and left for his three-day course on safety. Marion was also in an upbeat mood as she made her way to the office. Half tempted to hire a cab to take her there, she decided in the end to set out later than usual to avoid the rush hour crowds. The thought of someone accidentally barging into her injured arm made her feel more than a little anxious. As it turned out, the underground train to Holborn was no less crowded than her usual earlier time, but she recognised that more than one person was careful around her and smiled her thanks to them.

The in-tray on her desk was not as full as she had expected, but there were a number of e-mails from clients requiring answers. The usual weekly meeting had been scheduled for the afternoon, and her first task was to find answers to the various points raised last week. Thankfully it was not in her remit to deal with any that involved finance. Although she often had the final say as to which author should be offered a contract, the final commission was not her responsibility. Sometimes though, she was quite shocked at what was actually offered. Occasionally too much, and at other times far too little. Undaunted, she often challenged the decisions, and sometimes the final amount was changed, especially to those she felt were underpaid.

Jeanette entered her office with two mugs of coffee, sat on the edge of Marion's desk and said, 'Hi, I've brought you some coffee. Oh, on second thoughts, are you allowed coffee?'

Marion peered over her glasses at her friend before saying, 'Of course I can drink coffee and thank you very much.'

For a few minutes they discussed their work, their mutual friends and their colleagues. Marion told her about the picnic. Also discussed were Alex's Music Hall plans and Marion kept her friend amused by telling her some of his gags. All the while she was aware of Jeanette's unspoken curiosity about the pregnancy.

Finally Jeanette couldn't resist asking, 'How are you feeling Marion? You will rest up and do all the right things, won't you?'

'Oh, I feel fine. On top of the world,' she replied in mock seriousness, 'but I will be glad to get this plaster off. It itches like mad underneath.' The telephone on her desk rang, and glad of the interruption, she reached out for it.

'Cheerio. Catch up later,' Jeanette mouthed as she left the office. The telephone call was quickly dealt with and Marion returned to her various tasks.

It was nearly lunchtime when the office porter, smiling broadly and carrying a large bouquet, said, 'For you Mrs Knowles. From your hubby, no doubt, but there's no name on the card. Funny that.' Scratching his head, he said, almost under his breath, 'Something I can't fathom, not anyways I try.' He sniffed, and looked keenly at her. 'Probably another one of your grateful clients, I should think.'

Marion smiled to herself, knowing he'd given himself away trying to find out who had sent the flowers, and fishing for a name. She pursed her lips and shook her head.

'That's not his style and it'll be a first if it is. Thank you,' she said as she took them from him. Bouquet was a misnomer. There was no overall theme, no ostentatious declaration of anything about it. The flowers were mismatched and straggly, spilling over the cellophane wrapping. There were vibrant yellow Marigolds, white Marguerites and striking orange Montbretia, as well as out of season, Morning Glory of the deepest blue, its soft vine stems drooping over the sides. Also in the bunch were the small-headed mauve Michaelmas daisies and the whole ensemble was enhanced with dainty Maiden's Hair fern. Marion smiled and thought the untidy arrangement both simple and charming.

Curiously she turned the card over in her hand. The porter was right, there was no name. There was no need for one as she knew at once why the porter was puzzled. No one could possibly know who the sender was, but she knew. The double M beautifully illuminated like a monk's lifelong work in the past, explained better than his signature. Looking at it her heart did somersaults, she experienced the feeling of missing someone no longer a part of her life, nor, she told herself, could he be. Yet here were the telltale feelings of her love for him.

There was no particular scent from the flowers, but nevertheless she pulled them up to her face, allowing the coolness of the petals to touch her cheeks. For five or more minutes she sat holding them giving up the time to wondering where he was now, what he was doing, was he happy and recovered from their eventful weekend? Telling herself he was probably well on his way to Nigeria and, more than likely, flirting with the air hostess as he ordered a drink, she smiled to herself. The question of him being over her, she couldn't answer, but hoped with all her heart that in time he would find happiness with someone else. If she could be happy with Alex, and she was, surely he too could find happiness.

The trouble was that although she told herself she was over him, and there were times when he was not foremost in her mind, suddenly he was there, filling her thoughts and bringing an ache into her heart. As she sat there she remembered the last words he spoke to her – "Good night cariadon." The only clue he gave her on the telephone was that he had told her his last adventure was in Wales. She turned on her computer, searched for translations, typed in Welsh to English and then the word 'cariadon'. In a few moments she found the answer. There was a lump in her throat as she read: lover, sweetheart, darling, dearest.

There was a vase in the cupboard, and she put the flowers into it and she bent to check their meagre perfume. She stood them on her desk, and she grinned at their untidy display, but there was no way she was going to dispose of them in a hurry.

Saturday morning, and as Alex wouldn't be home until Sunday afternoon. She decided that after breakfast she would do a little shopping. There were some shoes she'd seen in an Oxford Street store, a lovely shade of gun metal grey with a fairly high heel and she was sure Alex would admire them too. After swilling some hot water into a bowl she began to collect her few breakfast dishes in order to wash them and gave only half her attention to the news programme on the television. She caught words like, 'visiting ambassadors,' 'alleged fraudulent activities of a banker,' some singing star or other visiting London, the sort of news reported daily. It was when she heard, 'Nigeria' and 'plane crash', that she was suddenly alert.

Quickly she wiped her hands, and went across to the television set and turned up the sound. She grabbed a chair and sat down to watch and listen to the newscaster, but was annoyed to find that she had missed the story. She began experiencing a feeling of foreboding as she turned on the radio for further news, but nothing was mentioned about a plane crash. There was tightness around her heart, and rising panic as she frantically turned back to the television, switching from station to station trying to find out more about the incident. Looking in the mirror she could see she had turned white, as fear had overwhelmed her. Matthew had warned her that once he had broken a Commandment, his death would follow and that it was usually shortly afterwards. 'Please no, God,' she murmured, 'don't let the Senate take him back so soon.'

It was nearly twenty minutes before the story was repeated on the News Channel. The newscaster in a neutral voice reported, '*A light aircraft has crashed shortly after leaving Nigeria's Sokoto Airport. The plane was on its way to Damatura in eastern Nigeria. It was two hours before local people were able to determine the exact location of the crash site, and they had difficulty making their way through the dense jungle to reach it. On arrival they found parts of the plane, the undercarriage and a wing, some distance from the site of the main fuselage, suggesting that the plane had broken up in mid-air. Reports say that the plume of smoke could be seen for miles around.*

There were four people aboard; the pilot, a male and female backpackers and an engineer from the United Kingdom. There were no survivors.'

Marion felt herself going cold as the man's voice went on.

'*The experienced pilot was forty-one years old, a local man, and leaves his wife and a family of five children between the ages of six months and sixteen years. Friends and neighbours say he was an experienced pilot, and a man with a sense of humour who will be greatly missed. It is believed the two young backpackers were from Germany. Their next of kin have been informed.*'

Marion had a hollow feeling inside, convinced that she knew what was coming next. The newscaster continued.

'*Matthew Hope from London also lost his life. It is believed Mr Hope, an engineer, was on his way to a village around a hundred miles from Maidururi where the people have little water. Mr Hope was to oversee the*

*installation of a well. Spencer Engineering, the company he worked for,
expressed their condolences to his family and said that Mr Hope was an
expert in his field, that his skills were invaluable, and that he will be missed
by his colleagues. Internal and United Kingdom crash investigators are
expected at the scene early on Sunday morning.'*

Whilst the accident was being reported a selection of pictures
showed the wreckage, and people milling around it.

Marion sat alone, gazing at the screen and seeing nothing, and
her hands were trembling. She clasped them tightly together, and
began weeping. There was no one she could turn to for comfort or
to tell how devastated or how lonely she felt. She was bewildered
by the ever changing emotions she was experiencing. She was
numb with grief, and wondering if she would survive the shock of
Matthew's death, believing her life would never be the same.

They had said their goodbyes, she knew nothing more was to
come of their meeting, but it might have happened. I might have
caught a glimpse of him in a crowd, I would have been satisfied
with that, but his death had made any such remote chance impossible. Guilt engulfed her. If only she had made it clear at the time,
that she did believe in him, and that they would meet in the next
life. Sadly, she convinced herself that he had died without hope of
gaining her everlasting love.

Marion stood up and turned off the television. Bright sunshine
cast shadows around the room. No one should die on such a
perfect day. She was angry, wanting to blame someone, and began
pacing around the room. Matthew loved his job, so there was no
use pointing the finger at his company. If the pilot had a sense of
humour as was reported, did he do something to impress the
passengers, and had he made a mistake? No, she told herself, it was
the Senate. Surely this time Matthew hadn't broken one of the
Terms? It was an easy mistake to make presuming she was single,
because the telltale wedding ring of marriage was not in view.
Inwardly she fumed, convinced that the Senate had spitefully, and
deliberately, arranged for Matthew to be misled. They had, she felt
sure, caused her accident in order to deceive him. She found
herself praying for a case of mistaken identity, promising that she
would give up all thoughts of Matthew if this was so. Guilt returned. If indeed Matthew were spared, some other wife, mother,
siblings, families and friends would be suffering the heartache she
was experiencing.

The telephone rang and Marion ignored it, knowing she was too choked to speak to anyone. Wearily she sat down on the sofa feeling hopeless and sobbed out loud, 'I can't bear this.' Overwhelmed and worn out by grief, she curled into a ball on the sofa, and slept.

It was close to two o'clock when she woke up. Immediately, she remembered the dreadful news and gave a deep sigh. Nothing was ever going to bring him back, she realised. On the table she saw the remains of her earlier breakfast. Less than half a mug of coffee, the crusts off the toast, and eggshells on the worktop. Immediately, she felt nauseated by them. Thirst, though, made her pull herself together, and she got herself a glass of water, taking sips as she finished clearing up the remains of her breakfast.

Marion looked in the mirror, and was shocked to see her drawn face with downcast mouth and smudged mascara. She washed, combed her hair and then stood gazing out of the window at the pocket size garden where she saw the montbretia in flower and remembered her bouquet. It was then that other memories began flooding in. She smiled as she recalled the first time she saw him, thinking him to be ordinary, but how extraordinary he turned out to be. At that first meeting there was an anxious look on his face, quickly replaced with relief, thinking he had found her. She remembered his spontaneous laugh when he heard her name, and hearing him saying it softly to himself again and again, 'Marion.' How gently he had helped her over the stile on last Sunday's walk and how they laughed when he offered help when she needed the toilet. There was another flicker of a smile when she remembered that he had upgraded her train ticket, and bribed the guard so that they had a compartment to themselves. What genuine pleasure he derived when he introduced her to his Italian friend, and the meal he had ordered for them. The hopeful expression after he had told her of each of his adventures, wanting her to be Magdalena, and wanting her to remember the time as well. Marion gave a quiet chuckle when she recalled, as if it were yesterday, he had teased her about stamping her foot. Where did he get that idea from?

Gradually, she felt calmer and more at peace with herself. It was as if Matthew had nudged her into accepting his death and reminding her she should be happy. That was always his intention, she told herself, that she should be happy. Hadn't he said it time and time again?

At around ten the next morning the telephone rang, and when Marion answered it, she was surprised and pleased, to hear a woman's voice.

'Is that Marion?'

'It is. Can I help you?' The line was quiet for a moment or two and then the woman continued.

'I think I can help you. I'm Rachel, Matthew's sister. Perhaps you've heard about Matthew's death?'

Marion felt a slight thrill at the sound of his name. At last, she thought, someone who knew him well, someone she could genuinely mention his name to, someone who was grieving as much as she was.

'Yes, I had heard. I am so sorry,' she replied. 'Matthew did mention you. He told me all about your trip to Italy.' Neither spoke for a moment.

Softly Marion asked, 'How are you?'

'Distraught, really, but he was doing his job, a job that he felt was so important. More to the point, Marion, how are you? Matthew told me if anything happened to him I was to get in touch with you. Funny really, it was as if he had a premonition of what was going to happen.'

Marion thought to herself, she doesn't know then, of the Senate's decisions.

'Do you think so?' she asked. There was a sigh at the other end of the line.

'Oh, I don't really know what he was thinking. He was certainly very strange, not himself at all when he phoned me from Amsterdam. I thought him a bit subdued, sad really, he was always teasing me, but this time ...' There was silence for a few moments and then she went on, 'He told me he'd met someone, someone special. He meant you, Marion. He also said that nothing could ever come of your time together.'

'I'm married,' Marion said quietly.

'Yes, I guessed that,' said Rachel. 'Nevertheless,' she took a deep breath, 'He asked me to tell you that he loved you, and told me that I was the only one he could tell of it, that he loved you beyond life itself.'

Marion felt herself choking on a lump in her throat and unable to speak.

'Are you there, Marion? I do hope that I've brought you some comfort and not distressed you further. I'm sure that in your own way you cared for Matthew.'

Pulling herself together, Marion said, 'Yes, I did care for him greatly and thank you for your message. He was very special. I'll never forget him.' Almost unable to say anything further, she whispered. 'Please believe me, I share your grief.'

'Thank you. I must go and phone others now. Dominic and Rosemary, she's your cousin isn't she? I'm sure they will be very upset at the news. Goodbye, Marion, goodbye.' Marion wiped away the tears that had welled up in her eyes, then threw the sodden tissues into the waste bin, and made up her mind to get on with her life. At that moment she longed for the comfort of Alex's love.

As soon as Alex arrived later that morning he folded her in his arms.

'I heard about your friend. I'm so sorry, darling. I know you cared a great deal for him. I thought you must have been terribly upset to hear the news here all by yourself. I did telephone, you know. I was thinking about you. When you didn't answer I guessed you might be out shopping or something.'

She clung to him for a moment then gently pushed him away. Turning so that her face was hidden and afraid it might betray her, she replied, 'It's all right Alex. Yes, yesterday was a bit fraught but, well today is another day and really I'm over it.' Though my heart never will be, she added to herself.

Sixteen

Alex drove Marion to work the day after their few days holiday together. When she arrived at the office, Jeanette noticed her pallor at once and that she was subdued. Concerned, she hurried over to her friend. 'Just look at you, Marion. What are you doing in today? You look decidedly under the weather. Why don't you just let the boss know about ...?' She raised her eyebrows hoping for an answer. 'You know what I mean? He'll understand, he's a family man, got three of his own.'

'For goodness sake, Jeanette, there's nothing to tell, and I'd rather be at work, thank you very much,' she snapped. If I keep busy, she thought, I'll get through the day. She must do her best to hide her feelings. It was lack of sleep that was making her look unwell. Last thing at night she had an image of Matthew. She kept reminding herself that he was gone. She was determined to get on with her life. At present it was hard to do so, but thankfully she had Alex to lean on.

Jeanette shrugged her shoulders.

'Just looking out for you, Marri, as a friend.' As Marion glowered at her, Jeanette took the hint, saying as she left, 'Call me if you need any help, all right?'

A mountain of post always accumulated after a few days away from the office, and it wasn't until well after eleven that Marion picked up a large envelope marked for her attention with a handwritten address. It was intriguing to find anything that was handwritten and, curious to find out where it had come from, she turned it over in her hands. The postmarks were smudged and, frowning, she finally picked up her paper knife and slit the envelope open.

There was no address at the top of the first page; instead the familiar MM design was drawn there. Gently she traced it with her finger, then got up from her desk and closed the door so that others would know that she wasn't to be disturbed. Sitting down again she stared at the motif, closed her eyes and relived the awful all-consuming news of Matthew's death again. Opening her eyes she picked up the first of many handwritten pages and began to read.

No need for me to start with affectionate addresses as you know full well what my feelings for you are, now and forever. As we will not meet again in this life, I thought I'd chat to you by means of a letter. I trust you and Alex are well and your arm is healing. When do you get the plaster off? Silly me, asking a question and knowing I shall never know the answer. So, what shall I write next?

Yes – did you like the bouquet? I had quite a tussle with the florist getting that lot together, I can tell you, but bless her, she managed to get at least five beginning with the letter M. Did you realise they all began with the letter M? She phoned me to say that Marigolds, Morning Glory,

Marguerites, Michaelmass Daisies and Montbretia had been included and something she called Maiden's Hair, all green and delicate she said, to compliment the others. Poor lady was beside herself, saying the flowers wouldn't look right together and that some of them never lend themselves to displays, but I persuaded her, I used my charm. Trust you're laughing at that last remark. I hope you liked it anyway.

As I was waiting in the airport, I took out my laptop and started looking to see if the flowers had a meaning, but perhaps you already know.

Marion shook her head and went on reading,

I was intrigued to find out more about them. I discovered that Marigold, quite unromantically I think, means 'riches' and for some cultures it means grief. Now I consider myself richer in life because of finding you, and if your happiness includes riches, then that's what I wish for you. I would definitely spare you grief, so I opt for 'riches'. Much more in keeping with my feelings, I found Morning Glory sadly states, 'Love in Vain', a tad too apt for me, don't you think? But only in this life I might add. On to Marguerite then, I suppose it's the white petals that give the idea of 'purity and innocence'. I must admit though, the daisies I picked from the lanes as a boy smelt absolutely vile! Did that make you smile, I wonder? Now, Montbretia was very difficult to track down, so I opted for Montbretia Crocosmia which, as it has a corm, might be close to the crocus family. The meaning that was nearest I decided was 'cheerful', which I am just thinking of you. Maiden's Hair, believe it or not, means 'discretion', very appropriate given the circumstances of our relationship. I still have your earring by the way. It is in my shirt pocket next to my heart.

A brief smile lit up Marion's face and she told herself, I too have a keepsake now. I shall treasure this letter all my life. She began reading again.

But what about Michaelmass Daisy, I hear you asking? Well, and I think the meaning of this flower sums up my feelings a hundred percent, Marion, would you believe that it means, 'declaration of undying love.' How about that? Just about perfect.

There was a knock at the door and Marion hastily thrust the letter into her desk drawer. It was Frank, the sub editor.

'You all right in there Marion?' he called out.

Guiltily, she hurried to the door, and opened it to find Jeanette with Frank, peering anxiously at her. Marion gave a huge smile.

'Sorry, sorry. Reading a long let ...' and quickly changed to, 'manuscript and didn't want to be disturbed.'

'Any good?' queried Frank.

'Hard to tell at present. I ...'

Jeanette interrupted, 'Time for lunch, Marion, and you're coming with me now. Understood?'

Marion nodded, and went back to her desk for her handbag. Returning to them she said, 'Right, no longer than twenty minutes then,' but seeing Jeanette's disapproving look, altered it to, 'thirty at the most.'

'I'll leave you women to it, then. Glad you're all right Marion,' said Frank and raised his hand as he said, 'Bye for now.'

During lunch Marion made it very clear to Jeanette that she was not pregnant, telling her only that she'd had a bad weekend. She could see Jeanette was disappointed and gave her a hug. 'Oh, I'm sorry, and you so excited.'

Marion patted her stomach, gave an elaborate wink and said, 'Watch this space Jeannie. As soon as I am, you know, pregnant, you'll be the first to know. Right?' She smiled at Jeanette, who said, 'That's a promise?'

Anxious to return to her letter Marion said, 'Yes, I promise. Now I must get on. See you later,' and hurried back to her desk. Picking up the letter she began reading it again.

I have asked Dominic to send me a selection of the wedding photos as soon as I'm settled and can give him an address. You are sure to be in some, hopefully all of them, as you were a bridesmaid. At least then I can look at You. It won't matter to the Senate as I've already broken the "Thou shalt not covet thy neighbour's wife" commandment. I'm sure they have no idea of love. I expect Rosemary will send you some photos as well.

Do you remember we talked about the commandment of stealing? I told you I believed I probably stole in nearly every life and, if all else failed, the Senate would use that as an excuse to have me returned? I never got round to telling you that in fact one of the times I was indeed a thief. It was like this:

You know, of course, about the dissolution of the Monasteries that Henry the Eighth carried out. During that time I was a soldier. The King ordered that his noblemen and anyone who owned sizable property were to have sufficient arms and trained men and be ready to muster when called upon. The practice musters were not unlike a drill exercise and lacked proper organisation, all very haphazard. However, it was an excuse for meeting up with others, drilling a bit with a few miserable looking muskets. At the end of the training session we would visit the local tavern. Not like the soldiers of today, but local gentry and yokels mixed together to serve the king in times of need. Never did I nor my friends ever suspect we would be called upon to do Henry's bidding.

During the early fifteen hundreds the Pope's authority over everything, including all crowned heads, was irksome to Henry. It was then that he decided to curtail the influence of the Vatican. We were not sure at the time whether the attacks on the monasteries were for a spiritual reason or to grab their accumulation of wealth. It wasn't just the monasteries that were destroyed. Included were the abbeys, priories and smaller establishments known as friaries. The personnel in closed monasteries remained entirely within its confines, rejecting the outside world, while others in holy orders in different religious houses worked locally among the sick and needy and in some cases became teachers and were highly respected.

The trouble was the closed establishments; they had become unbelievably rich. You could say that they were the fat cats of their time. At least thirty or more monasteries owned around thirty percent of the land in England and Wales and were thought to be richer than the highest ranking nobles. Land had been donated over centuries by those who thought they could buy their way into Heaven. By the way, the Senate will tell you that is not the way in. Henry had earlier declared himself supreme Head on Earth of the Church of England. He didn't do things by half, did he? It is said that Thomas Cromwell, one of Henry's advisers, whispered in his ear of the wealth of the churches, and between them they legalised the theft of the riches from religious establishments.

I was shocked and angry at what I and others had to carry out as militia men. We were ordered to collect the gold and silver plate, jewellery, oak doors, cloths and holy relics, along with the livestock; everything that was of value. There were some men who were more exuberant than others and used their axes and pikes to smash the wonderful stained glass windows and furniture. I was very involved with the local monastery at the time. As a boy the local monks of my village had taught me my letters. They cared for the poor and sick in the surrounding villages and were also hospitable to travellers.

My brother and I decided to see if we could steal something of value. Our plan was to make sure that now the monks were outcast, we would be able to contribute to their well-being. I had seen others secrete a small valuable item about their person and get away with it. That is what we did, steal what we could two or three times during the destruction of the Abbey in our neighbourhood. We buried our haul carefully in separate caches in fields two or three miles away. My undoing was keeping a small gold ring with a ruby, one I'd seen often on the small finger of the abbot. At the time I was thinking of my future, not, I'm ashamed, to say of the abbot's well-being.

I expect you are impatient to learn where the girl came in. Margaret was her name and she was on a pilgrimage to York. As there was no longer anywhere for travellers to rest locally, my mother offered Margaret a few days rest at our farm and being a lady of high birth she was well chaperoned. I was made acutely aware that I should never approach her. I knew at once, of course, that she was my eternal life's destiny.

It seems someone, the monks no doubt, kept an inventory of their wealth and it was soon established that I was one of the thieves. I returned most of the stuff, including the ring, but not all. I wouldn't be surprised if one day someone finds it if it hasn't been found already. I was whipped for the deed but never told anyone of my brother's part. I was lucky as others were put to death or had experiments carried out on their bodies. After the whipping my open back became infected, and despite my mother's ministrations, I was soon reunited with the Senate. Probably the monks could have saved me, but they were long gone. So you see, Marion, I have been a thief in all of my lives, but only as a secondary crime in most.

I still have half an hour to wait for my connecting plane and will end this letter now to post it here. Once I'm up country it will be weeks before any post is collected or delivered.

I know that you have enjoyed my telling of my lives and adventures. You once told me to write them down. I know I will not have the time in this life, so, my dearest Marion, I hereby give you permission to write and hopefully have published all my experiences, if it will not be too painful for you to take on such a task.

Until our meeting in the next life I will continue to love you, my beloved Magdalena.

Her eyes filled with tears, it was as if she could hear his voice as she read it again. Carefully Marion folded the letter and returned it to its envelope and locked it in her office safe.

The letter was definitely showing signs of wear by Christmas as she was unable to resist reading it again and again.

Alex's Music Hall presentation was a success and his adrenalin ran high for hours afterwards. It was in the New Year that he surprised Marion. He had been nervously pacing around the house for a few days, and had been making countless telephone calls. Patting the seat on the sofa beside him, he said, 'Come and sit with me for a few moments, Marion, I want to put something to you.'

As she did so, he took her hand and took a deep breath before saying, 'How would you feel about me leaving my work?'

Quickly she asked, 'And do what? I thought you loved your job, but if you're unhappy, well, of course, you must find something else. Have you anything in mind?'

Again he took a deep breath and said, 'Yes, but please don't laugh will you? I would value your honest answer, my love, and if you don't agree, then I'll forget it.'

'All very intriguing, Alex, I won't laugh, but for goodness sake say what you have in mind. Stop teasing. Am I such an ogre? Come on, don't keep me in suspense any longer.' She watched as he took another deep breath and swallow nervously.

'I've made a few enquiries and I believe I can make a fair living once I get going.' He looked at her and she could see he was anxious as to how she was going to react.

She squeezed his hand and murmured, 'Go on, I'm listening.'

'I'm sure I can be a successful comedian,' he blurted out.

Marion didn't laugh, but sat quietly absorbing his news.

Pulling her closer he said, 'Say something.' When she remained silent, he said miserably, 'You're not keen on the idea at all, are you?'

Turning to him and stroking his face she said, 'I love the idea. I'm sure you'll be very good, but how will we manage? I mean financially. You may not get many offers to start with you know. You have to be realistic before making up your mind.'

Feeling more confident now, he said, 'If it's okay with you, we could move to a smaller place, somewhere in the suburbs so you could get to your office.' He hesitated for a moment. 'House with a garden so that ... well, when you're ready, I did think we might have a family one day.'

Marion smiled and hugged him, 'I could work from home if needs be. When are you thinking about making these grand changes?'

'Beginning of March suit you? I have to give a month's notice to the company, for them to get a suitable replacement. If it doesn't work out after say, two years, I'll go back on the rigs. I'll make sure you never go without Marion, you know that.'

Marion was thoughtful for a moment before saying, 'Alex, I have had it in my mind for a few months now, to write.' She paused then added. 'To write Matthew's story. You remember, the person I met at Rosemary's wedding, and I have thought about having a family, but wondered how you would react to the idea. So, yes, let's start planning. It will be a change of direction for both of us.'

Her answer surprised and pleased him, and teasing her said, 'And I suppose you've named this family we're going to have?'

Marion gave an embarrassed laugh, 'Yes, Alexander Matthew for a boy and Magdalena Alexandria for a girl. What do you think?'

Seizing her face, he kissed her over and over again, 'Marvellous. Sorted, something less for me to worry about.' Snuggled up in his arms, Marion knew that she had come to terms with Matthew's death, and that the pain and sorrow had lessened. Alex had offered a way forward and, she realised, two dear men loved her in this life, and there was a promise of love in the next.

Seventeen

Marion made her way to the conservatory and sat down close to the window so that she could gaze out over the garden. She could see the tomatoes ripening in the greenhouse, and made a mental note to get the lawn cut. She welcomed the warmth of the sun as it seemed to ease her arthritic hands. It was her eighty-fifth birthday and she was waiting for her children to collect her and take her out for lunch to celebrate. Where, she pondered, had the last sixty odd years gone? Alex had died three years previously and she missed him dreadfully.

Feeling very tired she had slowed down considerably over the last few weeks. Even the smallest of chores took so much effort. She closed her eyes and wondered if this was her time. She wasn't afraid of dying. Something at the back of her mind convinced her it would be no more than a transition. Perhaps that's why she was able to let Alex go, she thought, glad that he might have found rest after such a long illness. She had been so lucky to have such a happy marriage she told herself, an ordinary life really, not like so many of her friends who had separated and suffered such loneliness as a result.

The past invaded her daydreaming as she sat in the sunshine. They, Alex and herself, had three wonderful children; boy twins, Duncan and Douglas, now in their mid fifties. Later, much later, their daughter Ruth had arrived. An accident, she had thought, Alex chose to say she, Ruth, was an afterthought, but was happy with their daughter's arrival. She had brought such joy into all their lives. It was Ruth, now forty-two, who had arranged today's treat for her.

Marion had chosen names for her children long before their arrival, Alexander Matthew for a boy and Magdalena Alexandria for a girl. But at the time of their births she had changed her mind. Matthew, still lurking in her heart, had been dead over five years when the boys were born, and she felt the names beginning with M would be a constant reminder of him.

There were times when she had felt so guilty. Guilty in her mind of being mentally unfaithful to Alex, but her feelings for Matthew had been so different. She hadn't told Matthew that she loved him, only that she cared, but had she cared too much, she asked herself? She could never put into words how she felt about their meeting, and of their parting, so how could she ever explain it all to Alex? At these guilt-ridden moments her eyes would fill with tears, and a lump would come into her throat. She would look at Alex, and knew without a doubt that she loved him, and that he loved her. All so long ago, she chided herself now.

They had bought a house in a tree lined avenue. There was a large garden at the rear with a mock-Edwardian summer house, a shed and a greenhouse, a perfect home for their planned family. Alex had put his plans into action and, after a slow start, was finally acknowledged as a comedian. His earliest audiences were the workers on the oil rigs. He was among his contemporaries who appreciated and encouraged him and gradually his confidence grew. It was when Alex's friend, Thomas Craig, got in touch suggesting that he could write material for him to perform, that his career really took off. Alex had been struggling to find new jokes and the arrangement with Thomas had worked well. Tom, as they called him, said he found a lot of his material in just observing and listening to people. Whenever they were out Tom and Alex would jot down anything they found marginally amusing and work on it until they thought it was acceptable. They were able to spark off each other, and together they would hone and rehearse every word before a joke was perfected ready to be told in public. True, Marion thought a great deal of the material was risqué, but as Alex had occasionally performed in dubious clubs, where crudeness seemed normal, she had not interfered, knowing that Alex was enjoying every minute. In every performance he managed to acknowledge Thomas's input, sharing the credit with his friend. True, Alex was often away from home, but it wasn't as if he was in the constant danger he experienced in the early days of their marriage. Her constant fear then had been that something dreadful would happen when he worked on the oil rigs, and she would lose him. He would be flown out to a rig by helicopter for his performance, and returned to shore when it had ended. He always phoned her once he landed so she knew he was safe and would soon be home.

It had taken Marion over two years to write her book. It had been a painful and difficult task, reawakening good and fearful memories. Quite often she found herself in tears as she recalled Matthew's hopes and disappointments time after time. As she wrote she had constantly felt angry and frustrated by the Senate's interference, and always longed for a joyful ending for Matthew.

Alex had read the book and said he'd enjoyed it. 'But is it all true?' he'd asked. 'I mean, did he declare his love for you? Were you in love with him at the time?'

Marion had burst out laughing. 'It's supposed to be a work of fiction, Alex. I have to ensure the reasons for Matthew's adventures, loss of love and continued returning to earth, don't I? Otherwise the story would have ended after the second chapter.' As she spoke, she was aware that she was being unfair to Matthew. However, writing the book had eased her pain, and when it was finally published she felt more able to get on with her life.

But there were moments when there were sharp reminders. More than once, soon after his death, she had seen his likeness in a stranger and her heart had constricted. Once, she remembered, she had seen someone ahead of her, and she couldn't believe what she was seeing. The man was the same height, had the same colour hair and the same easy stride as Matthew. A wave of happiness had come over her and she had hurried up to the man. She touched his arm as she said, 'Matthew?' and was aghast when she realised her mistake. Her face had reddened and she had stammered, 'Sorry, sorry. I …'

The man, seeing her distress, had murmured, 'Sorry to disappoint you, miss.' He'd smiled and jokingly added, 'It's something I do all the time in the supermarket when I'm looking for my wife. Some of the women from a distance seem so like her.' He'd walked on and casually lifted his hand as he'd said, 'Goodbye.' How could I have been so stupid, she had thought as tears filled her eyes? Matthew had gone. Sometimes it was no more than the smell of some Italian dish that wafted out from a restaurant, or the distant sound of a train. She had never told anyone of the love-bond between them, or that it was still secreted away in her heart.

The three children had all gained university degrees. Duncan, with his own family of three girls, was a consultant in a teaching hospital in Adelaide. Marion had recently returned from Australia, and, sitting in the sunshine now, she was wistful as she remembered. There was no hope that he and his family would be with her today and joining the rest of the family for lunch. She smiled as she recalled he said they would be over and spend Christmas with her. She was happy though, that her sister's extended family had made Duncan welcome.

Douglas was an architect. He had entered Bath University following his boyhood ambition to study architecture and civil engineering. He was living with his partner in London, how she hated the expression. Weddings were an old tradition that meant nothing to the young today, and only the very elderly remembered them, she mused. She was pleased to think that at least they were still together after ten years and thought of Jane as his wife, it was easier that way. They would bring their youngest daughter with them.

Ruth and her partner had twins, a boy and girl. Ruth had attended London University and gained an MA in Education where she had met Terence, her partner and father of her two daughters. She was now heading a research programme concerning the illiterate. Marion was surprised, and appalled, that despite many reforms to education during her life-time, there were still children unable to read or write. It was impossible to believe that there was still illiteracy in the world.

Marion hoped her grandchildren were having the same fun in their childhood that her own family had enjoyed. Warm summer holidays in Italy and France. It always surprised her how quickly the children were able to pick up the languages, but then she always welcomed her children's friends wherever they were, and they always travelled by local transport, so really it wasn't so surprising. Winter, for them was a wonderful time, spent mostly in Russia. Always plenty of snow to play with and everyone went to the hills for sledging. They made snowmen and igloos, and she smiled briefly as she remembered they always collapsed, usually on Alex. They also had plenty of spontaneous snowball fights and she could see, in her mind's eye, herself running away from three excited children, who had been coached by their father to pelt her unmercifully.

Marion eased herself into the cushions of the wicker armchair, smiled, and thought what a wonderful life I've had. There were ups and downs of course. Both boys had broken a leg. Duncan had fallen from a tree and Douglas had fallen when he was showing off his cycling skills with no hands on the handlebars. The children experienced all the childish, contagious ailments with high temperatures causing Alex and herself sleepless nights and worry.

There was a time when Alex had no bookings. As far as she was concerned it wasn't too difficult to manage. In fact, it was quite an exciting challenge to surmount the short-lived hardships. Alex had fretted, constantly blaming himself for, as he put it, 'letting her and the kids down'. Quickly, he had cheerfully taken up gardening, even thought he knew little about gardening and made mistakes. How they had laughed when he had pulled up a client's prize leek seedlings, thinking they were grass sprouting in the vegetable plot. He had pruned ornamental bushes at the wrong time of the year, over watered some plants and neglected to water others. Nevertheless, he had learned quickly, and kept them out of financial trouble. What's more, she now had a beautiful garden to look out on.

Her eyes felt heavy, it was warm and comfortable sitting in the sunshine. She put her hand up to her cheek to support her head. and closed her eyes. Just a little sleep before the family arrive was her intention. She hoped she'd dream of Alex, but it was Matthew who stood before her, smiling.

The two families arrived together and Ruth's daughter ran into the room then turned to her parents and putting a finger on her lips, said, 'Oh, nanna's asleep.' Together, Douglas and Ruth looked at Marion and then at each other.

Douglas frowned and pursed his lips. 'Not like mother to sleep in the daytime,' he murmured.

Ruth shushed the children and ushered them from the room. 'Go and play in the garden until we're ready,' she said, as Douglas crossed the room to his mother. He bent over her and gently took her hand.

Ruth's hand flew to her mouth when Douglas half turned and looked back at her over his shoulder. His shoulders had dropped and by the look on his face, she knew. 'She's gone, Ruthy,' he said.

Eighteen

Marion knew exactly where she was. Happily she moved forwards, sure that she'd seen Matthew in the distance. It was sixty years since she had last seen him. She acknowledged that during those years Matthew had come into her thoughts, and she was quietly glad of the memories they evoked. All he had told her was true after all. Yes, she was quite sure that she had passed over, kicked the bucket, gone upstairs, passed on and was in heaven, whatever, all the euphemisms that were quoted after Alex's death, and had partially amused her later. Convinced she was in heaven, she determined to seek out the Senate, reprimand them and insist they release Matthew from his tasks.

Her first experience in heaven was that of freedom, free of pain, free of all the roles life had subtlety imposed on her. Not that she was complaining, in fact she had enjoyed many of them, wife, mother, nurse, cook, writer, grandmother, the list was endless, but she loved them all. Now suddenly she was herself – young again and carefree.

There was someone ahead waiting with a welcoming smile, but she didn't recognise him. She smiled back as she walked determinedly forwards.

With outstretched hands, the man said, 'Welcome, Magdalena, so glad to see you here. I am here to escort you to the resting rooms.' As he took her hand he could see Marion wasn't at all surprised at his words. 'There are a good number of people waiting to see you, and wish you joy.' Seeing her give a little frown he queried, 'Is there something amiss? Anything I can do to help you settle until your return? Most people find it a little strange at first, even though they have returned many times.'

Marion was unsure how to go about her self-imposed challenge. She took a step away from him and looked around, bit her lip, then with an outward show of confidence, said, 'Yes. Yes indeed. There is something important I want to put an end to. I need to see the Senate as soon as possible.'

The man's mouth dropped in surprise, and he said firmly, 'Impossible, quite impossible. It is they who summon people before them. Usually those who have defaulted, and the number is increasing I'm sorry to say. So many are flaunting the Terms of Agreement. The Senate haven't had an assembly for a long time, but things are about to change.'

There was a determined look on Marion's face, and politely she repeated, 'I need to, in fact I insist, on seeing the Senate.'

The man shook his head, 'No, I cannot arrange that for you.' He was silent for a few moments and Marion waited patiently, then his face lit up as he said, 'Perhaps you'd like to see Matthew.'

At once Marion bristled and snapped, 'Of course I want to see Matthew. It is Matthew that I want to discuss with the Senate.'

Seeing the perplexity on his face, she said, 'You have no idea, have you, how ill-used Matthew has been at their hands?'

The man looked surprised. 'Something has gone wrong somewhere. You have somehow gained knowledge of another's destiny. That is not the intention of the Senate. Perhaps, after all, they might be prepared to see you. Tell me the facts and I'll do my best.'

Stamping her foot, how Matthew would love that she thought, she demanded, 'Just show me where they are. No need for you to get involved. Thank you.'

She realised he was ignoring her request as he pointed into the distance. 'You know how to get to where all your loved ones are waiting.' He added, 'Please make your way there. On reflection, I don't think I can ... In fact I'm sure the Senate will not see you.'

Smiling grimly, she muttered as she moved forward. 'Oh yes they will, and what's more they will listen to what I'm going to say.'

It really wasn't difficult to find the Senate building. Everywhere was clean and bright with colour, but the unobtrusive building of marble, discreetly built in a small copse area, could not be mistaken for anything other than the place she was looking for. Marion stood in front of the building, allowing the stillness and quiet around her to calm her nervousness and strengthen her resolutions. There were three steps up to the entrance and, as she stepped onto the first, she told herself that the rule was to be assertive, not aggressive. On step two she wished she was not alone and on step three she vowed not to lose her temper. The door was open and she peered in. Marion was pleasantly surprised. The hall was bathed in soft sunlight filtering through the stained glass windows. The floor was of marble and on the walls were scenes of nature. In a semi-circle were white upholstered chairs. She entered the hall and noticed that beside some of the chairs there was a clean, empty drinking glass. She picked one up, then checked the others. Each was engraved with the names of the owner. She wasn't surprised to see they were the names of the disciples. As she crossed the hall another man appeared. Marion was startled at his sudden appearance, but saw he was equally surprised to see her.

He crossed his arms and smiled as he said, 'Hello, have you lost your way? It's Magdalena, isn't it? I'm Peter.'

Peter, she thought, head of the Senate. Marion swallowed and began to tremble. Get a grip, she told herself, think of Matthew. Ignoring the questions, she asked, 'Is this where the Senate meet?'

Puzzled, but still smiling, Peter nodded and added, 'But it is no place for you, all the members are men of some distinction.'

Marion's face remained closed. How dearly she would like to walk away, but Matthew had suffered enough at the whims of these men. Looking squarely into Peter's face she said, 'Yes, and it's these men of ...' she paused wanting to say dubious, but instead continued, '... distinction I intend talking to. I have something I would like to say to them, something that has caused great suffering to a very dear friend.' Watching Peter gently wringing his hands, she knew she had disturbed him. Unable to meet her gaze, he looked out over her head and made short hmm-ing noises.

'I'm sorry, it isn't possible. They are informed well in advance of any meeting. Only in special circumstances can they be summoned at short notice.'

Marion could feel herself getting impatient, and replied sharply, 'This is important, important to me. How do you call them in an emergency? Surely there is some sort of signal – a bell perhaps, or a gong?'

Peter, without thinking, turned his head towards a curtain and began to say that it was impossible. Before he could stop her,

Marion darted towards the curtain and pressed the concealed button. A bell, with a loud, demanding ring disturbed the peaceful building. Peter was aghast.

'That bell hasn't been used since we had to discipline a young man some eight hundred years ago. That was our last emergency meeting,' he spluttered as he sat down abruptly.

Marion frowned, knowing in her heart who he was talking about. 'Emergency meeting yes, but what about the meetings held each time Matthew returned to you? Were they held just to mock him?'

Peter leaned forward and said, 'If you will allow me, I can explain. I ...' but the room was now full of men who hurriedly took their seats, and gazed around the hall. All were amazed when they saw Marion, and she felt as if she were shrinking under their gaze. She heard them begin talking and muttering amongst themselves.

'A woman!'

'How did she get here?'

'Broken protocol.'

'Needs to know her place.'

One called out, 'Peter, what's this all about? I mean, a woman in the Senate's presence. I was astounded at being called to an emergency meeting. Surely not by this ... this person?'

'Yes, Peter, can you throw any light on this intrusion?' another enquired.

Marion felt her anger rising, but curbed herself, waiting for Peter to speak.

He held up his hand and when all were quiet he mumbled, 'This is Magdalena, who wishes to address us on a matter of some importance – she believes.' He gave a little cough before adding, 'Something to do with Matthew.'

Everyone looked at her. At first she was embarrassed, then remembered how many times these men had tried to destroy Matthew. She lifted her head and heard their mutterings of disapproval.

'Matthew,' she heard one say, 'Always trouble, always will be.' She let them go on with their unfriendly criticisms, waiting and waiting, letting their grumbles wash over her.

After a short while Peter lifted his hand and everyone stopped talking. 'Shall we hear what Magdalena has to say?' he said. There were a few sighs but most gave a nod of assent. Peter turned to her and said, 'You have their attention now, Magdalena. Perhaps you'd like to tell us what your problem is.'

Marion took a deep breath, afraid of the outcome. Remember how they treated Matthew, she reminded herself. What if they decided to punish her? She wasn't asking for anything herself. All she wanted was peace and rest for Matthew. It seemed to her that the Senate's thoughts on women had been made clear, and she realised she had a daunting task ahead.

It was as if from nowhere she suddenly found the strength and confidence she needed, and shocked them all by asking, 'Why are there no women on the Senate? Where are the women saints whose sacrifices and dedication have been acknowledged, but do not have a prestigious place on the Senate?'

The men seemed at first to think the question was of no importance. Words like unable to cope, prejudiced views, their own specific roles, lack of intelligence were bandied around the room. Marion was amused by their spluttering excuses, and when they had settled down again, she spoke.

'You are living your lives as you did a thousand years ago. Indeed, you arranged everyone's destiny at that time and thought your duties complete. Believe me, gentlemen, you may not know, but many things have altered. No doubt you thought the universe would go on forever, never to change.' She shook her head and sighed. 'Yes, gentlemen, I agree there are useless, ill-informed women still, but no more than their male counterparts. Women now have a strong voice in the world you left long ago. Gender discrimination has long gone.' She looked at each of them in turn. Some appeared surprised at her words, others were sceptical. She thought how smug, how out of touch they all are. Bravely she went on.

'There are now progressive women in all walks of life. They have leadership positions, forward thinking and establishing new ideas for the betterment of all mankind. Health care and education are prime examples. At present there are women working alongside men, equal partners on ideas to end wars between neighbours and nations.' She breathed deeply, wondering where she was finding the words. 'It seems to me,' she went on, 'that you have never altered the traditions, rules or guidance established long ago. Nor do you want to. I'm surprised no one has ever challenged your blatant segregation of women.'

There was silence in the room for a moment or two, until Peter said, 'I had no idea, nor I suspect, did any of the members of the Senate, that such a change in women's roles had taken place. If there were more time, we would ask you for more details. However, perhaps later. In the meantime, you had better tell us your reason for invading our peace.'

But she hadn't finished and went on, 'It seems to me that you enjoy the prestige your position gives you along with the power it imparts, power that to my way of thinking is abused. How, I ask myself, do any of you deserve such an honourable appointment?'

The men were silent, and Marion waited for someone to speak up. Carrying on she said, 'Were you truly that perfect in life? You,' she pointed to one, 'what did you do?' and pointing to two more, asked, 'You? And you? Can any one of you answer me? Are you all blameless?'

Now a little out of breath, she watched as some faces reddened, others blanched white, while others dropped their heads, and she guessed they had memories they were probably ashamed of.

All was quiet for a few moments until an accusing voice asked, 'Do you think yourself without fault? You were married to Alex and yet you dared to ...'

There were nods of agreement from some of the members; others looked to see her reaction.

Swiftly Marion turned to the accusers and hissed, 'Don't you dare bring Alex into this. I made him happy, we were happy, wasn't that the destiny you meant for him?'

Another stern voice said, 'The secrets of your heart are known to us.'

Peter gave a little cough and, indicating a chair, invited Marion to sit down. He turned to the assembly. 'That's enough, my friends.' He smiled at Marion and asked, 'Is there more you would like to say, Magdalena? Tell us now, what has upset you so much that you feel you must speak to us.'

She looked around the room at all their expectant faces. Sitting down and clasping her hands in her lap she said, 'There are two questions that have troubled me greatly. Firstly, did none of you think the punishment meted out to Matthew was too severe? He is a fine person and has done his best to meet your almost impossible demands.'

Someone cleared his throat before saying, 'He altered his destiny and was given a chance to gain it back. We all thought it suited the ... the transgression at the time.'

Marion realised that she was at a disadvantage sitting in the chair and stood up so that everyone had to look up to her. 'But all his suffering, was it really necessary? What about the deliberate situations arranged so that breaking one of the Terms could only alter the outcome for the good of someone else?' She felt herself getting angry as she remembered Matthew's face every time he told her he'd failed.

There was hostility in the next person's voice as he said, 'Matthew was a disobedient child and took it upon himself to interfere with our plans.' The men turned to each other and there were murmurs and nods of agreement.

Marion whirled round to the speaker. 'That's it exactly. He was but a child and children are chastised and given another chance. You have made every one of his lives a punishment.'

The men shifted uneasily and Marion caught some of their words.

'True, he didn't think.'

'He knew the ways to conduct a good life.'

'He ran away, proof surely of his knowing what he'd done?'

On and on, each trying to justify their long ago decision.

Marion waited for them to settle and, when it was quiet said, 'I believe that someone deliberately made sure Matthew could not win. He told me that on one of his returns someone actually said something like, "You will never succeed." How he dreaded coming back to you, the jeering and smirking by some of you, undermining his confidence at every turn.' She paused for a moment. 'Is that the conduct expected of honourable, elected men?'

There was an uneasy shuffling of bodies, quick glances at each other. Someone gave a little groan, and another nervous laugh.

Peter held up his hand again for silence and addressing Marion directly, said, 'It was never intended as a punishment, Magdelena. What I had in mind was to test the possibility of living a life without breaking one of the Terms.'

Marion interrupted and, sweeping her eyes around the group, said, 'Did any of you in your own life do so? Live a completely blameless life?' All were silent, and sighing she said, 'No, I thought not.'

Peter began again, 'It was better if Matthew was given that chance. People who frequently default are left in limbo, unless there is an emergency and we need to send one of them back.' He hesitated, then under his breath said, 'Always a mistake, but we do our best.'

Marion was thoughtful for a while.

'So, you're saying that is where Matthew would have been sent? Into limbo, lost and forgotten forever?'

Peter nodded. 'But I agree with you. Basically Matthew is a good person. Everyone who is returned is given, shall we say, mental weapons.'

'Mental weapons?' Marion was puzzled, 'What do you mean exactly?'

'I mean that each have the gifts of empathy, tolerance, remorse, love, forgiveness of others, compassion and freedom of choice, to name a few. Those in limbo chose not to use any one of the gifts, thus causing pain and suffering to others.'

'Giving us a tremendous amount of work too, clearing up the aftermath,' a voice piped up.

Trying to keep her voice level, Marion said, 'You knew full well, all those years ago, that Matthew would do his utmost for the good of another human being.'

'Exactly,' exclaimed Peter. 'That is why I thought he was the right person for the test.' Marion was near to tears, and holding them back said, 'It was so cruel.'

'I know and I'm sorry for all of it.'

'But the others, these people here, knew of your intentions?'

'Not at first.'

'So even when they knew, they continued to undermine him?'

'Each time Matthew returned it was put to the vote. The majority still felt he ought to be punished, though admittedly some are now coming round to my way of thinking.'

'Shame on you. On all of you, for letting it happen.' There was no doubting the anger and disdain in her voice.

Peter stood up and went to her and put his hand on her shoulder.

'Truly we are sorry. Shall we move on? What was your second problem?'

'Before we discuss that, I want all of you to know that I intend to speak to the Higher Authority.' There were gasps all round. 'Oh, yes. Matthew told me about him. Does he know what you have done to Matthew and ...' she was surprised as a sudden thought came to her, '... and could there be more people suffering because of your spite? Yes, spite,' she reiterated as someone began to protest and others slumped forward.

'Please Magdelena, calm yourself,' Peter begged. 'Think again before you approach someone else. Much depends on his judgement.' The men roused themselves, hoping that Peter could alter her mind.

Marion frowned. 'What do you mean? Hopefully you will all be severely reprimanded, and learn a lesson in true forgiveness and humility.'

'It would be more than that, I'm afraid.'

'What more is there?'

'We could lose our positions and truly, on the whole, we do get things right.'

Marion watched as she saw him raise his hand as if to signal, and a few moments later a man discreetly left the room.

Turning back to the assembled men, she said, 'Here is my second question. When you decided to change Matthew's destiny, albeit temporarily, although I believe some of you would have made it permanent, when that decision was made, did anyone, anyone at all, think how it would alter my destiny? What suffering might unintentionally be inflicted on me? After all, Matthew told me, again and again, of his love and that our destinies are linked together.'

Peter gave a gentle smile as he answered, 'In every life, as you waited for Matthew to complete his ... his tasks.'

Marion interrupted him by snorting but he continued, 'I, we, made sure that you were given every happiness. Were you not content with Alex in this last life? That is how it has always been.'

It is true, she thought, I have been more than blessed with Alex and the children.

'That may be so in this life just ended, but only as you chose not to let me have a memory of past times with Matthew. He had to tell me, and that was a hurtful blow, to keep on reminding him that he had failed each time. That surely is unforgiveable. The memories were the more painful as they came to him only when he met me.'

Her question seemed to amuse Peter, and she demanded, 'Well?'

'We may have made foolish mistakes dealing with Matthew, but, and you will have to believe me when I say this, we are unable to map out disagreeable futures for anyone. It is of their own making if all goes wrong, hence the gifts I mentioned earlier.'

Marion felt the tension leaving her and as she sat down, Peter asked to be allowed to speak to the Senate in private. Marion nodded, and they all left the room. Inwardly she was appalled at how she had addressed these learned men. At the same time she was pleased that she had been able to put forward her views and, what's more, she thought, they listened.

For a few moments she closed her eyes, but was disturbed by the opening of a door. Glancing up she couldn't believe what she was seeing. In the doorway, with open arms, stood her beloved, Matthew. Marion's heart turned over as she rushed into them and said, 'Is it truly you?'

'Truly it is I,' he answered as he caressed the top of her head. 'I had a summons to report to the Senate at once, and thought I was about to be sent back, a little earlier than I anticipated I must admit. Instead,' he kissed her forehead, 'Instead I found you.'

They turned together as the Senate returned to the room, all of them smiling.

'I see you have found each other,' Peter said. Clearing his throat he went on, 'The Senate have now agreed that Matthew's term of redemption, as some are calling the events of his lives, is over. So, we are happy to inform you that your true destinies from now on will be fulfilled.'

There was joy on both their faces as they heard the news.

'Matthew will return to earth within ...' he looked at the shadows lengthening along the floor, '... the hour,' Peter said. The two lovers were instantly alarmed by his words. Peter and some of the men chuckled at their dismay.

'And you, Magdalena, will follow shortly. Of course, you realise that you will not meet each other until you are adults – we cannot send you back as adults, you realise that, don't you?'

Matthew and Magdalena looked at each other, embraced then together nodded.

'And that is how it will always be from now on. You will return here to rest for a while until we send you back to find each other,' Peter said.

One of the members pulled his cloak around himself and said, 'I, for one will be watching you very carefully Matthew. Should you make just one mistake, I shall see to it that you forfeit your destiny again. I think you have been let off lightly.' There was no mistaking the seriousness of his threat. For a moment there was a shocked silence. Peter looked sternly at the speaker, who shrugged his shoulders and shook his head indicating that he had little faith in Matthew.

Matthew put his arm around Magdalena and, facing the man, said, 'That will not happen, sir, I can assure you. I value Magdalena and our destinies.' There was a ripple of applause at his remarks and the group turned to leave.

Suddenly Marion's hand flew to her mouth. 'Wait,' she cried out. 'Wait, please wait a moment.' Everyone turned towards her, curious to hear what she had to say. 'Alex? Where is Alex? I must know he is well and happy before I can accept my fate with Matthew.' She stepped out of his arms and turned to him. 'You do understand don't you, my dearest?'

'Yes, of course I do. I met him recently and I know of his qualities and his love for you.' Looking at Peter, he asked, 'Can you tell us what will happen to Alex, sir?'

There were smiles and murmurs from the members. A voice said, 'I knew the girl was anxious about Alex.'

'A caring person, proved that beyond doubt as far as I'm concerned.'

'Always puts herself last.'

'Look how she's fretted over both Alex and Matthew.'

Peter held up his hand and, when all were quiet, he told the Senate members they may leave. He turned to the couple. 'You need not fear for Alex. He can pursue his own destiny now. Indeed, he left us some months ago and already we have sent his soul mate. He is and will be very happy.'

Marion sighed with relief. 'Oh, I wish him as much joy as I have with my soul mate.'

Peter silently left them when Matthew folded her in his arms and whispered, 'Soon, forever.'

'You'll find me, won't you?' Marion whispered back.

Nineteen

Magdalena lifted her head and watched the unmanned, silent skybus slowly glide overhead. She could see the excited children framed in the windows, turning to each other, and pointing to the sea sparkling in the sunshine. They were on their way to the undersea museum.

Today was her twenty-third birthday, July 2103 and it was her rest day. The ban on sunbathing had been lifted, and she kicked off her sandals and lay on a park lounger, letting the warm man-filtered rays gently tan her. She remembered her first visit as a child to the small, once-working, colonies on the ocean bed, considered a miracle of engineering at the time. The colonies were around four square miles she was told. They sat on the seabed at roughly one hundred and ten fathoms, about a quarter of a mile.

Each colony, or pod as they became known, was covered by a dome. People could freely walk around and they were able to venture into neighbouring pods through airlocks. The lighting mimicked that on land, including dawn and dusk so that work and sleep patterns were maintained. Most pods were comfortable homes, placed at the edges of the central pod, so that people could enjoy the creatures outside in their natural habitat, which was artfully lit up during 'daylight' hours. When Magdalena had visited, the homes had furniture dating back to the 2040s. In the central area were small parks, offices and a clinic for minor ailments, but severe illnesses were quickly sent to mainland facilities. Desalinated water, recycled air and heat were pumped into each pod by nuclear fusion power stations, a clean, cheap means of energy. A few of the pods were only of a basic standard and housed criminals. Deprivation of any comfort was deemed to be the best disciplinary action at the time.

Magdalena turned her head and shaded her eyes to watch the bus begin its descent to the platform in mid-sea, a short distance from the shore. The children would then enter the tourist submarine stationed on the platform, and on arrival at the seabed, enter an airlock to reach the museum.

It was the video games of the twenty-first century that had intrigued Magdalena on her visit. Her teacher had frowned and said, 'Those games you like so much, Magdalena, became more and more violent and there was much concern by governments. What's more, the children were mostly isolated when playing these games, rarely stepping outside their homes. When some did meet up with others, they were prepared to act out the fictitious brutality they had become addicted to, thinking that was how to behave.' Her teacher had gone on to explain, 'All digital machines, were good in their time and were useful, but as always there is a negative side.

'All of these components were banned for young people until the age of eighteen, so that children's lessons from that time on were of basic classroom teaching. And now you and your friends can read and write and do your calculations without resorting to electronic aids.'

Magdalena remembered that she had found an almost thread-bare teddy bear, and had cuddled it, and the teacher had suggested she find the history behind such a popular toy.

Another bus passed overhead as Magdalena settled back on the lounger. She lay there daydreaming of nothing in particular, and was startled when a man's voice, a voice that turned her heart over, spoke.

'There you are, at last. This time I thought I'd never find you.' Although he had a wide grin on his face and she could see his relief that now, finally, his search was over, he seemed puzzled and he frowned.

'And I've been waiting for you,' she answered. As she said these words her eyes widened, and she quickly covered her mouth with her hand, wondering where the words had come from. 'I'm sorry. I don't know why I said that,' she said.

'I have exactly the same feeling,' he exclaimed. 'As if I had no control whatsoever of what I said.' He shrugged his shoulders, 'One of those strange things that happen in life, I suppose. Think it was once called déjà vu. But now it's happened,' he turned and dragged an empty lounger nearer to hers, 'let's get better acquaint-ed.' He sat down on its edge and thrust out his hand. 'I'm Mat-thew, Matthew Hope.'

She took his warm, dry hand and was immediately overcome with a feeling of knowing he was special. Her hand stayed in his for longer than she intended. 'I'm Magdalena,' and both were aware of the frisson of tension between them. She withdrew her hand, took a deep breath and said, 'I'm not sure about this. I mean, well, your name is not familiar and I'm certain we have never met before. I go to a good number of parties so perhaps we were introduced at one of them, but I really don't remember meeting you.' She hesitated, 'But, I have this feeling, it is as if we have known each other before.'

'That's just how I feel, but I'm so glad to have met you now, Magdalena.'

They smiled at each other, unsure at this moment, how to move on. Time seemed to stand still. Magdalena swung her legs over the side of the lounger and faced him. Spontaneously and together they broke the silence.

'Do you like ...'

'Have you been ..?'

They laughed together and he pointed to her. 'Go on, you first.'

'No, no,' she protested, 'you go first.'

'I insist. If nothing else, my good manners wouldn't allow me otherwise. Besides, I want to hear what you were going to say.'

'I was going to ask if you have ever been to the underwater museum. I went as a child. and was reminded today when I saw two skybuses full of children on their way to the sea platform.'

'Yes,' he replied. 'I have. Fascinating history, isn't it? I mean, to think that once, and not so long ago at that, the earth was so crowded that space had to be used under the sea so everyone could have a home of some sort. My grandfather told me some people loved it, others found it claustrophobic.'

'I'm not sure I'd liked to have lived there myself, although there were no restrictions about coming to the surface, I believe.'

'Do you know why it is obsolete now?'

'Yes, I do. I understand that within two years, three-quarters of the world's population was wiped out by disease and as antibiotics no longer worked and nothing could be found to eradicate it, people died.'

'Quietly in their sleep, I understand.'

'How dreadful, don't you think, to go to bed wondering if you are going to wake in the morning?' She shook her hair and tweaked it into shape. 'My great grandmother told my mother, that long past, if the population was unmanageable – meaning space, food and water – then war, famine or pestilence, her word for disease, would happen. For instance the First Great War, as it is still called, claimed the lives of over nine million people. As if that wasn't enough, almost immediately after the war ended there was a worldwide flu epidemic. It is believed that up to 100 million lost their lives then.'

Matthew nodded. 'Well, now we have space, water and food for everyone – advances in science have ensured all of that, along with cures for all illnesses known. A hundred years or so ago, it was so different, governments were at a loss, not knowing how to overcome the problems. We are so lucky to be alive today.'

'Yes, I agree we are. So, Matthew, what were you going to ask me before I interrupted you?'

'Do you always come to this Tranquillity Park?'

'Mostly. It is so peaceful, I find.'

'It must be fate then. I always find myself in the music park. It is my favourite, out of all the pleasure gardens here, but today I find myself here. I don't know why, but I'm glad I did as I have found you. I mean, I don't think you were ever lost to me, but chance has brought us together. I have a feeling that I ought to add "at last". Are you comfortable with that thought?' He mused for a moment, 'It must be fate, I just can't understand why, perhaps it was ordained.'

'Well, we're certainly getting to know each other and it could be fate I suppose.'

'Have you ever been to the Music Garden? Early in the mornings cheerful, sort of marching tunes are played, followed by the classics of the 2020's. I avoid it in the evenings though. Music for the teenagers is pretty awful to my ears, but then my parents said that about my choice of music when I was that age.'

'I had the same problem with my parents, sort of rows over my choices. To be honest, I think they didn't like it being played so loud.'

'Nothing changes, does it?'

They smiled at each other. Matthew lifted his head and swept his arm around as he asked,' Which of these pleasure grounds do you like best?'

Magdelena gave a little laugh. 'Now, that's a difficult question.' After a few moments thought she said, 'I think each has its own merit. The perfumed one is particularly great for evoking memories. But I really, really enjoy the colour park – you know the one I mean? There are masses and masses of flowers and shrubs, an absolute joy.'

'Yes, I do. I believe that is the one voted the best in a recent competition.'

'I'm not surprised. I've noticed that no matter what time of year one visits, it is alive with colour, no matter how drab the day.'

'What about the Water Gardens? Have you been in there?'

'Yes, but I've never succeeded in getting to the other side dry. Someone was very clever arranging for water to spray from hidden sources when you pass by. Every time, a different place, so exasperating. My friends and I have tried often to avoid getting wet. I understand there is a prize for anyone who is dry when reaching the other side.' She was surprised to hear Matthew chuckling.

He stopped when he saw her mouth drop in indignation. 'Oh, I'm not laughing at you. I'm laughing because it can be done, stay dry I mean.'

'And I suppose you have?'

'I have indeed. It was when I was a teenager. I was with some friends and we thought we knew everything in those days. Anyway, this is what I did. I entered the park and put up a very large, a very, very large umbrella and strolled along the paths. I thought that we had solved the problem and the prize would be mine.'

'And was it? What did you win?'

Matthew shrugged his shoulders. 'I got nothing, nothing at all. I was told, although I was dry, I had cheated.' He laughed. 'They, the organisers were quite impressed with my ingenuity though.' He began to grin and Magdelena asked,

'What? What are you up to now?'

Still grinning, he said, 'Well then my friend decided to have a try. He too crossed the park and returned without getting wet.'

'And what did he dream up?'

'Nothing really, he just waited until the system was turned off at nightfall, climbed over the gate and ran both ways while the rest of us cheered him on.'

Magdelena laughed, 'Honestly, you definitely had a misspent youth.'

Taking her hand in his he pulled her to her feet. 'Let me take you across to the refreshment bar for a drink. My treat.'

She grabbed her sandals as he began running across the grass, dragging her along with him. It was difficult for her to keep up with his pace, but, struggling and panting, she did her best, laughing at the same time as she begged him to slow down. Halfway across the park she fell and dragged him down beside her. Matthew let go of her hand and rolled over to face her still form. There was concern on his face and in his voice as he attempted to lift her head.

'Sorry, sorry. You all right? Answer me, Magdalena. Please.'

'Yes, of course, you idiot. Let go. You went so fast I tripped over my own feet.'

Matthew withdrew his arm from her neck, leaned on his elbow and propped his head in his hands.

'Good,' was all he said.

He remained still and looked into her eyes, causing Magdelena a measure of consternation. She was very aware that her hair was tangled, that her face was red with exertion, and that her dress was grass stained and had ridden up over her knees. 'What?' she asked sharply, 'What are you staring at me like that for?'

A gentle smile, accompanied by the softest sigh, made her heart beat faster.

'What?' she asked again.

'I was admiring the softness of your skin, the way you crinkle your eyes when you laugh. Your tender mouth ...' Matthew hesitated as she began pulling at her skirt, sensing her agitation. He didn't add that it was a mouth he wanted desperately to kiss. Instead he said, 'And you have thirty-five freckles on your right cheek and twent ...'

'No I haven't.' she protested as her hands flew to cover her face.

He chuckled, 'I bet if we were standing up you would've stamped your foot just then.'

'I never stamp my feet, never,' but the tone of her voice through her closed fingers, said otherwise.

His unwavering stare continued and as she looked back into his eyes through splayed fingers. It was then for her, as if the world had stood still. Not sure how it had happened she was certain that she was in love. Suddenly she felt as if she had come alive and had no control over her feelings of happiness. At the same time she began to wonder what feelings Matthew might have for her.

'You have freckles on the back of your hands too,' he said but his teasing words did not spoil the joy in her heart. He stood up and offered her his hand. 'Come on, let's go and find some fruit drinks.' After putting on her sandals and pulling down her skirt, at the same time brushing away the grass, he tucked her arm through his as they walked towards the bar, displaying its beckoning awning, across the park. She had no control of the feelings that now engulfed her at his closeness. Magdalena chose freshly pressed pineapple and Matthew opted for orange. They quietly contemplated each other over the rim of their glasses.

'I suppose I've ruined your sun tan topping up?' he said.

'Perhaps you did me a favour. After all, you made some very pointed remarks about my freckles.'

'Sorry,' he mumbled, then sighed. 'I've to be at my workstation shortly, but I'll walk you to the gate first, if I may?'

She nodded and they sauntered towards the gate, the mood between them seemed to have an air of sadness, and for Magdalena an air of finality. When they reached the gates, Matthew turned to her and took both her hands into his. He cleared his throat.

Magdalena's heart beat a little faster – she had found her destiny, she was sure. Now she feared he was about to leave her, this was goodbye.

'Magdalena,' he began. 'I cannot, just cannot …' He let go of her hands abruptly and began muttering, 'This is ridiculous,' to himself as he strode three or four paces away. As she watched him move away, she experienced utter despair and slowly tears trickled down her face. She lowered her head and turned to leave.

He was beside her in an instant, snatched her hands and pulled her close. She sensed his agitation.

'Wait, please wait.' She lifted her head and, on seeing her tears, he wiped them away gently with his thumb. He took a deep breath. 'I feel that something special has happened today Magdalena,' he said. 'Don't you feel that way too? Every day I walk through the park, and today it was as if I were propelled into the Tranquillity Garden where I seldom go.' He hesitated. 'And then I found you.' He looked down into her face and saw that she was smiling and her eyes were bright with happiness. 'I cannot from this moment on, imagine a life without you.'

When she spoke her voice was choked with emotion.

'I have felt like that from the moment I saw you. I just dreaded you leaving me.'

He held her closer for a few moments and she knew she had found her true love. He looked at his watch. 'Glory be. I must go.' On seeing her crestfallen face, he added, 'I really must. There's a guy on satellite thirty-five waiting for me to guide him through a repair routine.'

'Will I see ...?'

Tonight, I'll meet you here at children's curfew bell and I'll take you to my favourite restaurant, Italian. They make all their meals from recipes going back over two hundred years.'

Magdalena laughed, 'Children's curfew! Is that what you call it? Eight o'clock old time, time for little ones to go to bed.' She grinned, 'Yes, I'll be here, Matthew, and I adore Italian food.'

He kissed her lightly on her forehead. 'I had a feeling you might. We'll go on from there, shall we? Make a pledge to be together forever.'

As he drew away from her he waved and she waved back, repeating softly to herself, 'Forever, forever.'

Beatrice Holloway

. . . is a playwright and author who has been writing children's stories since 2014. In 2015, Beatrice was appointed Children's Storyteller on Hillingdon Narrowboats Association which has led her to write about canal life.

Beatrice has written a number of children's books: *The adventures of Rhys* series, *Towing Path Tales*, *More Towing Path Tales* and *A Particular Year* as well as a number of science experiments for children – all available as ebooks.

The London Borough of Hillingdon library service has published two of her children's stories and awarded her with a Certificate of merit – 'In recognition of an outstanding contribution to the Arts'. Beatrice was also awarded a Lottery Grant to write a commissioned historical play: *Commoner to Coronet*.

Beatrice is a retired teacher and a member of The Society of Women Writers and Journalists. and the Society of Authors.